To Mike Kobre,
Thanks for buying
my book. I hope
you like it.

With best wishes.

[signature]

Ohio University
Athens, Ohio
May 25, 1989

STRAIGHT THROUGH THE NIGHT

STRAIGHT THROUGH THE NIGHT

Edward
Allen

SOHO

Published in the United States of America by

Soho Press, Inc.
One Union Square
New York, NY 10003

Library of Congress Cataloging-in-Publication Data

Allen, Edward, 1948–
    Straight through the night : a novel / Edward Allen.
        p.   cm.
    ISBN 0-939149-19-2 : $17.95
    I. Title.
PS3551.L39225S8   1989   88-26707
813'.54—dc19   CIP

Design and composition by The Sarabande Press
Copyedited by Margaret Wolf

Manufactured in the United States of America
FIRST EDITION

For my mother and father

Welcome

Coming home, the clouds
looked like patches of
fat in a lean sky, a day
spent trimming boneless
wedges of beef. Fatigue
is a blanket of frost
around the first day
on a new job, the wind
a cold handshake. In
my friend's car I kept
falling asleep, looking
at the clouds, trying
to trim them away with
a sharp knife. I dreamed
I cut myself, the blood
flanged into a sunset
with the same colors of
all the other sunsets
when light leans west
and November is just
another place to live.

Edward Allen

CONTENTS

TWO

THREE

PART
ONE

1
___

Cigarette Music

It was a private light: modest, unblinking, a cold eye pale and pasty above the silhouetted bungalows; and during the months that I drove in the dark to Manhattan, to my job at Denny Meat Packing Company, I came to think of the planet Venus as my secret morning companion, silent, untouchable, demanding nothing.

People with coats and ties and dogs and lawn mowers, people who got up at a normal hour to carpool by day in bright Toyotas, could never know such a light. The people I worked with on 13th Street all lived too deep in the City to see anything that low on the horizon; and those few meat people who lived up here in the northern suburbs could never have understood the difference between the twinkle of a star and the milky light of a planet. Somewhere in the parking lots of two-story apartment complexes with names like Cameo Gardens and Hickory Estates, young overweight meat managers getting into their low-slung, soft-springed Monte Carlos might see, through the blue smoke of their morning cigarette, that cold light pasted up in the sky, but nothing would register, like a dog watching television. It's a question of what your eyes are tuned to, and the way the skull has become accustomed to resting on the atlas-bone, configured to let a man look up at the sky, or down at his work.

I remembered a morning ablaze with northern lights, on a previous meat-business job, how all the way to work, in my rearview mirror, those ribbons of ionized particles in red and green and white had splashed across the northern constellations like agitated comb jellies, like the searchlights of a thousand grand openings of a thousand shopping centers, fading out opposite Yonkers as I approached the zone of light where the air never gets dark and the stars never come out. When I got to work, and tried to describe those lights to my cutting-line colleagues, nobody had any idea what I was talking about. Wet gray lumps of boneless veal drifted down the white rubber conveyor belt to be sliced into four-ounce portion-control cutlets. The other butchers didn't even look up from their boards.

But I knew better now, as I pulled out of the driveway of my apartment building, past the crooked mailboxes, knew that Venus was mine alone, cold and private, under whose eye I turned right onto Cresent Drive Spelled Wrong, and left onto Get High Street, which would take me to Route 59, which led to a ramp which led to another ramp and another, which was the entrance to the New York State extension of the Garden State Parkway. It was a warm, moonless December morning, my first day on my new job.

Get High Street was actually called High Street, but kids had changed the sign to Get High Street so many times that the Village of Spring Valley had given up trying to replace it. Cresent Drive Spelled Wrong was spelled right in the phonebook and in Hagstrom's Suburban Road Atlas, but all the street signs were missing the *c* in the middle.

My old yellow Volkswagen hummed along through the deserted hours, down streets where cold blue streetlights shine for nobody, where traffic lights flash their sequences all night to control the flow of traffic that isn't there, down through the darkness of bedroom communities where everybody was still asleep, digital alarms set for six or seven. At Paramus the Garden State bends west, and Manhattan-bound traffic merges onto Route 17, whose northbound and southbound roadways are separated only by a steel partition, and the land is all squeezed together, houses butting up against the edge of the road; and here the traffic seems to go faster, gathering speed like water passing from a wide river to a narrow channel, empty trucks booming all night over the broken pavement.

These townships at the edge of the marshland are a different territory, and these hours run on a separate clock. Chemical companies stand floodlit, tiny figures walking on catwalks between pressure tanks. All-night diners have been enclosed in Italian stucco, lit by floodlights that shine through a slowly turning wheel of gels.

It was warm. I had my window open. I was tired. Halogen headlights were ringed with bright coronas. I could smell hydrogen sulfide and the sweet brackishness of low tide in the mud flats, the decomposing stalks of cattails. Strange to think that the shapes we know by day stay up all night every night, that places never take a rest from being places; nothing is dismantled; the round faces of tower clocks glow, with chimes shut off; and McDonald's leaves the flag up all night, which is proper as long as it's illuminated. Cars scuttle past with a sibilance of tires, going to work, or coming home drunk. I'm talking about banked fires and smoke and darkness and control rooms full of dials from which electricity is distributed, a haze of brightness over exit ramps, gas stations forming islands of light in the night. I used to hate this land. I was so serious about everything in those days, thin and scraggly, on my way to Oregon years ago in a previous Volkswagen.

On a bluff overlooking the Hudson, from the ramp that curves around and down under itself into the Lincoln Tunnel, I could see the skyline of midtown Manhattan, at this hour a browned-out city with just a few lights here and there among the jagged dark of skyscrapers, a city still on the graveyard shift, run by skeleton crews, a city of janitors and dispatchers.

Ninth Avenue was already busy with low-slung sedans hurrying downtown to work in the meat business. At 39th Street, just south of where elevated bus ramps cross the avenue into the Port Authority bus terminal, a few black streetwalkers stood in front of an all-night greengrocer's stand, flagging down cars with a fluid waving motion of their arms. One girl opened her mouth wide and waved her tongue from side to side like the clapper of a bell; another threw open her leather coat to show that she was naked, her dark nipples looking as big and round as coffee saucers, then thrust her hips toward the traffic, and twiddled a finger in the shadows of her loins.

I felt a flicker of desire, in the darkness, its sharpness muffled by the ruff of new flab around my waist. In the three months since I had been laid off my previous job, I had gained twenty pounds. I like hookers, even though I was in love with someone quite the opposite, a cartoon character named Pepper, who was part of a junior detective agency on a Saturday morning kiddie show called "Clue Club." She was beautiful, all porcelain blond, with soft hair seeming to move as one alive unit, big cleanly penciled eyes; and she would stand with just the right tilt to her hips, and her designer jeans at the perfect height, chaste and voluptuous.

When the traffic was caught by a light at 34th Street, I could see in the cars around me the tips of cigarettes growing bright and fading, like lights on top of a radio tower, and I could hear E-Z-Listening music on a car radio, soft strings and muted trombones, before the light changed and the harmonies were drowned in the whoosh of automatic transmissions.

I parked in the outdoor Kinney parking lot and walked down 13th Street to my new job. My head buzzed with fatigue and fear and financial arithmetic, a first-day-on-the-job sort of feeling. The air was filled with a blue diesel haze from dozens of tractor-trailers, one of which was unloading dressed hogs at the corner of Ninth Avenue and

13th Street into the front door of a company called Pork Packers, whose own trucks, parked nearby, carried the trademark of the "Pork-Pak Twins," two smiling copies of Porky Pig, each a mirror image of the other, each with a little blue waistcoat and bow tie, each holding a breaded pork chop in its front trotter. An extension of the overhead railings inside the building had been swung out to connect with the railings inside the trailer. The naked pigs, without bow ties and without heads, came sailing out of the trailer and down the inclined rail into the front door while the square-shaped Peterbilt tractor hummed at a fast idle, the hinged rain covers atop the upright exhaust stacks jiggling and bouncing in the engine's hot wind.

It was 4:35 AM. The streets were already full of people. White-coated butchers hurried along, their cigarettes glowing in the night air. A few gays, slim in black leather, cruised the streets with long strides. On 13th Street a fire blazed in a garbage can, and around it stood a group of black butchers drinking tea from Styrofoam cups, the lines of their faces ancient and meditative in the flickering light.

Denny Meat Packing Company was a narrow little establishment, sandwiched between Interstate Poultry and Gingold-Fudim Provisions, with two truck bays recessed back from the street and a narrow glassed-in office overlooking the loading dock. Two luggers were unloading legs of veal from an Imperial truck as I walked up the ramp beside the truck bays and reported to Sandy, the man who had interviewed me last Friday.

"Where's your hat?" he said.

"I didn't bring one. I figured you had one for me."

"You didn't bring a fucking *hat?*" Sandy was a wiry little man with pigment-deficient blue eyes shaded by the brim of a heavy red vinyl hunting cap. His face, elongated somehow, with too much space between the nose and mouth, was a wintry shade of red, as if slapped awake.

I followed him upstairs to the locker room, up metal stairs so old that they had hollows worn into them from so many years of so many feet. The last place I had seen steps worn like that was in front of the main academic building at Hotchkiss, smooth foot-sized concavities, which my father, and most of my classmates' fathers, including novelist John Hersey and Governor William Scranton, had worn down with their own shoes; so that every morning on the way to study hall we walked literally in our fathers' footsteps, a continuity of Florsheims.

"I can't *believe* you didn't bring your own hat!" he said. I followed him into the locker room, where the butchers were waiting to start work, and pipes and tufts of Fiberglas insulation and BX cables sprouted from holes behind the green lockers, and rags of peeling green paint hung from the concrete walls. He gave me a white butcher's coat and an apron, and found me an extra hat, a heavy construction worker's helmet that shifted back and forth on my head; then he hurried out the door.

The butchers were clustered together, some sitting on a bench, others leaning against lockers, all facing the same direction, ranged in three tiers like the lacrosse team pictures we used to pose for at Hotchkiss. They were discussing the World Situation, stabbing the air with their cigarettes for emphasis.

"You know what I heard is gonna happen?" said a tall red-haired man with a sunken chest and a top-heavy haircut. "I heard the freakin' abadoolla of I-ran gonna take all our hostages and shoot them. On freakin' *Christmas Eve!* And they're gonna show it on television, live, for the whole freakin' world to see!"

In the space above where they were sitting, wisps and rings and tendrils of smoke twirled and stretched and blended in the churning air.

"They're gonna have a fuckin' *nukular war!*" somebody said. "Send them a fuckin' IBM rocket with a hundred fuckin' megatons!"

"What the *fuck* are you talking about?" said an old man with long white hair. "We shoot one fuckin' missile at the ayatollah, the fuckin' Russians gonna wipe us off the face of the fuckin' *planet!* And they got the power to do it!"

"Let 'em all hostage die, see if I give a fokkeen' shit," boomed the baritone voice of a fat-faced man whose European accent I couldn't place. He turned to me with the secret inquisitiveness that I had begun to notice that fat people have toward one another. "Should kill that fokkeen' shah bastard, what you think, my friend?"

I told him I thought we should stand by our friends.

"*What fokkeen' friend?*" he roared, swinging his arms so the loose sleeves of his white coat fanned the twirling smoke. "That guy a fokkeen' piece of *shit!* He torture everybody, he steal all the money from his people!"

"I'm not saying he's a great person," I said, wishing I had kept my mouth shut, "but I don't think we should just walk away from somebody like we walked away from the Hungarian freedom fighters."

"Ho *HO!* You tell me about Magyaria, you tell me about Budapest, my friend the professor. Where you think I come from?"

"Where, Hungary?"

"*Noooooo!* I'm refugee from Helvetia!"

"Helvetia? Where's that?"

"It's the fokkeen' Swiss-land! They chase me out because I work in a Swiss cheese factory and I take a shit in a hole in the cheese. So you tell me all about history, yes? What's you name?"

"Chuck Deckle. What's yours?"

"You Chuckie Deckle, I'm Heckle and Jeckle."

"Where're you from really?"

"From my fokkeen' *mother,* where you think?" Everybody laughed, a dry, rustling mirthless laugh beneath the dark skylight, and puffs of smoke were launched skyward. "My mother, she's a French gypsy live in Finland, and my father, he's a Chinese Jew priest and he teach Turkish language to Iran students in the fokkeen' Rome University. So you give me good lecture, my friend."

It was stupid to let myself get drawn into discussions like this, especially on my first day. Being serious and fervent about things, being intent about getting my point across, all that belonged to

9

another part of my life, back in Quinnipiac College, when I was skinny and knew things beyond question and wore blue chambray work shirts to demonstrations. It had been fun, the joy of the chant, the luxury of marching to the cadences of rage.

One April we chartered two Greyhounds to Boston for "Bring the War Home Day." As we double-jogged in time to the referee-whistles of the SDS parade marshals, we passed an old man who wore a makeshift khaki uniform with the words POLISH FREEDOM FIGHTER felt-markered onto the shirt. He held an American flag on a tall pole, and lower down on the pole was tacked a cardboard sign reading STAMP OUT COMMUNISM WHEREVER IT APPEARS. People were shouting at him, people were spitting. There was a scuffle. I punched him in the face, hard, and as he went down and his flag fell on the pavement, a full set of dentures came flying out of his mouth. Everybody was chanting, "*ONE, TWO, THREE, FOUR!*" I remember how bright and clean and pink those dentures looked lying there on the pavement of Tremont Street in the spring afternoon.

Ever since then, whenever I hear voices chanting, I see that old man lying on the ground. I was a hero. My friends were patting me on the back. Whenever I hear voices chanting, I see again those upper and lower plates gleaming in the sun. He must have kept them very clean.

Later that same spring, I saw those same colors again. My high school girlfriend, Cheryl Bergman, had come to visit me for the week end. My roommate was in New York. We were drinking beer mixed with Ripple, a combination not nearly as bad as it sounds. We had all the lights on; and the colors she showed me that night, there in the hard light of my bare-walled room, made me remember those flying dentures, and I had a problem.

From that time on, I've felt a sort of loyalty to whomever the slogans are chanted against, have believed that anybody hated so ferociously by the slogan-chanters can't be all bad.

"So you give me good lecture, Professor Chuckie," the fat-faced man who wouldn't tell me what country he was a refugee from was saying. "You tell me what you think about a man who take CIA money to make electric shock machine put on somebody's *prick!* What you think about that?"

"I think he's a hero as far as I'm concerned."

"Ho *HO!* You see what they do you fokkeen' hero!" He was beaming and his face seemed to be getting bigger. It was almost time to go downstairs. "They cut his fokkeen' ball off, they drag him through the street on a rope behind his own fokkeen' Cadillac! You fokkeen' hero look like a Denny Pack hamburger! You see. Fokkeen' hero ha ha."

2

Butcher Noises

In white-coated procession we moved down the stairs, to the time clock, through a pair of green canvas flap-doors, through the main cooler and order-assembling area, where a tall young man shouted orders from a stand-up lectern at helpers who bustled from shelf to conveyor to pallet, putting up the morning orders. A conveyor inclined down from the ceiling in the middle of the large room, like the escalators in Bloomingdale's.

We moved deeper into the building, as through the vaults of a many-chambered cave, through another pair of flap-doors, through a room lined on both sides with galvanized aging racks filled with boneless sirloin strips sealed in Cryovac plastic.

The cutting area was a bright white room with white plastic cutting boards set into stainless-steel frames all around the walls. Rounds of beef and legs of veal hung from stainless-steel rolling hooks on a system of overhead rails. Soon I was busy cutting four-ounce tenderloin steaks, weighing them on a Chatillion Portion-Master scale, and laying them out neatly on a white plastic tray. Refrigeration units hummed. The hamburger grinder groaned and crackled, spewing out bursts of meat through the perforated grinding plate. The air was filled with the voices of butchers, some singing, some analyzing the World Situation, some just releasing the puffs and grunts that all butchers make as they work.

"Fuckin' stupid jerks . . . right outside your fuckin' house . . . goddamn politicians a bunch of *crooks* . . . freakin' hoor business . . . line 'em up against a wall . . . should resign like a crook Nixon president . . ."

Silvery knives flashed in the seams between muscles, and everything was white and silver and red, the knives, the coats, the cutting boards, and the red meat. I was cutting steaks as fast as I could, but I could tell it wasn't fast enough. Bob Dragoslavic, the portion-control foreman, was looking back and forth from his cutting board to mine. He was producing twice as much as I was.

The problem I've always had in the butcher business is that I was never any good at cutting meat. Somehow I could never make my hands learn fast enough. People would demonstrate for me, once, at lightning speed, how to cut a particular piece of meat, and I could never seem to catch on.

"My friend, you must do faster now," said Bob Dragoslavic. The muscles around my neck were getting stiff. "He see you work so slow, he chase you away. You lose you job, my friend."

I worked and worked, in the brightness of the cutting room, as the butcher voices droned into a midmorning lull. On the white wall I could see fatigue patterns dancing, dark shapes rushing together. As we walked up the stairs for lunch at nine thirty, I could hear Bob's words ringing in my ears: "Lose you job . . . Lose you job . . ."

After lunch, as I was slicing eight-ounce sirloin strip steaks, Sandy came around to check on my progress. I could feel his eyes on me, staring at my slow hands.

"See me in the office before you leave tonight," he said.

After work, I waited in the office for him to get off the phone. I kept a smile on my face. I was determined to be fired with dignity. I would look him straight in the eye. I would shake hands with him. Butchers filed past the window. Paper was everywhere, scraps and flimsies, file cards, invoices, manila folders. Sandy had his hat off, and his short brown hair was evenly streaked with gray. He looked serious, almost intellectual.

"Has anybody ever told you that you can't cut meat for shit?"

"Everybody's always told me that."

"So what are you doing in this business?"

"Trying to improve, I guess."

"Well, I asked you to come speak to me because maybe we can use you in the main cooler putting up orders. The pay's not as much as a butcher, but with the way you work you're not going to find a steady butcher job. You don't have another job in the afternoon do you?"

"No."

"Because you'll be working later than this. Two o'clock, three o'clock, whenever we get done."

"That's okay with—"

"See Chris tomorrow at five o'clock."

"Who's Chris?"

"At the *desk!* In the *cooler!*"

"Okay, that'll be—"

"*G'night!*"

There's a special weary joy in driving home from the first day on the job, in the light afternoon traffic; and there is a sort of warmth in not having been fired on the first day, as I was sure I was going to be when Sandy called me into his office. In Paramus, Bamberger's was girded by two red ribbons, like a Christmas present, and where the ribbons met, a bow the size of a small airplane was pinned against the blank brick windowless wall.

The Volkswagen engine hummed and purred, the world seemed

afloat. I was happy, in a way that college graduates might never know, because you don't appreciate a job until you've lost them over and over again. On worn tires you feel closer to the ground, and there is a weariness, a jangling, wounded kind of weariness, that only people who did not finish college can feel. I was thinking about all the accidents that had brought me into the meat business, trying to figure out how one accident influenced the next. The question of "why" comes up. I suppose I could say I was at Denny Packing because the phone call from the union representative had come the day before I was to start looking for a job as a telephone salesman for commodity options; and that I was looking for a commodity option job because I had quit the sales department of my previous job and asked to be transferred back to the cutting room from which we had all been laid off; that I had quit the sales department because the double chins of Italian meat salesmen ballooned like tree frogs; that I was in the sales department in the first place because I saw a grown man cry when he lost his job; that I was in the meat business instead of the advertising business because one snowy day I saw Huckleberry Hound hammered into the ground by a falling tree and it was beautiful; that I had dreamed of the advertising business because of the way a man's suit hung one night when he raised his arm to hail my taxi; that I was in the taxi business for no reason at all except that I found myself back in New York; that I was back in New York because of the mottled Christmasy brightness of an Idaho snowball that Jim Ludwig dabbed his nose with after being beaten up by my friends at the old farm that I lived in after I decided not to go back to Quinnipiac for my senior year; that I didn't go back to school because of the way the warmth of a girl's body transferred itself through the aluminum of an empty Maxwell House coffee can; that I was there that night with her in the back of Goose's pickup truck because that's where I spent the summer with an incomplete in English rattling around in my head; and on and on, cause and effect, A equals B, until we get to the stars I was born under and the day my parents met, on and on, the ascendancy of mammals, the death of the dinosaurs, back, back all the way to the Big Bang, which, if you're stoned on acid in a gingham-wallpapered living room of a broken-down farmhouse on a rainy day with so many leaks in the roof that the kitchen had not pots and pans enough to catch them all, which theory is thoroughly explained by the Grateful Dead's lines, "Ripple in still water / when there is no pebble tossed / nor wind to blow . . ." being the exnihilation of matter, a disequilibrium, a glitch in the quantum stability of nonspace, and God said, "Let there be Chuck Deckle, and let him have such a ridiculous career that he shall sit in the ashes and scratch his ringworm with broken shards." I commend that song to astrophysicists.

Anyway, that's how I ended up at Denny Packing, some years after having driven west in a previous Volkswagen, a weary green '61 model with one black fender, and all gray and soft and frayed on the inside, a magical car that ran without repairs. I spent the summer in Brewer's Bend, Idaho, at a bankrupt farm that some friends of mine had bought. I built a teepee out of clear plastic. There was a girl named Sparrow, a ridiculous name, but a beautiful girl. One night we were riding together in the back of Goose's pickup truck on the way home from visiting some freaks in Yakima, Washington. We sat huddled in the lee of the cab, drinking Red Mountain Burgundy from a gallon jug; and then I was kissing her and touching her soft breasts, and we held each other in the deep and private warmth of the night, under the blazing, abnormally bright western stars in the middle of nowhere. We both had to go to the bathroom. I knelt at the gunwale of the truck bed, but the wind caught the spray and blew it all over the sacks of potatoes we had bought in Moses Lake. I was so full I couldn't stop. I tried to walk aft on my knees, on the rusty ridged steel of the bed, spouting all over my pants. We were both laughing. Then I held a coffee can beneath her as she squatted in front of me, braced against my knees, her long brown hair blowing all over my face; and when I felt her warmth through the aluminum, I knew I was in love, with Sparrow, with the night, with the soft motion and howling of the rear axle through rolling open cattle country with not a human light in sight, nothing but the cold white stars, shapes of cattle among patches of vegetation, the Milky Way so clear we could see its bright patches and dark mottlings where the light is blocked by interstellar dust; and her tongue was all over my mouth, her warmth between my hands in an empty Maxwell House can; and I knew I could never go back to school again, that my Incomplete would become an Administrative F.

In my teepee, we lay together on my sleeping bag. She was breathing heavily, with a tremulousness to her inhalations; and the colors she showed me, by the light of my flashlight cradled in a mound of dirt to point upward; those colors made me think again of the Polish Freedom Fighter's dentures, like the night Cheryl Bergman had lain beneath the ceiling lights in my dorm room, and I had the same problem I had then. I stroked her with my finger, and she kept catching her breath and losing it, and I buried my face in her dark, moist hair, and her whole body arched and stretched as she moved herself around the other way. Through the burgundy numbness I could feel the high vibrations as she keened and squealed; and when she became quiet I could hear the coyotes yipping and singing far away, and my wind-up Big Ben alarm clock was standing in the dirt, its tiny voice going *chink-a-chunk-a-chink-a-chunk.*

"What's the matter?" she said.

"I don't know. I guess I'm kind of numb from all that wine. You know, 'It provoketh the desire but taketh away the performance.'"

"What?"

"Shakespeare. Macbeth, I think."

That was as good as Idaho ever got. Soon it was winter in the main house, after I had abandoned my plastic teepee, long after Sparrow had caught a ride back to California with a couple named Bill and Emily Harris, soon to be famous revolutionaries. Missy's ex-husband Jim, who with Missy had been one of the original owners of the deed, had filed a claim against his share of the property. One evening when he arrived for dinner and negotiations, Morgan grabbed him and held him in a headlock while Maggie screamed with rage and spit in his face, and the rest of us stood around watching.

"Stinking fucking money-grubbing *bastard!*" she said, as Jim and Morgan struggled round and round the gingham-wallpapered living room in the twinkling of Christmas lights strung behind the couch, and the floor shook. Both dogs were barking. Jim was much bigger than Morgan, and he had most of the leverage. He lifted Morgan up in the air and they went waltzing around in the colored lights with Morgan wrapped around Jim's head like a cowboy in a calf-roping contest, until Maggie pulled Jim's feet out from under him, and they went down with a crash, and ashtrays flew off the mantelpiece. Morgan had him under control now, Jim's flushed, constricted face wedged against the faded Oriental rug, with extra skin from his neck pulled up in folds around his face, like one of those Chinese dogs.

"*Bastard!*" Maggie shrieked, "Stinkin' greedy *BASTARD!*" She pulled her thin arm back and punched him in the face again and again. The sound of her little fist hitting flesh was barely audible above the bullish wheezing of the two men. Jim's nose was bleeding all over his blond mustache.

Later, dabbing his nose with a bright red and white snowball, he agreed to relinquish his claim. "I wouldn't want to do anything to interfere with the high consciousness you folks have going here," he said.

In January I drove back east to my parents' house in Airmont, New York. I hooked up with some old friends from high school who were sharing the rent on an old farmhouse in Blauvelt, and I moved in.

I got a job in New York City, driving a taxi on the evening shift for Ding-a-Ling Service Company. I was a terrible taxi driver. The first time I tried to get to the World Trade Center, I ended up taking a furious passenger through the Brooklyn Battery Tunnel.

There was a night, in rush hour, when I picked up three well-dressed young people, two men and a woman, and took them from 39th Street to a bar on 86th Street. What I remember most is the way the man's suit jacket hung when he raised his arm to hail the cab, still symmetrical, perfect, sophisticated.

They all worked for Young and Rubicam. The men were account executives, and the woman, in her tailored tweed blazer-and-skirt combination, was a copywriter. It turned out that she had written the Sonny the Cuckoo Bird commercials for Coco Puffs, a campaign for which I've always had great respect.

They talked and laughed as I drove up Park Avenue, as crowds of suits and Burberry trenchcoats steamed across the walkway in front of us; plumes of vapor rose from under the sidewalks, as if the whole city drew warmth from the ground below. I thought about how the City smiled on these passengers, flagging down a cab after work, riding to Upper East Side watering holes where I knew there would be baskets of pretzel nuggets floating, gratis, around the bar. I thought about how the City might smile the same upon me, if I should make that leap of faith into the advertising business.

They tipped me five dollars. I turned on the off-duty light and went cruising down Fifth, all the way past the Plaza Hotel, which lights Plaza Square with its Parisian lightness, past dozens of lit-up airline offices with models of jets hanging on threads in the windows, some with lights inside the fuselage, the tiny windows bright above a terraced hillside of travel brochures. There are moments when desire and possibility intersect, when saxophones play one perfect solo, when men can fly and dreams become flesh, when taxi drivers may be transformed into account executives, if they dream hard enough and dress correctly. There are dreamers who have dreamed the same dream for years, and those dreams have firmed into steel and stone and electronics, into tailored worsteds and wing-tips so shiny that they sparkle with the flame of many-branched candelabra, in restaurants where overpriced drinks gleam in polished glassware, infrared heat lamps beneath the canvas awnings.

I quit the taxi business. I got up a three-page résumé and had it printed on beige textured paper. At Barney's I bought my first suit, a sort of European-cut gray plaid with wide lapels and built-up shoulders. One day I took the train into the City to do research at the New York Public library to find which advertising agencies to send my résumé to. As I raised my hand to hail a taxi, when I struck that classic pose, I could see, from a reflection in a restaurant window, that the jacket hung all wrong, ballooning out crooked and clumsy.

And there came a day, watching cartoons in the farmhouse with everybody else away at work, in which Huckleberry Hound, in black and white, was hammered into the ground by a falling tree, the classic Hanna-Barbera sight gag, and windows turned white with a sudden snow flurry, and the whole room was without color, and everything was beautiful, the raggedy wallpaper, the snowy lines across the screen, and I realized I couldn't leave that part of my life behind. I didn't even send my résumé anywhere. In the microfiche files of the New York State Employment service I found a listing for an apprentice portion-control meat trimmer at a company in Haverstraw that prepared meals for airlines. I looked the owner straight in the eye, called him sir, and got the job, my first in the meat business. Three months later I was laid off.

Through the union I found a similar portion-control job in Manhattan, and soon was commuting by Volkswagen to 14th Street, to Jak-Pak meats, from which I was laid off and then called back. I spent an interlude of five weeks working in the Jak-Pak sales department before asking to be returned to the cutting line, from which I was laid off again, this time permanently. I had already moved out of the farmhouse to my little basement apartment on Cresent Drive Spelled Wrong, and had bought another Volkswagen, bright yellow, reconditioned from a crash, with a rebuilt engine and four new retreads. The car had only one serious fault. It tracked crooked on its bent frame, pointing eleven-o'clock to the left of where it was actually headed.

I got a job at a restaurant supply house in Paramus, New Jersey, and was let go at coffee break. I worked for a week at Passaic Wholesale Meats, where the owner, a seventy-five-year-old man named Mr.

Pressburger, went charging around the cutting room all day yelling at people, his red face blazing.

"Boocha you are *not!*" he said as he fired me. He was right. I was terrible. My hands seemed to have a learning disability. I tried working outside the meat business, in a factory called Fasco Labels, that made the little latex-coated labels for underpants. My job was in the mixing room, blending solvents, pigments, latex, and diatomite, into the smooth chemistry that was used to coat the cloth so that the label could be printed clearly. By my second day I had a rash all over my arms. I was allergic to methyl-ethyl ketone, one of the solvents we were using.

I was just about to start looking for a job as a high-pressure telephone salesman for a commodity options firm, when I got the call from Tom Chambers saying that there was a job open at Denny Packing.

"You don't look like a butcher," Sandy said on Friday when I introduced myself to him, "but I'll give you a try."

And now I was home from my first day at Denny Packing in time for hot soup and Heckle and Jeckle and a walk in the leafless woods across the brook from the house. I could feel the fatigue rolling over me like surf, could hear the low hum of afternoon traffic, a slight buzz from the power lines that ran through an overgrown cut in the woods near my apartment. I kept checking my watch so I wouldn't miss "The Mickey Mouse Club." This wasn't the original show from the fifties, but a whole new production, with an ethnically mixed troupe of youngsters doing disco dances in their leisure suits, and today taking a field trip to a glider school where Ricky and Jennifer got to ride in a glider above rolling California scrubland while Joni Mitchell's song, "Wings of Wind," played; and then they sang "The Good-bye Song."

Chimes rang softly. This was always my favorite moment of the day: when they all sang how it was time to say goodbye to all of them. And then they went into the part about M-I-C, and how they would see us real soon, and then K-E-Y. And then Lisa, my favorite Mousketeer, beautiful Lisa, all softness and kind eyes, just a touch overweight, appeared on the screen, as she always did, flashed a dazzling smile, and pointed directly at me, and in response to the letter Y, she said it was because she *liked* me!

And then I answered, aloud, as I always did, "And I like you, too, Lisa!"

"M . . . O . . . U . . . S . . . E!"

3

Dogface Discipline

The next morning I reported to Chris Karbo at the desk in the main cooler. Soon I was bustling around helping to assemble the morning orders with three other workers, Joe G, a tall stooped-over man in his sixties, and Wilfredo and Herman, two young Puerto Rican men who kept up a rapid Spanish conversation. Chris stood at the lectern, his cheeks ruddy with cold, wearing a gray felt hat that looked as if it belonged on Wall Street, calling out items to be added to each of the orders.

"YO!" he would say. "City Squire! Fifteen pounds Uni-bacon! Thirty pounds franks!" and Herman and Wilfredo and Joe would go bustling over to wherever the item was stored against the walls, which were lined with boxes of frankfurters, and bologna, smoked tongues, pickled tongues, boneless Shattuck hams, knockwurst, bratwurst, liverwurst, all the preserved and processed meats known in the business as "provisions." I had no idea where anything was.

"YO!" said Chris, "Get moving! Open your fucking *eyes!*"

After several minutes of yelling and hurrying, the early flat was ready to be pulled out to the loading dock. Joe showed me how to hook the wheeled handle onto the flat. The flats we were using were wooden platforms two feet wide by five feet long, with wheels on one end and steel pontoons on the other, and on the pontoon end was a protruding steel lip with a hole in it into which the spur of the wheeled handle would fit, so that the handle could be levered under the lip, lifting the pontoons and acting as a steering bar. As I pulled the flat through the green canvas flap-doors onto the loading dock, I could hear Sandy yelling at the men who were loading the truck.

"YO! *HEYYYYYY!* What the *fuck* are you *doing?* Wake UP! This ain't fuckin' nursery school!"

"This is Lido and City Squire!" I shouted as I pulled the flat into an empty space between two other flats at the edge of the loading platform.

"*YO!*" said Sandy to me. I looked at him, but I didn't know what he wanted. "*YO!*" he said again, with such force and seriousness that it seemed I should instantly understand, the way foreigners are supposed to understand English if you shout. His small eyes were fixed on my face. It was just beginning to get light, a secret dawn of blue diesel haze.

"Look at the other *flats!*" I still didn't know what I was doing wrong. The traffic noises got louder, and I could hear blood rushing in my ears. Clerks behind the office window looked up from their invoices.

"I don't know what you want," I said, but my voice hardly carried across the loading dock.

"I can *see* that!" he said and came charging toward me, puffs of vapor steaming out of his small mouth. He grabbed the shaft of the handle with one hand and with the other snatched my hand from the cross member, and threw my hand aside as if it had been a piece of trash. He moved like somebody in an old-time movie. My hand went swinging around behind my back. He pulled the flat away from the edge of the dock and wheeled it around the other way and backed it in, wheel end against the dock.

"Okay," I said, "Now I see how you—"

"Fucking *dummy!*" I turned away and hurried back to the cooler, my face numb and burning in the cold air.

"*YO!*" his voice rang out again in the sharp air. "YO! *ASSHOLE!*" he held the wheeled handle off the ground like a prize fish he had caught. "The *HANDLE!*" He was yelling directly into my face, and I could feel the warmth of his breath. "*TAKE THE FUCKING HANDLE!*"

Back in the cooler, I could feel my face tingling as I weighed Cryovac-wrapped ribs for the Ponte Vedra Club in Florida. In the shiny stainless-steel pan of the scale, I could see that my moonish and overweight face was red. It hurt to be yelled at. I was a grown man, and I'd been in the meat business for three years, and it hurt.

"What the hell is wrong with that Sandy character out there?" I said to Joe. "Has he got some kind of *problem?*"

"Ahh, don't let him get to you," Joe said. All the skin on Joe's neck hung loose beneath his chin like wattles, and his rheumy eyes looked off into the distance as he spoke. He looked as if he had lost weight very fast.

"What I don't understand is why they would hire a guy like that in the first place."

"*Hire?* What do you mean hire?" Joe was almost smiling. "He's the fuckin' owner! With that guy Marty Cohen. They're partners."

The butchers came chugging through the main cooler, on their way to the locker room for coffee break.

"Hey, Chuckie! How you fokkeen' hero shah today, my friend?" The white coats bustled toward the far door. I could hear their voices as they puffed up the stairs.

". . . fuckin' jerkoffs . . . gonna get lay-*off* . . . fuckin' peanut butter farmer . . . key inna fuckin' door . . ."

It was terrible to think that I had already been spotted as one who was vulnerable to needling. I remembered a documentary I had seen about prisons, in which an inmate explained how important it was for prisoners always to "dogface," to keep a completely blank expression, to stay invisible within themselves. I didn't want to lose this job. I was afraid that Sandy would start to pick on me, like a white leghorn chicken does when it sees a spot of blood on another chicken's feathers. I don't like to be chased out of places, not by angry supervisors, not by Slavic predictions for the future of the Free World.

"Are you planning to *finish* weighing those ribs?" said Chris.

"Barring any complications," I said, "I certainly intend to."

"We don't need no *sarcasm* here!" he said, and I went back to work, my face beginning to tingle again. I was thinking about sarcasm, about my favorite song, "Bricks in the Wall," by Pink Floyd, in which a chorus of angry cockney children rail against dark sarcasm in the "clawss-room." I loved that song, its wounded dignity, the notes of the guitar solo swelling and soaring, sustained and distorted above a wash of angry minor chords. It had been on the radio this morning, in the darkness of the West Side, as I drove through the space beneath where the Henry Hudson Parkway was condemned, past pillars and stanchions and traffic lights and pylons and Day-Glo orange plastic impact attenuators, past the mooring of the *Queen Elizabeth II,* her white superstructures cold and floodlit, her dark bow jutting over the roadway, where chandlers' vans were queued up, revving and honking while yellow-gloved supply officers shouted and waved flashlights, frantic to get the Great Lady reprovisioned and out on time.

The cockney brats chanted that they didn't need "naow ed-u-*kai*-shun!" as I turned onto 42nd Street, where wispy figures were blown like weeds beneath the few movie marquees that were still lit.

There was a day when I saw my parents off on the Queen. I was collecting unemployment insurance. I came into the City and met them at their hotel, the Sheraton Centre, and we rode by taxi to the pier. I was crazy in those days. I used to smash things. It was a beautiful spring day. I watched the ship swing slowly out into the Hudson. Departure had been delayed so that the Queen could wait for slack tide, because the tugboats were on strike. Waiting at the bus terminal for the bus back to Spring Valley, I smashed my sunglasses, and people edged away from me.

Louie the porter was drunk. He dropped a barrel of waste fat from the barrel-jack, and it rolled all the way across the main cooler, spilling scraps of fat onto the floor. Sandy appeared and spoke very quietly, smiling, as the rest of us pretended not to listen.

"Don't bother to pick that up, Louie," Sandy said. "You've been warned before. You don't work here anymore. You'll get your check in the mail."

Later, when I went upstairs for coffee break, Louie was still there, silently cleaning out his locker.

I've always hated watching people clean out their lockers. At Jak-Pak, there had been a helper named Harvey, a small man in his thirties from Harlem, who had been hired under the federal government's "New Beginning" program, in which the government, the union, and the company had together pledged to find jobs for a quota of disadvantaged workers.

Everybody at Jak-Pak liked Harvey. He helped pass the long conveyor belt afternoons with jokes and banter and ghetto stories, like the story of one of his friends who, in attempting anal sex with his girlfriend, could find no suitable lubricant. Later, when coitus was finally achieved, the girl sniffed the air, saying, "What's that smell?" He had lubricated the act with Hellmann's Mayonnaise. From then on his friends would tease him with the story. "YO! Johnny Mayonnaise!" his friends would yell across the street, "Bring out the motherfuckin' Hellmann's!"

There was always something to laugh about; even Harvey's near murder, when the McDonald's he was working in was held up, became a funny story. He always called me "Chuck Berry," and would get me to sing "Memphis" while he sang along in perfect harmony. Then he got laid off. He worked his last week, after the standard one-week layoff notice, in silence.

On Harvey's last day, the foreman sent him home half an hour before the rest of us stopped work. Gently he lifted the red plastic hard hat off Harvey's head, a sort of de-coronation. When the rest of us came downstairs, Harvey was still in the locker room, cleaning out his locker. He was drunk, and he was crying.

"I love you guys," he said, his voice cracking. "I'll never forget you guys." Outside it was a precise September afternoon, so clear we could almost make out the individual windows of the World Trade Center against the blue sky. From the locker-room window I could see Harvey swaying slightly in the sunshine as he walked up Little West 12th Street, toward the A train, back to Harlem.

That was when I first decided to go into the sales department, to see if I could bring in some steady business to protect my friends from these relentless layoffs.

Mr. Packard was impressed with the letter I had written to him. He sent me into the field under the instruction of Carmine, a salesman so fat that his company car, a two-door Buick Regal, had to be specially modified so he could fit behind the steering wheel. He wore brown double-knit suits, and his favorite tie was an iridescent palm tree embroidered on a black velvet background.

In my second week of training, we called on Paradise Gardens, a catering house in the Bay Ridge section of Brooklyn. Carmine kept dozing off in the anteroom as we waited to see Tony Napolitano. All over the textured red velvet walls hung framed wedding pictures, young men in powder-blue tuxedos, timid virgins in white. It seemed as if everybody in the world was Italian.

Tony Napolitano was a young man who seemed to have gained weight so fast that the fat hadn't had time to get up to his face. Most of his face looked normal, but below his chin his neck was a great swollen ruff of flesh, as if he were wearing around his neck one of those foam rubber dougnuts that hemmorhoid sufferers have to sit on.

As I sat there in Tony's office, sandwiched between the two fat men, who talked about meat and weddings and jewelry and credit terms, I began to realize that I was prejudiced against Italians. The office walls were covered with pictures of the Powder-Blue Tuxedo Crowd, young men with amaretto-reddened eyes, a portrait of a young girl so Mediterranean that I knew the photo had been retouched to erase the wispy mustache and downy black sideburns.

The two men waved their arms. I could hear their gold bracelets jingle. As they spoke, their throat-fat seemed to bulge like the resonating air bags of mating prarie chickens; and I knew at last that I was a snob, and that if I stayed in sales I would become Italianized, would start swinging my arms as I talked, that my silk ties would become orlonized strand by strand, and I would end up driving a deodorized two-door Monte Carlo with soft music on the stereo.

The next day I asked to be returned to the cutting line. There at least I had a sort of privacy. I could pull my plastic hard hat down over my eyes and be far away, in Protestant-land, among the green lawns devoid of glazed ceramic ornaments. I could think about the girl I loved, Laurie Partridge of "The Partridge Family," played by Susan Dey, her face so calm and waxlike, her sculptured lips at rest beneath a well-defined philtrum, and I would know that I was the only person in the building, perhaps the only person in the whole 14th Street Market, who knew what a philtrum was.

4

Isis Bars

By my third week at Denny Packing I felt as if I had been there for months, driving in the dark, with the cockney children on the radio railing against dark sarcasm, followed by crisis-bulletins, and Deborah Harry of the group Blondie, her clear throaty voice ringing through the dark above the hammering triplets of the backup band. "Roll me in designer sheets," she sang, with a sort of raunchy absent-mindedness, a passionate insouciance. It would be nice to roll Debbie in designer sheets, her blondness lighting up Halstead patterns on satin.

The first hour was always the hardest. From five to six the order department was a snarling pressure cooker. Chris and Joe would be yelling at each other, Herman and Wilfredo speaking Spanish in ominous low tones, the voices of the butchers whooping and swooping in the cutting room, shouting about the World Situation.

I was having a serious "Over There" problem. Whenever I asked Joe

G where to find something or where to put something, he would always say, "Over there," without pointing in any direction. I couldn't make him understand that there was no such place as Over There.

"Over where?"

"Over *there!*"

The money was good. A fifty-dollar bill accompanied each paycheck. They liked me.

"Learn to manage!" Sandy used to yell. Often I was called out to the loading dock to read off the weights on a pallet of boxed beef that had just come in while Sandy checked off the list of box weights on his clipboard. His eyes were so fast that he never had to ask me to stop while he found a particular weight on the list.

The first time he had me read off weights, a Monfort tractor-trailer was unloading in the middle of 13th Street. The forklift tottered across the cobblestones, carrying the pallets of boneless shells of beef from the tail of the trailer to the edge of the shipping platform. Horns raged. Drivers stuck behind the trailer were leaning out their windows and shouting and shaking their fists. Sandy yelled at the howling horns. He jumped around and waved his arms. He yelled at the traffic, he yelled at Freddie on the forklift, he yelled at his partner Marty, he yelled at a pigeon that flew into the open space of the loading area.

"Read 'em off!" he told me.

"Seventy-eight point four . . . seventy-eight even . . . eighty-one point one . . . seventy-six point five."

"Don't read the decimal points!" he said. "Just read the numbers!"

"Okay. Eighty-one, six . . . eighty-one, three . . . seventy-six, nine . . . eighty, four—that's eight-oh point four . . ."

"You read the decimal point! I *told* you, we don't have *time* to fart around with the decimal point!"

"Yeah, but that number could be ambiguous. I didn't want you to be confused."

"Do I look confused?"

"No."

"*You're* the one that's confused!"

"So how should I read that number so it's clear?"

"Don't ask!" he shouted. "*Learn!* Learn to *MANAGE!*"

Sandy used the word *manage* in a way I wasn't familiar with. I always thought that managing had to do with theories and formulas, such as those presented in the seminars offered by the American Management Association, whose catalogue had been sent to me because I once filled out a card from a display in Penn Station. The association listed hundreds of courses, with titles like "Flexible Negotiation Strategies," and "Delegating Responsibility: The Challenge of Trust." I used to read that catalogue in the evenings when it was too late to make phone calls looking for unskilled jobs.

But now I saw that it was all nonsense anyway, that the MBAs who wrote those courses had never dealt with a cash-flow crisis or sweated out a recession while companies died all around them. That Denny Packing was an angry little establishment, that Sandy was a nasty little man; none of that was important anymore. This was the most stable company in the market.

"Nobody ever get lay-off here," Al told me one day, after he had finished describing the things that were going to happen to my hero, the shah of Iran. "Most people have your job in the cooler he chase away the first day, or they get mad and shout in his face he's a stupid Jew bastard. You stay here thirty days and you got a safe job."

I thought about my last day at Jak-Pak, when fifty people got let go at the same time, and how nice all the supervisors were as they shook my hand and wished me good luck. I thought about all the kind and gentle and bankrupt owners putting the key in the door for the last time. The market was littered with abandoned meat companies, some boarded up, some converted into gay bars. I liked my job.

It was really just a matter of taking a step backward when things got too crazy, a matter of not taking things personally. At Christmas at my aunt's house in Baltimore, my cousin Charlie, on leave from the marine base at Parris Island, told me about the moment in which he realized that the drill sergeant who was browbeating him was just playing a game, and the only important thing was to play the game with gusto.

At Carrol and Cantwell, a small lamb and veal distributor where I was often sent with a handtruck to pick up breasts of lamb, I learned, almost by heart, the elaborate economic scenario that the father-and-son team who managed the place loved to talk about.

"Credit," said the old man to me the first time I was sent there. "Fucking credit's gonna kill this business."

"How so?"

"You don't *know?*" The son was at the back of the cooler getting the boxes of lamb breasts. They looked alike, both with scraggly unwashed hair and drooping mustaches, the father's white, the son's black, both with baggy exhausted eyes and loud, hollow, whinnying voices. "You mean you haven't heard about the *credit crunch?*"

"I've heard of *Captain* Crunch."

"Comes a time when the big companies are gonna refuse credit to their customers, and those customers are gonna refuse credit to their customers, all the way down the line, and the whole fucking meat line gonna fall down like a freakin' house of cards!"

Something must have set them off that morning in the dark as they drove to work from the Bronx, some bulletin on All-News Radio 88.

"You wait and see what this fucking street gonna look like in six months, with the union predicting sixty percent unemployment by the end of the year," said the son as he piled the two boxes on my handtruck.

I had almost forgotten to bring the handtruck with me when I left Denny Packing. "Handtruck!" Sandy yelled into my face, "*HANDTRUCK!*"

"I hope you got some money in the bank," said the son "'cause your job ain't gonna be worth shit. It's gonna be a fucking *wasteland!*"

There was probably some grain of truth in what they were saying. An aide to President Carter had warned of a major economic catastrophe, much worse than the Great Depression of the thirties, and had cautioned all Americans to stockpile at least a year's supply of canned food.

"You could be right," I said.

"*Could* be right?" roared the father, coughing up menthol. "You better fucking believe he *is* right! This street's gonna be a wasteland! Gonna be *unreal!*"

They were in love with the word *wasteland,* even though I knew without asking that they had never heard of T. S. Eliot.

"So you better read the writing on the wall," said the son. "It's gonna be unreal."

"Well, I appreciate the information," I said. "I'll have to see what my broker says about all this. You see, my broker is E .F. Hutton, and—"

"Gonna be a *wasteland,* my friend, gonna be *unreal,* and I just hope you're freakin' prepared!"

Then I was out in the street again, hurrying back to Denny Packing. From the doors of meat companies, the cigarette-wounded larynxes of overweight men shouted utterances such as, "We gotta hurry the fuck up and get these fuckin' boxes on that fuckin' truck or we're all gonna be fucked!" The language of 14th Street is so dependent on the all-purpose word *fucking* that it can't really be called English; rather a separate dialect best referred to as "Fuckinese."

The words of the father-and-son team still rang in my ears, and for a moment I was afraid, of panicked stockbrokers, of chanting voices and refineries in flames; and I knew that everybody needs a little nest egg, knew at last that Campbell's in the cupboard is like money in the bank, while far away across the desert, the Crisis is moving its slow thighs, closer and closer to the gridlocked streets of the market, where all around reel shadows of indignant pigeons. White coats went bustling everywhere, under the brown fog of dawn. Unreal city, the S & M gay bars closing, discharging the market's other population, lanky black figures moving among the butchers on coffee break. The two populations move among each other without seeming to take up extra space, like ghosts among mortals, or vice versa. They hate each other, of course, but any razzing or insulting would be out of the question.

It was strange to be a part of nothing, to see both populations of the market simultaneously by virtue of being part of neither, by virtue of living among my own private loves, in the purity of television. My favorite show was now the "Isis Adventure Hour," featuring Joanna Cameron as Isis, spectacular in her sun-goddess outfit, across her forehead the amulet that she carried in her mundane identity as Miss Greenwood, young high-school science teacher and counselor to troubled students; until there would come a crisis—school on fire, school bus over cliff—and she would hold the amulet between her breasts, and a bolt of lightning would transform her into Isis, demure in a sort of heiroglyph-embroidered Cheopian tennis dress, thong-calfed, bejeweled, glossed lips and black hair shining; and trapped students would be saved, amid the flashing of serpentine bracelets and the cascading of hair. Isis! Finest of all my television loves, lovelier than Laurie Partridge, more chaste than Mousketeer Lisa, more sensual than Pepper of "Clue Club."

And it was all mine, immune to Crisis, luxuriously private, and I trundled my handtruck through a sunrise in which there was nothing to discuss with anybody else, nothing to congregate around, a world devoid of Laurie Partridge social clubs, a land whose cocktail lounges are blind to the transcendent eroticism of Isis.

I'm not complaining, although there were times I wished I had a wife and a normal life. There were times when being above everything got tiresome, but there were just as many times when it didn't. In my heart I was a snob, and a moderate Republican, and an atheist, and the world's worst bridge player, let it be known, and a cook and a captain bold, and I can judge a good man by the pattern on his tie, and my shoes were a personal gift from the Shah of Iran, and I have made death-threat phone calls, gone without eating, without sleeping, have known the secret of ex-nihilation on a scratchy stereo, have raided

Safeway dumpsters out of love, have looked at clouds from above and from below, have seen both ends of the blue and secret dawn, and the lights of Albuquerque, and the Commodore Hotel, and it was all beautiful, roads that shimmered with fatigue, a roomful of telepathic eyes.

The voices rang out up and down 14th Street, in Fuckinese, pressured, constricted, like the voice of Mr. Pressburger at Passaic Wholesale Meats, where I had lasted only a week, trying frantically to bone out fresh hams, while behind the office window I could see Mr. Pressburger on the phone, his rapid stressed syllables ringing off the glass.

"Ya-da-da-da-da-da-*DA!*" he shouted into the receiver, his face blazing red beneath an old fashioned snap-brim cap.

As I pushed my handtruck through the streets, back to Denny Packing, I thought about the time Mr. Pressburger had called me into the storage cooler to help him move some meat. When I pushed some hanging rounds onto the wrong rail, he became furious.

"I tell you other side!" he said. "*This!*" His English was so poor that I couldn't make him understand that I didn't understand. I pushed a tree-hook full of ribs in the direction he had waved his arms.

"*NOOOOOOOOOOO!*" he roared. "You not *listen?*" His face was so red that I thought he would have a stroke on the spot, and that it would be my fault, despite the fact that he was seventy-five years old and had never taken a vacation in his life because he didn't trust anybody enough to be able to delegate responsibility. How can one delegate responsibility if one doesn't know what the word *delegate* means?

I took things personally in those days. My meat career in those days was like a ship on war alert, everything burning, with desire, with correct attitudes, with dreams, with financial arithmetic, which itself was burning, a wheel of fire, faces burning with hypertension, sermons of fire, the torchlight red on sweaty faces, and I made a mistake with a leg of lamb, and Mr. Pressburger was mad again, and he plucked me out from my cutting table and fired me, and I drove home with my face burning.

And now Sandy's watch was burning, evidently, as he fanned it and pointed to it, jumping up and down in his little glassed-in office where clerks scurried among a hurricane of invoices. He bounded out onto the loading dock.

"What the fuck *happened* to you?"

"Those guys at Carrol and Cantwell seem to have some inside track on the economy, and they spent a lot of time giving me financial advice."

"Oh, those monkeys! They're always like that. Ignore 'em!"

"I'd like to ignore them, but I really do need advice on managing my investment—"

"We do things with a little *speed* around here."

". . . portfolio."

5

Blood Wine

We were busy, rain came down in bright steaming sheets, Denny Packing rang with sound. Butchers' voices rang off the walls of the cutting room. Every morning the three-tiered steel cart came squeaking through the door, loaded with the early cutting orders wrapped in peach paper and tied with white cotton butchers' twine.

The hall outside the locker room was piled with black umbrellas, drying out in a stiff-spined heap, like dead birds. Above the skylight in the locker room, spring was a quality of light, a new adjustment for diesel injectors, a young and hanging, wet, half-burned petroleum vapor that blended with the river smell, a breeze in from Hoboken, a churning of soupy mud molecules, full of richness and dirt and life and disease, breathing its complexity into the Lower Manhattan meat district, from which the Hudson, now a rain-dulled battleship gray, was visible beween the blond brick Marine Sanitation Terminal and the patchwork corrugation of an abandoned pier.

The air was rich with smells, sweet and bitter and sour, smells frozen for months, the sweet breath of fried onions in the steam tray of the Sabrett hot dog wagon that stood most days at the corner of Washington and 13th, run by a twelve-year-old boy.

"Freakin' social workers wanna put me out of business," I heard the boy say one day as he dabbed the mustard brush onto an old man's hot dog. "And here I am supporting my mother, but the freakin' city wants me in school five days a week so I can learn what the fuck is two and two; as if I didn't learn no arithmetic from this cash drawer! But they'd rather see me in school and my mother on the welfare."

Between Ninth Avenue and Twelfth, 14th Street runs one way, west toward the river. All along that wide thoroughfare, lined on both sides by ancient meat companies, the trucks park diagonally, angled like the fletching of an arrow pointing west. Steel awnings, held by steel cables, hang over the sidewalk, allowing trucks to be loaded and unloaded in the rain.

On the south side of 14th Street, in front of a pork-processing house called Charles White Provisions, the head of a large hog is mounted on a wooden plaque, above the words THIS IS NOT CHARLES. It's a jolly hog face, easygoing and slaphappy. I always enjoyed walking past it, smiling back into its intelligent eyes, while all around the horns howled and tired and angry men shouted in Fuckinese from the doors of tired and angry meat companies. But the hog face, which is not Charles, just grins, ears perked up, cheerful, not even caring that he's dead.

In the meat district in the spring, when the ground turns warm, a peculiar odor sometimes comes lifting up from between the cracks in the concrete, beneath which the earth is all porous with forgotten passages and cable lines and abandoned gas conduits; something rich and round-edged and fruity, a bubbling warm floral flatulence breathing up from the tunnels and catacombs underground; a sweet and fulsome yeastiness, as if somebody were operating an illegal underground winery; or perhaps the excess blood from a dozen meat packing companies was running down and collecting in a great natural pool, as in a limestone cave, where yeast was processing the glucose into alcohol and CO_2, a sort of transubstantiation in reverse.

When it rains in New York, something happens to the colors. They gather into points of greatest concentration, leaving all else washed-out and gray. The pastel colors of cars are lost, all their intensity transferred to the paint of taxis, so that all traffic is a rain-dulled monochrome, except for the taxis, which blaze up and down the avenues in a hard yellow light. All the muted tones of a ten-story apartment building will be gathered into a poster in a drugstore window, concentrated in the lips and eyes of an aging Catherine Deneuve; and a girl, returning home in a lime-green plastic wind-breaker, may find all the colors of a street of brownstones, and all the infant green of a tree's first budding, concentrated upon the green of her coat. When it rains in New York, the pavement shines through a glaze, and tires go hissing through a world of dust and water, in the cruelest month, when the voices of woman crisis-announcers are soft as milk in the dark morning, reporting more executions, which will be duly noted in the debates of butchers waiting to start work, white-coated arms gesticulating in the locker-room air, the glowing tips of cigarettes forming French loops and figure eights in their lingering brightness.

There are some people whom the rain makes happy, and there is a theory about negative and positive ions in the synapses, an electrochemical explanation for the wild looming excitement that children feel just before the lightning starts. There are some people whom the rain makes angry, old men who have forgotten their umbrellas, old men with lopsided black loafers, men with white hair stained from cigarette smoke into a kind of yellow that, like the yellow of taxis, gains intensity on a rainy day. Such men invariably spend their entire lives in the meat business.

It was strange to listen to old men being angry when I was not angry myself. As Harry, a wiry little truck driver in his sixties, told me about how much he hated the food and beverage manager at Charlie

O's in the World Trade Center, I pretended to be interested, but actually I was far away, thinking about the key moments that had defined my own personal relationship to rain, thinking about the colors of popcorn in the rain, about Woolworth's in downtown Stratford, Connecticut, when I was six years old, the cheese flavored kernels bright against the corner of the glass popcorn bin at the front of the store outside of which plump domestics waited under the overhang for the local bus and stared into the color-drained traffic through a bright curtain of rain. Black umbrellas crowded along, their blunted rib-ends rustling against one another. A newsstand flashed with comic books.

"Freakin' asshole has to weigh every fuckin' piece of meat I carry in there," Harry was saying. "And I got to wait for fifteen minutes while he's looking for one ounce too much on the invoice!" Blue veins bulged among the sunken muscles of his pale arms, and I knew without asking that he was from the Bronx. I was thinking about the amber light, about the blazing intestines of neon tetras in the Woolworth's pet department, about the woody smell of hickory shavings in the birdcages, where green and orange parakeets fluttered and screeched.

"It's a fucking *joke!*" he said. "And you think he'd send some kitchen helper to help me carry those boxes down the stairs, right?"

"It would be nice if he did."

"Well, he *don't!*" He pulled his belt tight with great jerks and lurches. I could smell the rain, a touch of ozone, like the smell of the rain from inside Woolworth's, the wet wool of carcoats, the damp stretched fabric of the piled umbrellas. I could smell just a touch of the round-edged sulfur smell of the cutting room, a smell with a slight sharpness to it, a thin, limey sourness. Most people think the meat business smells bad, but it really doesn't. It's complicated, and it changes with the seasons, and it's sharp and exciting and full of work and anger and effort. Some women who work in the meat business are afraid of the way they think it might smell; and they cover themselves with perfume so heavy that it lingers on the street long after they have gone home to the Bronx.

"And then you should see that fuckin' walk-in they make me put the meat in. Poo-hoo-*HOOF!* Fuckin' rat wouldn't eat off that floor. And the smell in there enough to gag a maggot!"

Rain surged against the wired glass of the skylight, lightning flashed, and I was happy, for no reason but the congealed light and the negative ions. I wanted to buy a giant black umbrella and walk, singing in the rain, leaning into the slanting drops, among a crowd of windblown figures surging up the sidewalk, hard against the downtown flow of traffic marshaled by progressive lights, the avenue blazing with taxis. Harry slammed his locker shut and hurried out the door, all elbows and angles, skin mottled with liver spots; and I was alone with the rain and the light, among the sad old shoes, gnarled and gouty, among the lockers full of wet wool jackets, cigarette butts pointing in all directions on the floor.

As I weighed primal ribs and hung them on a tree-hook according to their weight range, I was thinking about age and anger, the way serious thought runs tight and purple around aged lips. My cousin Charlie in the marines referred to such people as "whiteheads," and as I drove him to the Philadelphia airport on my way home, we had laughed at how many of them there were in the cars around us, and how sad and frightened their little faces were. I knew it wasn't nice, but it was fun to be prejudiced against them.

There was a time that I almost ran an old man over with my car. I was driving home from the unemployment office, listening to All-News Radio 88, where they were interviewing the president of the Iranian Students' Organization of Columbia University. When I heard the joy rolling in his Moslem throat, and his precise, surgical diction, I felt the left side of my scalp tingling with rage; and at that moment I saw an old black man walking by the side of Route 304 with a bag of groceries. I swerved toward him and he scrambled in panic, dropping his shopping bag. In my rearview mirror I could see him stooped over, picking up the groceries. He looked like Uncle Remus.

I was ashamed. To think that overseas crises could cause a young man on unemployment to terrorize an old man on food stamps. As I drove the rest of the way home, I tried to keep telling myself that I had nothing against anybody, that I had no ax to grind—yet I couldn't seem to stop grinding it, any more than I could stop grinding the car's gears as I rattled up Parrot Hill Road, home to an afternoon of cutting little chits of print out of the Help Wanted section and Scotch-taping them together on a piece of paper. I've seen the faces of houses in my neighborhood all toothless and humiliated with the Crisis, have seen people shoveling snow who refuse to look me in the eye. I've seen in the post office President Carter's face, careworn, frightened, etched with rivulets of failure.

As I was weighing the ribs, I cut my hand on the edge of a bone. Joe G helped me clean and iodine the wound. I went back to work, and it seemed to be all right, although as I drove home my hand began to throb.

The next day it was worse. My hand was red and swollen, and I felt feverish. I called in sick. After I had cleaned and treated the wound again, I couldn't get back to sleep, so I watched television in the morning darkness. It was too early even for cartoons. The only thing on besides news bulletins was a public service program called "Senior Health Update." Today's show was about senior citizens who have trouble moving their bowels.

I was laughing, though it made my head throb. Whitehead B.M. troubles! Such things are not supposed to be funny. I took my temperature, and it was 102 degrees. I remembered that night's dream, a fever dream, a dozen little old men scrabbling around in the Woolworth's popcorn bin, their faces convulsed with rage. Something was wrong with my right knee. It was swelling up like my hand.   All my hair follicles were sensitized, my chest was congested, my knee ached. When I heard the little voices who phoned into the health program, it made me laugh, and laughing made me cough. I was thinking about fresh oranges, about a world without whiteheads, about prostitutes, smiling prostitutes in front of the all-night greengrocer's stand behind the Port Authority bus terminal, how sharp and parakeet-green the kale and spinach glowed beneath the arc-lights.

I like prostitutes. An old guy named Red, who was the butcher foreman at Denny Packing, had told me about a Japanese prostitute he used to visit. She was studying diagnostic radiology. I would have liked to meet her. I, who know a few words of six languages, would have said, "*Anata wa watakushi no onna no ko desu ka?*" which means, "Are you my girl?" and she would have answered, "*Hai!*"

And then I was thinking about whiteheads again, about senior citizens, side-wheelers, crutch-monkeys, about how much fun it was to be prejudiced against them, as long as I never did anything about it. It hadn't been fun to remember knocking the dentures out of the Polish Freedom Fighter's mouth, or to make an old man who looked like Uncle Remus drop his groceries. Still, it was amusing to think of those tight white coifs in the back of sedans, being taken out for Sunday dinner from Bader's Retirement Community at the other end of Cresent Drive Spelled Wrong, being ambulanced around, prim as poodles, on a suburban Sunday to quaint gingham-wallpapered restaurants where the air is filled with perfumes so strong that one can't taste the boiled carrots.

Infinitely timid, with nothing to live for but the fear of losing what few days they have left, they have visited their decrepitude upon themselves, trundled their accents from neighborhood to neighborhood, and neighborhoods have passed from accent to accent in a heirarchy of sugared urine, until even the rats complain. And there are loads of airmailed garbage that have not yet reached the ground. I'm talking about the Bronx. Everybody's from the Bronx.

Being sick is a luxury, even though it's something my family has always disapproved of. My father, in eighteen years at Prudential, never missed a day of work, except for the morning between Oradell and River Edge when a vandal's rock smashed through the train window and hit him in the side of the head. My mother hated it when I stayed home from school. Bacteria were for the sort of people who blew their noses all the time and talked about it, people who kept a blue-and-white box of Kleenex, which they called "tissues," on the rear window ledge of their sedans.

I turned on Channel 9 and watched the 6 A.M. sign-on film. The battleship New Jersey's nine-inchers lit the night sea. A Polaris missle breached in a spray of white from blue water. A radio-controlled Scorpion fighter plane, caught by a heat-seeker, burst into flames; and then, Felix the Cat.

Between cartoons, there was a commercial for Coco-Puffs, in which Sonny the Cuckoo Bird was locked in a phone booth to keep from going cuckoo for Coco-Puffs; and I remembered the night that the girl who had developed that series of commercials had ridden with her two associates in my taxi. That was long ago, years and layoffs and hirings and firings and walks in the woods ago.

I seemed to be getting worse. The swollen slit on the heel of my hand made me think of a young girl's vulva, clean and modest, with the inner lips hidden politely inside the outer, completely different from the fold-out poster that Red, the butcher foreman, kept on the inside of his locker door. This was a pimply-faced, drugged-looking girl with her mouth hanging open and her legs spread wide to show a most unusual set of pudenda: the labia minora splayed out, extending way over the edges of the labia majora. It was a strange picture. It looked surgical somehow, as if a piece of freshly sliced liver had been sutured between the young girl's legs, a brown and red butterfly of moist tissue.

When I thought about girls, I preferred to think of the curve of a tight-clad leg, softly kohled eyes, the glossed lips and shining black hair of Isis when she would hold the amulet between her breasts and lightning would flash and wind would blow her soft hair like seaweed in the surges. My fever was up to 103 degrees.

As I was walking back from the bathroom with a glass of water in my hand, everything started to get all paisley-red. I woke up on the floor. In one hand I was holding a half-spilled glass of water. In the

45

other I was holding the needle-arm from my stereo, which I had evidently grabbed at as I fell. The rest of the turntable lay upside down on the carpet. I called the Pascack Valley Community Hospital, which was a mile from my apartment, and told them how sick I was. They told me to come right in to the emergency room.

It was strange to drive with a 103-degree fever. I kept thinking I was going backward. It was a beautiful day, full of willow branches waving in the wind like the hair of a young girl in the animated Clairol Shampoo commercials.

I lay in my clean underpants on a hard, paper-covered bed. It was nice to let go, to be helpless and insured, ministered to by kindly nurses. The doctor, a young Pakistani with a soft musical voice, palpated my neck and my hand and my knee, auscultated my chest, and shined lights into my eyes.

"You're a sick man," the doctor said. "I'm veddy glad you have come to us." He said I had blood poisoning, and that the bacteria from the cut had made my knee septic. The hand and knee would both need to be opened up immediately. I signed the consent form in a left-handed scribble, and told the nurse that she could find my union medical card in my wallet.

"Tell me, Doctor," I said, remembering the question I'd wanted to ask for years, "Will I be able to play the piano after this is healed?"

"Oh, yes yes," he said. "Surely you will."

"Hey, that's great! I never could play it before."

"Most funny," he said. "*Most* funny!" and put the funnel over my face.

I woke up in the recovery room, surrounded by silent white asleep shapes, like beached whales, my hand in a gauze mitten and my knee in a white muff. I was wheeled through the white halls. It was night, a soft evening buzz of activity, like the streets of an indoor city, with stainless-steel carts of linen and hot food passing one another on the main thoroughfares. A clear plastic bag of yellow liquid connected to a needle in my arm swung gently with the motion of the rolling bed. I was wheeled into a room with two other men, both of whom had visitors. A nurse gave me a needle, and everything was warm and bright, and the soft voices of my roommates' visitors drifted away like a boat out to sea in a gentle breeze.

Then it was morning. The windows were a wash of cold light. A woman in white gave me a glass of water with a flexible straw and changed my glucose bottle. She gave me a blue plastic thunder mug that looked just like a Howard Johnson's coffee pitcher. All day I drifted in and out of sleep. In the evening a young girl came around with a form to fill out if I wanted to rent a television set. She wheeled the set in and showed me how to use the remote control. I fell asleep in the middle of "Name That Tune."

In a hospital, as on a long-distance bus, time takes on a different shape, a drifting weary mildness, neither fast nor slow, because there are no clocks but the light and the meals and the comings and goings of white uniforms.

In the middle of the day, after the bells and buzzers of the game shows have gone silent, the day sinks into a lull, and time is padded and packed with cotton and air and milk, like the light of hospital windows when the sun has gone behind clouds. At last I understood the slow pace of the afternoon soap operas, how they drifted within the rhythm of weekday afternoons. Nothing ever happened. Doctors' wives, beautifully dressed and elegantly coiffed, poured coffee or sherry, and talked, for clockless hours, about people I didn't know, with only the change of shows and the appearance of new, equally elegant faces, to show that time was passing at all.

I was feeling much better. A nurse's aide brought me my first solid meal of soft-boiled eggs and limp toast. My doctor, Dr. Feinerman, told me I'd be out of the hospital in a few days, although I would be on crutches for at least two weeks. Nurses came and went in the changing light of clouds outside the window. The nicest nurse was named Miss Clifford. Although she was fat, she was very pretty, with blond hair and soft, cleanly outlined eyes.

I like nurses, their kind hands and strong, sensible shoes. I used to be in love with Kate Jackson, in her first major role as the beautiful Nurse Danko on "The Rookies." Whenever anybody in the show ended up in a hospital, anywhere in the city, it was always Nurse Danko's hospital, and Nurse Danko was *always* there.

As Miss Clifford daubed the purple disinfectant on the incision in my knee, she started asking me about the meat business. She seemed genuinely interested, even though she was a vegetarian herself, "except for the odd carnivorous episode," she said. Her first name was Jill, just like Nurse Danko. She lived with a roommate, another nurse, in the Cameo Gardens apartment complex.

I like garden apartments. I like to think about nurses coming home at all hours on a warm spring night, all their little Toyotas, their starched whites, their clean, nursely kitchens. As she reclosed my knee bandage, she told me how much she was looking forward to her upcoming vacation.

"My parents have a house on Block Island," she said, dabbing with an alcohol swab the spot where the intravenous needle had been. "And they're not going to be there. I'll have the place all to myself for a whole week. It's going to be great." I told her about the house my family used to rent on Martha's Vineyard for two weeks every summer, and about how much I missed it, now that I was a blue-collar worker.

The next morning Nurse Clifford told me that the nurse's aides had gone on strike. Just after "Huckleberry Hound," she wheeled the sponge-bath wagon in and pulled the privacy curtain shut. This was a job usually done by nurse's aides. My skin tingled at such good fortune, to be bathed by my favorite nurse. I had been sure they would send some tough old broad. However, it was essential that I remain a gentleman.

I remembered the last time a girl had given me a sponge bath. It was under rather different circumstances. It had been mandatory at the beginning of a massage session in the Venus Leisure Spa on 42nd Street. I was celebrating the raise that Sandy had given me. My hostess was having a fight with the girl in the next cubicle. They were throwing things back and forth over the partition.

"Listen, *bitch*," she shouted, her hand taking over the task from her mouth. "You get the fuck outa' my *face!*" Later, just as I was about to bring the session to its conclusion, a wet towel landed on my back.

With Jill, my objective now was the opposite of what it had been with my hostess of that night. It was imperative that I spare her the embarrassment of having to use the spoon. I could feel the cool water running from her sponge. I had to think about something other than the girl who was soaping my stomach.

I decided that I must think about playing tennis, about the long rhythm of a backcourt game on red clay, among the weathered gray shingles of the Vineyard Yacht Club where we used to play, although we had no yacht. I needed to think about that sound, the long lost and classic summer sound, the *fwopp!* of a ball hit solidly with a wooden racket, on a court surrounded by green canvas screening with little half-moon shaped wind baffles, a sound within range of which people will be drinking gin and tonic at the club's outdoor lounge; and when the wind is right, the people on the courts—where the dress code specifies white only—can smell the lime and juniper on the soft air and hear the clinking of glasses. I've always loved the laminated-wood note of a well-hit ground stroke, as different from the cheap Taiwanese *punnngg!* of a steel racket as the Vineyard or Block Island is from 42nd Street.

On the Vineyard, as on Block Island, nobody yells "*YO!*" across the cobbles of Main Street, where bicycles are walked through the wiggling shadows of oak leaves, where bright red and green Izod shirts move in and out of the light, where the open doors of gift shops give forth the fragrance of expensive blue and yellow soaps wrapped in porous paper. On Sunday everybody lines up outside the Island Stationery Store, waiting for the *New York Times,* which arrives at the airport in its own special plane, chartered jointly by the island's four newspaper vendors. Nobody reads the *New York Post.* The last time I'd been to the Vineyard, some years ago, there was a man on the plane reading the *Post,* whose headline that day read HOLIDAY TERROR BLASTS FEARED. I wanted to tell that man that such a paper didn't belong on our island, that it would poison the air, and ladies on bicycles will yell at one another, fighting for the right of way outside the Island Dairy Bar, and people's voices will get all sharp and constricted. People will yell *"SHUT UP!"* and other people will yell *"SHUT UP!"* back at them.

Let it be known that I succeeded with Jill, in the same way that I succeeded with my leisure spa hostess, though at the earlier episode the identical response, by the cruelty of a mood-destroying towel, had been counted failure; let it be known that, undressed in the company of a beautiful nurse who knew the rolling moors and gray shingles of a similar island, islands whose tennis courts would in a few months be filled with my Hotchkiss classmates, that despite the Isis-like shine of her hair and her kind hands and her face with the same silkiness as Nurse Danko, despite the angel white of her uniform and her soft isopropyl fragrance and the clean lines of her eyes; let it be known that I remained a gentleman and an intellectual and a professional and a Protestant, late of Hotchkiss '69, ex Quinnipiac '72, visitor by Volkswagen to all forty-eight contiguous states, spiritual adventurer, moderate Republican, watcher of the moon, lover of the light of the sun on the sea of a Vineyard morning, how it glares and sparks, and all it promises, another perfect day in a perfect land of weathered wood and combed cotton, and sun and wind and sand and wild bright water.

6

___

Hexagon Perspective

Nobody had ever called me a *New Yorker* sort of person before. That's what Jill said when she brought me the latest issue. It is my favorite magazine, although I never read it. Just seeing it on the newsstand between the martial arts magazines and the hot rod magazines, the cover a clear and sensible watercolor of a clear and sensible suburban afternoon of Audis and antiques, has always reawakened my faith in my own future. I have known lost souls in the meat business with their faces buried so deeply into the *New York Post* that they forget that the Dreyfuss Fund even exists.

On adjustable crutches I went maneuvering around the empty room, in the hard light of the windows. Both my roommates were gone. When my knee started to throb, I got back in bed and flipped through the pages of Samsonite attaché cases, Mercedes, Lancia, Shearson Loeb Rhodes Financial Services. I skipped the "Talk of the Town" because I knew what it would be: a soft and erudite observation of the hopelessness of the World Situation. That's the one part of *The New Yorker* I can't get serious about, because beautiful merchandise is beautiful merchandise whether or not one spends a few paragraphs feeling guilty about it; yet for some, even those paragraphs are not enough. I have known people who refuse to read *The New Yorker* because they are offended by the luxury of such advertisements in a world where moral issues rise with the sun each day and shine in monochrome down over summer cottages.

It's hard to get serious about such things. There will always be a World Situation. And as we grip the textured padding of Volvo ignition keys, we will always have the luxury of reminding ourselves of those who have no cars, no shoes, no feet. I've known neighbors who fasted for Christmas at our house, sitting pure and correct at our table, out of duty. With Duty comes Meaning, and with Meaning comes Truth, and with Truth comes Duty.

All my life I've had a problem with the word *duty*. It always sounds to me as if it should be spelled "doody."

Let's all get serious. Let's get so serious that a pall falls upon the zoysia, a curse upon the milled handles of lawn rakes.

I remember a game I saw at Yankee Stadium, a twelve-inning thriller of a hot night with moths fluttering in the floodlights. At midnight we thronged in victory down the steel corridors, to the exit arches, and our feet were all marching in unison, and we were chanting, "YAN-*KEES!* YAN-*KEES!* YAN-*KEES!*" Outside in the night some boys were burning a Red Sox banner, and the flames lit their faces; and I knew at last what the Truth was all about, that the cadence of the chant is the thing itself and the words can be filled in later, that burning moral issues burn chiefly in the soles of the feet, in the ecstasy of dog-voices in the night.

When Jill came back again I thanked her for the magazine and told her how much I loved that issue's cover illustration. It was a picture of the hexagon-tiled sidewalk surrounding the Museum of Natural History, painted from a vantage point close to the ground, the fitting-together of hexagons forming primary rows of perspective, and secondary rows, and tertiary, as when you look out a train window in a cornfield.

"I love that neighborhood," she said. "I lived on West Eighty-first street for five years until I moved up here." Jill was fat, but not with the sad fatness of some nurses, who become puffy-armed and hard-faced. I saw that Jill could carry her weight as if it weighed nothing, graceful and loose-limbed, in an easy-going Gloria Vanderbilt sort of way.

"Why'd you leave the city?" I asked her.

"Zabar's," she said. "I had some serious Zabar's issues, and a major Häagen-Dazs problem." She smiled and looked up at the white ceiling, and I could see the pure whiteness of her eyes, set against blue irises. There was something secret and vulnerable and un-nurselike in her smile.

"There are some people," she said, "who must not allow themselves to live within walking distance of Zabar's. Those were crazy days. It was like being in a war. When I walked to Broadway I had Zabar's on my right and Häagen-Dazs on my left, and Pastry King on the opposite corner. It was ridiculous. Sometimes I'd go into Zabar's and end up spending fifty dollars on things like hickory-smoked chicken livers and dilled crabmeat. And Häagen-Dazs was open twenty-four hours a day. I used to have dreams about 'I.C.'—ice cream, that is—and I'd wake up and get dressed at three o'clock in the morning and call a taxi, hating my own guts the whole time."

"Do you like living up here?" I said.

"It's nice, but I do miss the West Side. I love to go down to the museums whenever I can. If I could just hire somebody to follow me around and keep me out of Zabar's, I'd move back in a minute. There's not much to do up here. I'm in the Lakeview Tennis Club, but I'm not very good."

I told her that we'd have to get together and play sometime, and then she left, still carrying her large shape and her immaculate uniform with grace and lightness. It would be nice to play tennis with her, a sheen of perspiration on her slightly flushed skin, in the indoor courts of Lakeview Tennis Club, where there was no lake and no view, just a big metal building in which all the sounds were muffled by curtains and carpet, where a soft bell, like the paging bell in Bloomingdale's, announces the end of each reservation period.

I knew it was crazy to let myself become attached to my nurse. I suppose they get used to it. I suppose they can quell an invalid's crush as quickly as with the spoon, as gently as they change an I.V. Still she was a special person. Perhaps if I had a better job, perhaps if I joined the tennis club myself, if I became a frozen-food salesman with a company car; perhaps I could make myself worthy of her, and we could read *The New Yorker* together and play mixed doubles with other overweight couples. Perhaps I could be the bodyguard she had spoken of, to follow her around the West Side and stop her when she tried to go into ice-cream shops, to hold her large body in my arms and protect her from the spiced and vinegared air that breathes out of Zabar's from a special fan that exhausts onto Broadway.

Let's be the right sort of people. Let's have good jobs and good shoes, and let's not take everything as seriously as everybody else does. Let's wear long and expensive coats on a gray winter day in the great gray city.

Let's have a light lunch. Let's be rich. Let's join the snobbiest, snootiest, WASPiest, most exclusive tennis club we can cajole and name-drop our way into, a club that doesn't have a golf course. Golf is a game one plays in beltless plaid polyester slacks, while smoking cigarettes. I do not own a pair of plaid polyester slacks, belted or beltless, and I do not smoke cigarettes.

Let's flag down a taxi, on a cold New York afternoon of bright scarves, the sidewalks all crowded, puffs of steam rising from everybody's mouth. Let's have it be the Christmas season, all the windows bright with gifts, chestnuts roasting in a vendor's cart. Let us hear *Messiah* at Lincoln Center; and when the fierce organ pipes announce the Hallelujah Chorus and everybody stands up in a rumbling mass, you shall hold my arm, and together we might sway slightly in the roaring of pipes and voices, and we can think of all Christendom before us who have stood up at this same moment, and of the King, whichever King he was, who first stood up, the tradition we are part of, world without end, and a roar of applause so loud that our hands will tingle for hours. Let's shout *Bravo!*

It will be dark outside. We can take another taxi, I can afford it. We'll ride to Rockefeller Center, where the Season lives, the epicenter out from which the quality called Christmas radiates, where the tree stands like a vertical city of light above the skating rink. We can tell the rouged and cheap-bearded Hindu Santa Clauses soliciting funds for the Hare Krishna Community Center to get lost. We can stand above the rink and watch the skaters going round and round on the scuffed whiteness of the ice. We can look up at the tree, and at the landings and terraces below it, where every year in a videotaped holiday greeting, Chuck Scarborough and Sue Simmons and the whole WNBC News staff link arms and sing a Christmas song, a different song every year, swaying back and forth in their beige coats and their gray coats and their Burberry scarves and Russian hats, swaying beneath the lights of the tree, fifty thousand pinpoints of light against the dark backdrop of Thirty Rockefeller Plaza, and we can let our eyes be trick lenses through which we can look into the lights and see out the other side, into all the other Christmas seasons past and present, lights covering every promontory of foliage on the great spruce, skaters going round and round counterclockwise, and all the lights bleared and smudged and multiplied.

There was a telephone book in my room, and I opened it and found that Jill was listed. A few days after I was sent home, I worked up the nerve and finally called her up and asked her if she would like to have dinner with me sometime that week. She said yes.

We went in her car, on Thursday night, to Pepe's Taco Garden, where I had made reservations. She helped me get my crutches out of the back seat of her blue Chevette. We walked, arm in crutch, between the gas torches of the front door. I was *Mr.* Deckle.

She was even fatter now than she had looked in her nurse's uniform, but I didn't care. I wouldn't have cared if she were as big as an old round-sided Dodge ambulance. The restaurant hummed with soft voices and the clink of spoons against earthenware, in the light of hurricane candles and flaming Mexican desserts; and I knew I was in love, with her face, and her voice and her easygoing Kate Smith shape, and I would be proud to be seen with her anywhere, even on the beach, where my own blubbery paleness would be in plain view. I would walk with her anywhere, around any chlorinated swimming pool, any health spa, any tennis club, through any theater lobby where people are smoking Benson & Hedges, along the sloping sand of any beach in the world, even that special beach in St. Tropez where the only thing they wear is Bain de Soleil.

I told her about dark mornings in the locker room, about hand-trucks and flats and pressure-cooker mornings and going to bed when it was still prime time, with the theme music from "Little House on the Prairie" sifting down through the ceiling.

She told me about the nursing profession, about the nurses' refrigerator, where she was having an ice-cream problem. Her blond hair, free from her nurse's cap, fell soft across her forehead, and she pushed her chair back and laughed. She told me about the Coronary Care Unit, about the practice known as "stagecoaching," in which a nurse, if she finds a patient dead near the end of her shift, will leave the corpse in a lifelike sleep posture for the incoming shift to discover and deal with.

"It's weird," Jill said. "I feel as if it's my job to be as nice as I can to everybody, even when I feel lousy. Because I'm the last person that some of them will ever see. When I was going through nursing school at Rochester Institute of Technology, I worked part-time as a receptionist at Kodak. Now I think of myself as sort of a de-receptionist."

She told me about the moment when she looked into a cow's eyes and realized she had to become a vegetarian. She told me about Jane Brody's *Guide to Personal Health,* which was the only nontechnical nutrition book worth reading.

"But there are some *glaring* errors," she said. "There's a chapter called 'It's Hard to be a Fat Vegetarian.' *Wrong!* In a world where there are frozen Sara Lee chocolate cakes in every supermarket, and a Häagen-Dazs on every corner, it's the easiest thing in the world." She was smiling in that distant and unfocused way that people smile when they're talking about something that hurts.

"I smashed my roommate's scale once," she said. "The day I first went over two hundred pounds I just sort of lost control. I grabbed the Girl Scout hatchet that my roommate kept beside her bed to protect herself against rapists, and I just started chopping and hacking at the scale, and I smashed the window where the number showed through, and I was crying, and I just wanted to smash it to pieces. It was a fancy scale too—a hundred-dollar Detecto, and I had to replace it." She swirled the margarita glass around, and part of the rim of salt washed down the side of the glass.

"And then when I bought a new scale and weighed myself, it turned out that the old one had been ten pounds off anyway, I didn't weigh two hundred pounds after all.

"That was back when I was in group therapy. What a joke. We used to 'Work on Issues.' Boy, did I ever Work on Issues. I talked to a pillow that I pretended was my mother, and then I talked to another pillow that was my father. I cried all over the place. We were encouraged to 'Get in Touch With Our Feelings.' I punched pillows, and I 'Primaled' and I 'Gestalted,' and it was just *Issue City!* I should have gotten a Ph.D. in Issues."

I touched her hand across the table, beside her half-finished Vegetarian Special. I wanted to hug her, there in the middle of Pepe's Taco Garden, among the soft voices and the plates full of brown jumbled masses of food.

"Well, I'm still fat, and I still hate it, but the one thing I learned from five thousand dollars' worth of therapy is that I shouldn't bend the rest of my life out of shape just because my body has a tendency to store more nourishment than it needs. A year ago I would never have come to dinner with you. I would have been too embarrassed about my weight."

"Well, I'm glad you've made peace with yourself."

"Not peace," she said. "Just a cease-fire."

We skipped dessert. She insisted that we split the check; and then she was driving me home in her little blue Chevette, from Route 59 to Get High Street to Cresent Drive Spelled Wrong, and then we were outside my house.

We sat in the dark, in the little car, and the motor was ticking and clattering. It was a diesel, a tiny Japanese unit, and it sounded as if loose golf balls were rattling around in the cylinders.

"That was really fun, Jill. Let's do it again sometime."

"Yes," she said. "Definitely." Her face was soft, illuminated by the red emergency brake light. I kissed her. She let me linger there for a proper interval.

"Sometime when I'm not an invalid," I said, and kissed her again, and hugged her as well as I could in the cramped car. She pulled the hatch cable, and carried my crutches to me, and then I got out and she got back in, and I crutch-walked over to her side and touched her cheek through the open window, and her face was all soft and bright and vulnerable, and blood throbbed in my knee, and the world hummed in the dark, and she let off the brake and the engine clattered louder, going "*tickety-tockety-tickety-tockety,*" and she curved around the parking loop, her headlights sweeping across the front of Building A, and when she pulled out onto Cresent Drive Spelled Wrong, she gave a little "*toot-toot*" on the horn and clattered off into the dark. I could smell the lingering sweetness of the diesel fumes, pure and soft, like a Greyhound bus whining off into the long darkness of the night.

7

Cadillac Oath

A first day back at work is like a first day at sea. The Jersey Meadows seemed to tilt and roll with fatigue as my Volkswagen hummed southward on its crooked frame, into the land where houses huddle together as if for warmth, and smokestacks pump clouds of steam into the orange night of a thousand lights.

I like those gray-and-yellow clouds. I like the fierce landscape of iron scaffolds, back-lit by the soft light of downtown Newark. Even from the northern spur of the New Jersey Turnpike, where it passes the PSE&G coal-fired power plant, even from five miles north you can see that Newark is a troubled city: something about the lights, something in the way they steam and simmer in the spring darkness, far away beyond the flatness of mud and water and factories.

I could feel the fierceness of this land, stretching out waterlogged, gaunt and dangerous, on both sides of the car; and beneath that fierceness, in the decomposing saturated loam, I could feel something sweet and fecund, green with poison, bursting with weeds and vines. There are times it would be good to share this geography with somebody, to conduct a private tour of old and friable roads with moss growing up from cracks, secret roads, almost abandoned, that slip under the turnpike. Perhaps my friend Jill could understand something of this joyful poisoning. Perhaps this could be our secret land to explore, because everybody else hates it, on which to walk hand in hand in no particular direction, perhaps to see the light of commuter bus taillights shining in the eyes of muskrats.

This tract of marsh, from Linden to Hackensack, from Secaucus to Clifton, lives by its own measurements, and those that live with it carry a light in their eyes beyond love or hate, a light blurred with rainbows of glaucoma around ochre security lights. The ground tilts like a floating island on a duff of decomposing reeds. It has the country's highest rate of juvenile cancer. It shines through the night with a formless hum of well-tuned vehicles, as if light were sound and sound light; and cars that come loose from its grip will lie rotting on their sides like dead animals. Show me a city. Show me the outskirts of a city, where the city meets the land, the peculiar angles where broken roads intersect in a five pointed star of Super Discount gas stations where attendants carry no cash after dark and all the signs say NO AIR.

I'm talking about air and light, the long ringing yellow light of the Lincoln Tunnel, and the secret light of cars in the hours before regular people get up, the way skin glows under the cold blue streetlights, where bus ramps bridge weightless overhead, the painted skin of harlots on Ninth Avenue. I like the word *harlot,* the harlotlike movements of their lithe and drug-addicted arms, as if dancing to the rhythm of traffic, among the synchronized lights shepherding the low-slung cars south to the meat business; and in that word you can hear the sin, the abandon, the exercise of their harlot mouths, and the fallen state of their harlot orifices.

In the locker room, I shook hands with everybody. Al, the Eastern European butcher who wouldn't give me a straight answer about what country he was a refugee from, shook my hand and spoke to me.

"Yo, Chuckie," he said gravely. "I see in the paper you friend the shah is a very sick man. You send a card for you fokkeen' hero to get well?"

"I sent flowers," I said, smiling into his red stubble. "And I drove to work with my headlights on."

"Well, I tease my friend Chuckie no more. I must tell you to be prepared that you hero is going to die, and I hate to see a grow-up man cry."

I'd forgotten about the smell, the sharp dry sourness of fat and meat and sulfur and detergent, serious and businesslike, the cold harshness of hanging rounds and full loins and short loins, the sweet and wooly fragrance of hanging lamb loins, like tiny saddles, hanging from the tines of the stainless steel tree-hooks. On my way to the main cooler I passed the open door of the dry-aging room, where three giant stand-up industrial fans blew the air across the galvanized iron shelves filled with bone-in shells and ribs. I could smell the hard black crusts on the aging meat, dusted with a touch of metallic blue-green mold. Before the meat was to be shipped, the moldy crust would be trimmed off, revealing the meat inside, firm and tender, partially dissolved by its own enzymes, toothsome and smooth, with a hard beefy undertone to the taste.

I shook hands with Chris and Joe, and soon I was bustling around again, putting up the early orders. Sandy shook my hand and went charging into the cutting room, shouting a stream of attention signals.

"YO! HEYYYYYYY! Let's *GO!* Wake *up!* YAH! YAH! *YO!*" I could hear the slamming-down of pallets on the loading dock, and the howling of blocked traffic.

"Where does Town Tavern go?"

"Over there."

"Where?"

"Over *there!*" Within five minutes I felt as if I had never left.

"Yo, Chuck! Let's go!" said Chris. "I need those lamb loins *now!*"

"Where are the lamb loins?"

"The lamb loins are *with the lamb loins!*"

I was thinking about Jill, wondering about the bad parts of her job, the nasty doctors with unintelligible accents, the hard-faced nursing director. It must be strange to be yelled at by somebody with a master's degree.

We found two cases of boneless beef on which the Cryovac seals were defective. Oxygen had turned the meat green, and it gave of a gassy sweet rotten-egg odor that filled the main cooler with its warm and sulfurous flatulence. We hung the meat on three tree-hooks to let it air out in the breeze of a fan that we borrowed from the aging room. After a few hours in the wind, the gassy molecules on the surface of the meat would have bonded to the nitrogen in the air and the meat would be good enough to be ground and formed into breaded patties.

While the beef was airing out, Sandy's partner, Marty Cohen, whose name on the P.A. system was such a source of hilarity for Hispaniphones, appeared in the cooler with a dozen well-dressed men and women from Eastern Airlines food service department whom he was showing around the plant. As they filed into the main cooler, their colognes and perfumes clashed with the gassy meat smell, all the esters and aldehydes and ketones fighting for space with the hydrogen sulfide molecules. The executives wrinkled their noses and stared at the green meat.

"How come that meat is all . . . green like that?" asked a young man in a gray pinstripe suit.

"Oh, that. That's just airing out," Marty said. "You get that color sometimes."

"You mean somebody's going to eat that stuff?"

"It's perfectly wholesome. It's just discolored. The USDA has a field office right in this building, and they watch everything we do."

After the butchers had gone home, as I was eating lunch alone in the locker room, Red, the old red-haired butcher foreman, came in and started changing his clothes. On the inner door of his locker I could see the sad and slack-jawed girl and her splayed-out calf's-liver vulva. Red was standing closely against the open locker, and as he began to tell me about his house and his car I could see that he was loosening a system of trusses.

"Should see the work I've done on that place," he said, and let out a long, constricted breath.

"*Ksssshhhhhhhhhhhhh* . . ." he said. "Fuckin' ruptures." With the loosening of each truss he let out a long grunting sigh, not of pain or exertion, but as if each truss held its own store of stale air.

"I refinished the whole basement with a bar and a rec room . . . *Ghhhhzzzzzzsssshhhhhhhh* . . . Replaced all the outside sofits . . . *hhrrugghhhssshhhhhh* . . ." The poster girl seemed woozy with drugs, her mouth dry, as if all her bodily moisture had drained into her dark labia. I wondered why he was telling me all this. I don't care about sofits. I don't even know what sofits are.

He told me how often he changed the oil in his Dodge pickup, and that he had his eye on a two-year-old Cadillac his neighbor's widow was selling.

"I don't know any more if I should get that Caddy now . . . *ksshhhh* . . ." he said, ". . . with the gas . . ." By "the gas" he meant the current oil shortage resulting partially from the Iranian crisis.

He was finished with his trusses, so he changed his shoes, and the drugged girl was swung back into the dark, and Red slumped out the door. I could hear his feet on the hollows of the stairs.

Before I went home that day, Marty Cohen sent me to get a box of order forms out of the trunk of his car.

"It's a white Caddy parked over on Gansevoort," he said, handing me a set of keys whose handle ends were padded with white rabbit fur.

As I carried the order forms back to Denny Packing, I thought about how I've always hated the term *Caddy*. It seems to undermine everything that a Cadillac is supposed to stand for: the quiet, the elegance, the restfulness of achievement. And the people to whom these qualities should be most important, the Cadillac owners who had worked and shouted and bullied their way up from the production line, didn't seem to care. They yelled out their Cadillac windows at other drivers, used the word "fucking" as an intensifier, which I like to call the "lower-class adjective," let their ashtrays overflow.

I'm not saying that the Cadillac is an intrinsically tacky automobile — far from it — only that a Cadillac deserves to be spoken of in a continent vocabluary, without diminutives; and that one need be vigilant about avoiding decals, bumper stickers, and especially those waving hands that wobble back and forth on the rear window ledge beside the box of Kleenex.

That night, as I thought again about Cadillacs, I decided to make a promise to myself. I pledged that I would never, ever, use the word *Caddy* except in reference to the person who carries golf clubs; and I decided to cement that promise with the sacrifice of a dollar bill.

I turned off "Charlie's Angels," found the newest, crispest single I had, and folded it into a little pup tent on my TV Dinner tray, in the section where the square of cherry cobbler had been. I turned off all the lights and lit the bill.

"I, Chuck Deckle, shall never call a Cadillac a *Caddy*," I said out loud. "By the light of this burning dollar I swear that I shall never call a Cadillac a *Caddy*. . . . And when I have a Cadillac of my own, the day I refer to my Cadillac as a *Caddy* shall be the day I park it with the keys inside, in the middle of Harlem."

In the dark of my apartment, the bill burned clear and bright. In the television screen, where a dot of blue light lingered, I could see my face, illuminated from below, spooky and Karloffian.

After the flame went out, the crinkled ash was covered with live embers, worms of orange light scrabbling with a tiny rustling sound across the wrinkled surface on which I could still make out the printed scrollwork, all the frills and embellishments like the tailpieces of a dozen violins grown together. The smoke of the bill smelled like a driftwood fire on the beach at Martha's Vineyard in the night.

After the last of the worms of light had winked out, I tried to imagine myself back on the Vineyard, on the beach in front of the house that my family used to rent for the last two weeks of August every year. Somewhere out along the moors, in the soft light of gray-shingled cottages, my former Hotchkiss classmates discussed their progress through the ranks of J. Walter Thompson; and current Hotchkiss students in another cottage, with parents out at a cocktail party, would be losing their virginity, or perhaps they had lost it long ago. It's not such a big thing anymore, not like it was to me in those long nights of wind and desire with the sky like an umbrella of stars and the beach dotted with little wounds of light, before beach fires were outlawed; but surely it must mean something to someone, among the silent houses; somebody must still be young enough to care about something so important that everything else disappears, in the deep and private night, summer almost over, the Pleiades rising out of the sea after midnight, rising a few minutes earlier each night, the katydids louder, not much time left; somewhere boys and girls, hiding in the bristly dune grass, are going all the way for the first time or the last time or the only time before the great white steamer pulls out, loaded with cars, before the fall clothes-shopping excursion, before school starts again in shades of maroon and gray, and adventures become escapades and remembering becomes bragging, and everybody is equal in their dress codes and curricula, though some are already on academic probation, some have neglected their summer reading lists, some wear jerseys from Phil Esposito's summer hockey program; and here among the rolling scrubs and rose hips and rhododendrons, where the night is a thing, where the night has a physical geometry that the young can feel in their throats, here the houses are so far apart, so private, that the voice of the richest meat man on 14th Street would not carry from one to another.

I hadn't been to the Vineyard in five years. The closest I had come was watching the movie *Jaws,* which was filmed there. There is a moment in that movie, when Captain Quint's boat is at sea in the night as they stalk the shark, and a point of light goes streaking across the clear sky. The shot was filmed in slow motion for better light detail, and the airplane that happens into the picture is speeded up into a flickering meteor speeding horizontally above the dark water and the warm cabin-cruiser lights. It is the most beautiful thing I have ever seen.

And I was far away, in a world of night and water and feet on the sand. It was already past my bedtime. I thought of Jill's blond hair. With the driftwood smoke still hanging in the air, I called her up. She had spent the day in the C.C.U.

"It's so good to talk to somebody who's not dying," she said. I told her about my first day back at work, how everything was the same, only more so. She laughed. She'd been having appointments with a clinical nutritionist who was custom-designing a megamineral weight-loss program for her.

"The first thing this guy wants to do," she said, "is evaluate my current mineral status. So I have to furnish him with a hair sample. Most people when they go to a hairdresser say they want an inch cut off, or they want a certain look. But then . . . we have the case of Jill Clifford, who is the first person in the history of Hair Dimensions to go in and ask them to cut off a *tablespoon* of hair.

"So anyway, now my tablespoon of hair is on its way to the lab, and this shrimpy little nutritionist who looks like he just recovered from scurvy has me lie down naked on the table like a stiff in the morgue, and he's taking Polaroid pictures all over me from about six inches away. Then he's got me standing on the scale, naked, and he's marking everything down on this schematic body diagram on his clipboard, like I'm a prize heifer. This guy has a special set of calipers to measure the thickness of the fat-covering in my breasts and ass. I mean . . . real personal stuff." Her voice was getting high and flutish, halfway between being upset and being amused.

She said that because of the strictness of her diet she would have to pass on my idea of going to the Gasho Japanese Steakhouse, which was one of Denny Packing's best customers.

"I've got an idea," she said. "Why don't you come over to my place on Sunday and I'll cook dinner."

"Sounds good to me."

"Great!" she said. "Let's do it. We can eat health food together and commiserate about our crazy lives."

8

Ventricle Wheel

Jill's eyes were all red. I had been waiting in the wind, which hummed through the railing of the cloistered walkway on the second floor of her apartment building. I was just about to give up when she opened the door.

"Oh . . . Chuck," she said, her voice weak and quavery. "Hi. Come on in."

"Do I have the wrong day or something?"

"Oh, that's right. I forgot. We were supposed to have lunch. I'm sorry." Her hair was stringy, the whites of her eyes pink above red-rimmed lids. She was crying.

"Jill, what's the matter?"

"Oh, nothing," she said. "You've just walked into Issue City, that's all." She tried to smile, and her chin was red and crumpled.

"I've been having some diet-compliance problems," she said, looking down at the floor. "I'm supposed to eat nothing but shrimp and raw spinach and canteloupe and mineral supplements. But last night, when I was driving home from my appointment with that little twit of a holistic nutritionist, I saw this enormous cheesecake in the window of Cake Masters, and I just *snapped.* I went in and bought it, and I ate the whole thing in the car. It's like I was a goddamn *zombie* or something! And ever since then I've just been bingeing out, Roman style."

"Roman style?"

"That's when I make myself throw up so I can eat some more. In fact, I just did a spoonful of Ipecac syrup before you rang the doorbell. So make yourself at home and excuse me for a minute while I go puke."

I stood there, alone, in the deep blond carpeting of her living room, and listened to her retching and coughing, the sound echoing off the bathroom's hard tiles. Somehow it wouldn't have seemed right to sit down, to thumb through her magazines. So I just stood there, looking out the window, listening to her throw up.

"Almost finished, Chuck," Jill said. "Be out in a jiff'! *Hocchhhh! Hocchhhh! Hchkkk! Pttchhoooiee!*"

"This really *SUCKS!*" she said as she flushed the toilet and came out of the bathroom. "Want some coffee?"

She poured two cups from the drip brewer and carried them on a tray to the coffee table in front of the couch. "I'll bet you've never gotten a reception like that before."

"I guess I haven't," I said.

"Well, consider yourself initiated into the arcane knowledge of the Jill Clifford Syndrome, Roman Dessert department. I hope you're taking notes. A Roman Dessert is what happens when Jill Clifford tries to deprive herself."

"I've heard about that condition."

"Not really. You're thinking about bulimia, which is actually a variation of anorexia. I don't puke to starve myself; I puke to make room for more food, because I like to eat. And I don't have a distorted body image. I have no delusions. I know I'm a fat pig, and I'll probably always be a fat pig." She sprinkled Sweet 'n Low into her coffee. "Cream? Sugar? Ipecac?" she said.

"Jill, that's not funny at all," I said, but I knew as I said it that the damnable thing, the thing that made us both so helpless, was precisely that it *was* funny. "I really hate to see you doing this to yourself. I'm not a doctor, but I know that you can get dehydrated and all screwed up."

"I'm all screwed up already, so who the fuck cares?"

"I care, Jill, that's who the fuck cares. And I'll tell you something else, even though maybe you don't want to hear it. I like you even though you're fat."

"Yeah, but I *don't*." She was crying again. "I don't *like* fat women. I don't even feel sorry for them."

"What do you think about fat men?"

"You're not fat. You don't know what fat *is*. You're just flabby. Fat is from the inside out. Fat involves the whole body and the whole mind and the whole *life*, and I'm just sick of it. That's why I had to quit Weight Watchers, because I couldn't stand listening to the other fatsos in the group begging for somebody to feel sorry for them. It's just so ridiculous. I mean I'm thirty-one years old, and I aced every biochemistry course I ever took, and I understand the whole cellular mechanism of glycogen storage, and I still feel like a fat little twelve-year-old girl. The more I understand, the less control I seem to have. It hurts, Chuck. It really fucking hurts."

Tears were running down her face. We sat together on the textured couch, and I put my arm around her, and she cried some more. I could see the outline of her breasts beneath her checked jersey.

"It's okay, Jill," I said. "I like you just the way you are. I think you're terrific, and I just don't want you to hurt anymore."

She cried and sobbed, and caught her breath and lost it again, her face against the hollow of my neck just above the collarbone. I could feel the wetness of her tears against my skin, and the warmth of her breath made my body tingle. Suddenly she was kissing me. I could taste something sour on her lips, and I realized it was the hydrochloric acid from when she had been throwing up. She was giving me big wet kisses. As she fastened her mouth on mine, I could feel how clean her teeth were, and then suddenly, almost violently, she pulled her checked jersey over her head, and her breasts were bare, and she pulled off her sweatpants with her underpants still in them, and she was naked in my arms, there on the clean and well-upholstered couch, and the windows blazed with the motion of wind and clouds and sun outside in the landscaped courtyard. There was a light in her eyes, wild and bright, as she led me by the hand into her bedroom. Her legs were fat, like barkless logs, but she didn't have any of those mushy dimples around her knees the way some fat girls do.

The whole sequence of events, from my ringing the doorbell, to listening to her throw up, to coffee table, to where we were now and what we were suddenly doing, had happened so quickly that in those five minutes I hadn't had time to remember about how I needed to make sure that I didn't start to worry about Performance Anxiety. Plus, it was early in the day and I hadn't had a thing to drink. It made a big difference. Her spine arched and her head tilted back and her breaths were frantic. She rolled her eyes upward, and I could see the slightly reddened eye-white tissue, soft and vulnerable, and everything felt good, like cold fire.

We lay panting on the sheets, as if we had just climbed several flights of stairs, both of us pale and blubbery, like beached whales. The hard light streamed in a shaft through a gap in the curtain. On the wall opposite the bed, next to her framed R.N. certificate from the Rochester Institute of Technology, was tacked a poster with the headline, FAT IS BEAUTIFUL, showing a huge, obese, rust-colored mother orangutan holding a baby orangutan half hidden in the fold of flesh where her pendulous breasts draped over her belly.

Jill told me about the time her mother, all for a good purpose, had concealed a loaded jack-in-the-box inside the tin cookie container, with a little note taped onto his clown face saying "Lay off the cookies,

Fatso!" The top of the clown's head had broken a tooth when it sprang into her face. She showed me the capped tooth, hardly noticeable among her flawless natural teeth.

"It's funny how things fall into a pattern," she said. "Working at the hospital is almost exactly like being a kid in my family. It seems that my main purpose there is to be criticized. And the more I understand about the psychology of the shit-hole countries that those doctors come from who have so many suggestions for how we Americans should be doing our jobs . . . the more I understand it, the more I hate listening to it. I should be above all that. But that's the story of my life, the more I understand things, the less I can do about them. Do you know what I mean?"

"Yeah, I do," I said. "You, me, and President Carter."

"So how do you cope with the bullshit?"

"I guess it's easier for me," I said. "The people I work with are so patently ignorant. I don't know what I'd feel like if I had to get yelled at by somebody who don't make no grammatical errors." She smiled. I told her about the locker room, the way ethnic arms sawed the air and made the smoke go swirling around, the way I liked to drive up Tenth Avenue on my way home in the rain and watch everybody leaning against the wind with their umbrellas. I told her about the sad and drugged face of the girl in Red's locker, and how her vulva seemed sculpted into an unusual configuration.

"Like this?" she said, taking my hand beneath the covers.

As we toweled each other off in the bright steam of her white tile bathroom, Jill decided that we should go to the Grand Ventricle, which was the nickname that everybody at Pascack Valley Community Hospital had given to the newly-completed Grand Atrium Mall.

We walked across the parking lot, through the light and shadow of clouds scudding across the sky. Jill was wearing black slacks and a pink blouse. She had covered the puffiness in her face with a light application of makeup. We walked toward my car, whose dusty yellow roof domed high above the low-slung Toyotas.

"There's something I have to explain about my car," I said. "Don't be scared if it looks like we're going to crash into something. The frame's all bent, and the car doesn't go where it's pointed."

"Who the hell does?" she said. We drifted crabwise, past real-estate offices and medical group buildings, around cloverleafs, past the new General Electric office building, whose sleek boomerang shapes towered above the intersection of the Thruway and the Palisades Parkway in the triangular space whose hypotenuse was the outer traffic ramp.

Jill insisted that we have lunch at McDonald's. "I'm officially putting my fat issues and my vegetarian issues on hold for the rest of the day," she said. "Today I'm going to eat like an American. And I hope we run into that little worm of a holistic nutrition counselor. He lives right near here. I'd like to take a goddamn Quarter Pounder with Cheese and smack him right in the face with it."

I like McDonald's. I like the lights and the soft warm smells and the casualness of it. I've long noticed that it's impossible to have overly serious thoughts in McDonald's. There have been times I've gone into McDonald's in a rage about the latest hostage bulletin, and have left as if through clouds of ordinariness, with the soft voices of ordinary Americans ringing in my ears. Perhaps there's something in the meat, some kind of emotional saltpeter, perhaps a tranquilizing mist in the processed air. Families are there for an inexpensive meal. Kids are jumping around in the padded wall seats.

The air was thick and sweet with hamburger smells and moist bun smells, alive with soft voices and the yipping of children, parents telling kids to sit down, the gurgling of plastic straws at the bottom of chocolate shakes, the hum of the shiny processing machines, the piezoelectric warbling of the french fry timer, and the light pizzicato of strings in the background music.

Jill and I sat at a window table, in padded seats, and the wind and changing light played over the creamy colors of parked cars. We had the tops of our containers counterweighted with fries, and all was bright, and traffic flashed past on Route 59, past the gas lines at the

Hess station, past where Korvette's had closed down and become a Service Merchandise Catalog Center.

There is a part of a land that can never be held hostage, a Miracle Mile irrelevant to the pleadings of a weakling president or the ultimatums of a strong one; and life goes on, and the voices of children, gathered in their glittery hats for a McDonald's birthday party, are the same from crisis to crisis, on the miniature merry-go-round and the spiral slide, under the gaze of a huge flat-relief color mask of Ronald McDonald, although there are serious voices hovering in the parking lot, and there is a cult for this and a cult for that; and the leaves come out as usual, this year strung with white hammocks of tent caterpillars; and there is a spot in Nanuet, at the Four Corners, wher radicals have vigiled since I was a child, and they were still there today, serious goatees, carefully stenciled signs, and there are Concerned Citizens about this and Concerned Citizens about that, and I have heard voices raised concerning the gypsy moth, and a grim scenario of defoliation, with the loss of Rockland County's watershed, in which there will not be enough water to keep McDonald's clean, a loud-voiced epic of the desertification of my green and pleasant county of lawn sprinklers and landscaped banks with red cedars growing from a mulch of wood chips, my county in which teenagers lounge in McDonalds' outdoor picnic area, among the hard tables, in their denim jackets and denim pants, all blue and casual and brass-riveted, in the changing light of clouds and sun and looming gray thunderheads, and buffed cars shining with a nimbus of wax. I suddenly noticed that Jill and I were stirring our thick shakes in unison.

"You know, Jill, I feel kind of strange about sitting here and eating fatty food with you. I don't want to feel like I'm collaborating with your fat problems, but I don't know what to do. Should I have refused to bring you here?"

"Hell no," she said, rubbing her ankle against mine beneath the table. "It's not your job. You're my friend, not my supervisor."

Suddenly it was raining outside, and the denimed kids scrambled under the overhanging roof. It rained so hard that the picnic tables were clouded with a halo of spray, and cars were turning on their headlights, and windshield wipers wagged like metronomes in time to allegro violins of Steve Allen's "Gravy Waltz." People were running with newspapers over their heads, families sitting together in station wagons, waiting for the rain to stop, as forks of lightning flashed in the distance behind the Caldor department store, its windowless stucco building white as a cube of sugar in the rain, never to melt. I touched Jill's cheek, and she smiled, eyes Visine-clear, across a table of plastic foam containers.

When the rain let up, we drove to the Grand Atrium and walked in through the upper level entrance. The Grand Atrium was the world's largest and most beautiful shopping complex. It had won dozens of artistic awards. The central part of the mall, where the three prom-enades came together, contained its most remarkable feature, the atrium pool, which was so large that you could rent little foot-pedaled boats and go paddling between islands of rock and under arched footbridges, under the skylight, beside the tall birdcage.

At the far end of each concourse stood a major department store: Penney's, Sears, and Bamberger's; and hard by the hub of the three walkways stood Lord & Taylor, with entrances leading to the ground-floor garden and to the second floor, where, overlooking the pool and the forest, stood a ring of international food shops, their stand-up eating tables overlooking the Japanese garden that surrounded the atrium pool where paddle boats went clunking around in the water among the greenery and the redwood walkways.

We walked around and around, from Sears to Bamberger's, up stairs and down stairs, up an escalator that ran through a ribbed cater-pillarlike tube of glass. We filled out our tickets to win a new Buick Riviera. A glassblower with a bushy black mustache had set up a temporary stand near the lower entrance to J. C. Penney. With a tiny blowtorch he was transforming old mayonnaise jars into swans, mold-ing Coke bottles into long-necked green storks. He said hello to Jill as we passed.

"That guy is my roommate's boyfriend," she told me as we walked along the concourse. "He's a nice guy, and he makes good money, and they have fun together; but somehow, beneath all that suaveness, I personally think he's kind of a jerk. And she's such a wonderful girl, I just wish she'd find somebody more substantial. I mean, he caught his mustache on fire twice with his blowtorch, but he still doesn't have the sense to shave it off."

We went into The Big Sound, and Jill bought an album by a guitarist I'd never heard of named Boomer Williams. We stood at the railing and looked over the leaves and the water. Rills splashed on both sides of where the glass elevator capsule emerged from jungle greenery. On the other side of the pool, in the three-story birdcage, bright macaws hooked their bills over the black mesh and chattered and screeched, and the light changed, the sun coming out again in the ribbed and frosted skylight above the lights of all the food shops: Tico Taco, Greek Garden, Hong Kong Express, Pizza Time, Arthur Treacher's Fish and Chips, and Ice Cream Emperor.

"Someday I'm going to get this goddamn weight thing together," Jill said. We walked and walked and ate big soft pretzels from which we had scraped off as much of the salt as we could. We walked around the upper level of the south concourse where walkways ran along either side but it was open in the middle so that you could look down at the stores below. Families were strolling, swinging their shopping bags, past the Sport Runner Shop and the Well-Tempered Kitchen. Teen-agers walked in denim trios. Monkeys screeched in the Sun-Ray Pet Shop, parakeets fluttered against the wire cage. A crowd of children watched through the glass picture window, behind which German shepherd puppies sprawled on shredded newspaper.

Next to the pool, beside the booth where you could pay two dollars to rent a boat, the doorway of Lord & Taylor breathed out its linen-white light, and we could hear bells inside, the soft two-noted chime of department codes. Around the pool ran little walkways and redwood landings where people could stand and smoke cigarettes in the rainless forest of oiled leaves.

There didn't even seem to be a World Situation today. Nobody carried newspapers; no headline shrilled from a yellow vending box. The negligeed mannequins in the window of Frederick's of Hollywood smiled, eyes lined in black, and husbands in beltless slacks from Sears would take a long look until wives tugged on the husbands' arms. As we walked around the Japanese garden we could smell the sweet cumin of taco meat steaming, caught in a downdraft through the processed air.

We stood among the waxy rhododendron leaves, among the holly and rubber plants and mountain laurel and ivy and acacia; and I paid two dollars and we found a pedal boat that was dry inside, and we went pedaling around in the surprisingly clean water. No cigarette butts floated; ribbed scuppers at the surface drank the water and cleaned it; and over the side of the boat we could see golden carp trailing willowy fins, some with white pigmentless mottlings among the orange, like those people upon whom progressive albinism advances.

Pennies shone in the light, in the shallow water, with a round bronzy sheen. At the edge of the pool stood teenagers in groups of three, all smoking cigarettes, all slim and clear-skinned, and it occurred to me that they were all thinking about sex, all thinking about getting naked with somebody, as Jill and I had been less than an hour ago; and that's what the mall was for, as much as for spending money, a boulevard of primates, because I've read somewhere that primates are the only animals who are in heat all the time, and it influences everything primates do, and each primate moves within a sphere of sexuality as within a soap bubble whose surface brushes against all the other spheres of sexuality up and down the bright primate promenades where young girls walk, their eyes outlined in blue, and boom-boxes were blasting out Led Zeppelin, and I knew at last that Jill and I were no different from them, we were all part of the rich busy crisisless day, part of the land, part of the mall, part of the sweet and steaming earth out of which dreams of future nakedness rise like mushrooms in the night; and I knew at last that the kids were all right in their denims and brass rivets, knew at last that there was nothing in the world worth worrying about. Everything was being worried about by consummate professionals of the worry industry and the indignation industry and the moral fervor industry; and I knew there were fake clocks without machinery, set at three minutes to midnight, and serious goatees made serious phone calls, and mailings went out by the bin, announcing, "I am writing to you about the survival of the Human Species," and I knew that some of the serious ones might be here among us at this very mall, buying a sensible pair of shoes for long vigils, but that was all right, because that's what the mall is for, and their money is just as green as mine, while their waxless cars stand unshining in the parking lot, brightened only by the colors of the bumper stickers announcing whatever it was they were up in arms about, in a world where those less fortunate than you and I are not permitted to dredge the pennies from the atrium pool. I happen to know that the pennies in the pool are collected each week by volunteer workers for the Rockland County Infant Nutrition Program.

As we paddled around in the little boat, I thought for a moment that I could see those invisible spheres of primate sex around everybody, even the girls with glasses, even the old women in walkers, even the dull-shirted bumper sticker people walking within a sphere of modest sexuality that respects the equality of genders and frowns upon the lace bikinis of the Frederick's of Hollywood mannequins, and I knew that Jill's sphere and my sphere intersected, here in the boat, side by side, as we went paddling like a mallard around in the filtered water, and our tangent spheres made music as they touched. We pedaled past the white waterfall and the cascading rills, in the rubbery green of leaves, where teenagers chattered like bright marmosets among the redwood rambles, and I put my arm around her, and I knew I loved her, and I knew I loved this place.

At the center of the pool there was spot from which we could see down to the end of each of the mall's three main concoursi, all the way to Sears, to Bamberger's, to Penney's, and I turned the rudder all the way to the right, and slowly we went round and round, and slowly the mall turned around us like a three-spoked wheel, and we were at the very center of it, at the very center of Rockland County.

"Let's try to imagine," I said to her, "that we're standing still and everything out there is turning around us. And if we can do it, and make ourselves believe it, I predict that we'll be able to solve all our problems, because hey . . . at the center of the universe, there are no problems. I'll be rich and you'll be thin."

So around and around we went, and the great wheel of the Grand Atrium turned slowly around us, and the voices hummed and the soft waterfall hissed, and we were at the heart of it, the mighty ventricle from which streams of oxygenated people were shunted in tides, an enormous heart, a great three-spoked wheel, a heart like a wheel, beyond which a pulsing aorta of brake-lighted traffic pumped out streams of cars on which water beaded cleanly, the ejection fraction rhythmically controlled by the valves of traffic lights, into the traffic arteries, while the chattering bright primates brushed their spheres of sexuality against each other, blond girls with eyes edged in blue among the redwood walkways, the music of the spheres, of the three spokes, the Atrium and ventricles, while oracles voiced the grim scenario of tent-caterpillar infestations, of trouble past or passing or to come, blood and flesh and water and sun and light and air and the wax patina of leaves; and far away, down at the end of the Bamberger's concourse, beside the children's carousel, stood an exit door thirty feet wide, a great vomitorium, and I thought of the sour cider taste on her lips before lunch, and her potassium troubles, and her borderline anemia, her iron-poor blood, and I could feel the traffic around us, the arteries humming and pulsing with the pumped red brakelights of Turtle-waxed cars among the rolling hills, the green of the rolling suburbs, and here we were at the very center, the hub of the wheel, among the hubbub and the soft noise, and the water and the air and the color and the ding-dong of Lord & Taylor's signal chimes, ringing for us alone and everybody else, and we were going round and round, and I touched her cheek and our legs were pedaling like mad and I asked her to marry me and she said no.

9

Quantum Popcorn

Beside Chris's stand-up lectern, Sandy was waiting for me. His voice was hushed as he motioned me into the aging room, where hundreds of bone-in shells and 109 ribs in various stages of aging lay on the galvanized aging racks, some with the beefy red still showing, some crusted with a black layer of jerky, in the whirling dry air agitated by three huge industrial fans. On Friday, in a desperate hurry, he had instructed me to pack up two dozen ribs for Gallagher's Steak House.

"I told you which ribs to pack up," he almost whispered. "In fact I told you twice." That was true. The first time, when I hadn't understood, he became furious and began speaking in pigin English. ("Meat! Take! Box! Pack! You *sabbee?*" he had said.)

"And you went right ahead and packed the wrong ones. You fucked up." His voice was beginning to get louder.

"Oh, shit, I'm sorry. I guess I misunderstood."

"*MISUNDERSTOOD?* Is that all you can fucking *say?* We don't have *time* for misunderstandings in this business! You know what would have happened if Joe G didn't catch it before it went out?"

"I'm sorry, Sandy, I—"

"Do you *know* what would have happened?" He was speaking loud now, his small eyes shiny. "And do you know what's going to happen if you fuck up just one more time?" My ears were ringing, and I could feel the flush of my face in the dry breeze.

"I made a mistake," I said. "I'm sorry."

"One more fuck-up, asshole . . . *AND YOU'RE FIRED!* One more fuck-up and you're out of here on the fucking *STREET* with all the other *jerks* who don't have the brains enough to work for me! Do you fucking *understand* that, *ASSHOLE?*" He was yelling directly into my face, so close that if he had been a baseball manager arguing with the umpire, he would have turned his cap backward.

It was strange to be yelled at like that. It hurt. That was the terrible truth. Even with all my years in the meat business, even with a color TV to come home to, even having been kissed good-bye this morning as Jill reclaimed her share of the blankets, despite everything, it still hurt.

It was strange to come to work and get yelled at with such fervor on a morning that had begun with Handel's *Water Music* on Jill's clock radio so loud that her roommate had pounded on the wall in the other bedroom, a morning begun with a wifelike kiss in the warm dimness of Cameo Gardens, strange to have Sandy's face raging into my face on a day when I was already a hero of sorts. That Friday Wilfredo had said that I had appeared in a dream of his. He asked me to pick a number for him to play in the daily lottery. I chose 3-1-4, corresponding to my initials, Chuck Albert Deckle, and thought nothing more of it, until Monday morning when I walked into the locker room and a cheer went up.

"Chuckie, my friend!" Herman said. "You hear what the fuck happen? Fokkeen' three-one-four come out in the *number!* We each win *fie thousand dollar!*" They were laughing and hugging me.

Herman explained that they weren't going to forget who had given them the number. He explained, however, that it was very bad luck to give money as a form of thanks. They had agreed instead to take me to a store and buy me something that I wanted.

"So what we buy you?" Wilfredo was saying. "You need a stereo player? You need a new suit? A new television? Anything you want, it's yours, Chuckie."

"I could use a nice suit, I guess."

"Okay, *Chuckie,* you got a fokkeen' *suit.* The day we get paid we take you in a taxi to Barney's and we buy you any suit you want!"

And immediately after getting that news, when I went downstairs to work, the yelling incident took place. For the rest of the day, with my ears ringing and my thoughts in a hurry like a butcher with a deadline, I bustled around and policed the area and rotated stock and fetched legs of veal. Why did I not feel more protected? It was strange to have a girlfriend, strange not to be able to complain that I had nobody to complain to. I wondered if Jill was perhaps getting yelled at by some Bangladesh radiologist at this very moment. Identical twins can feel such things, some people say, but friends are on their own. Besides, she was leaving directly from work for a nursing conference in Philadelphia, and I wouldn't be able to talk to her.

There is something about being yelled at that is hard to forget. Voices ring in my ears. I wish people's voices would ring in my ears when they said nice things, as when Jill said I was the smartest person she knew who didn't have a Hindustani accent.

I could understand her not wanting to marry me. We would drive each other crazy. She'd get fatter, I'd lose my job. It would be fun, though; we would hold hands in front of the television; she would hear jokes at work and tell them to me over the Formica dining nook.

It suddenly occurred to me that I never heard any jokes at work, here in the zone of seriousness, with the transit strike locking up the traffic around us. It's a different sort of territory.

Why did people in the meat business have to yell so much? That's what I couldn't understand. Tradition, I supposed, as in the song from *Fiddler on the Roof.* Perhaps fifty thousand years ago the first Cro-Magnon ever to pick up a sharpened rock and start hacking apart a decomposing mastodon was in a bad mood, snapping at his helpers in Proto-Indo-European. Perhaps all bad butcher-moods are an extension of that original mood, the father of all moods.

Tradition! There are hours in the morning when people shouldn't have to get up, and there are hours in the evening when grownups shouldn't have to go to bed, like children being punished, in prime time, with the theme music from "Little House on the Prairie" lilting through the apartment upstairs, where they are serving popcorn. Sometimes lying in bed I could hear children's stocking feet thumping across the ceiling, could smell popcorn cooking. Sometimes, drifting off to sleep I could hear the corn popping, and I would think about the invisible threads that hold houses and hindquarters and careers together, about quantum physics, and the idea of random distribution that keeps all the kernels from popping in the same instant with a great *BOOM* and blowing the house down.

Tradition! There are young music students who make a hundred dollars a day at weddings, playing the violin on sombody's roof; and we are all of one meat-eating tribe, all with genetic instructions for maximum cholesterol storage, all descendants of the first angry butcher in the Late Stone Age to say, "Damn, this freaking copper knife won't stay sharp for shit. Why the fuck don't somebody melt copper and tin together and see if it don't hold a freaking edge better!"

Tradition! Ethnicity. Ethni-city, city of yellowed fingertips, of calf's-liver labia, city of gold teeth, of fat men with sleep apnea whose grandmothers, toothless, babushka'd, cursed the tzar, the land of quickies, land of the *New York Post,* whose headline today was BECAUSE SHE CRIED! the story of a two-year-old shot to death in a bodega holdup.

After lunch, as Joe G and I were putting together a Florida order, I mentioned that I was looking forward to baseball season starting again.

"I can't watch baseball no more," he said. "Our boy was a baseball player." Joe seemed to be looking somewhere far away, past the partition that separated the main cooler where we were from the storage cooler, looking off away somewhere past the frosty banks of fluorescent lights that shone on hundreds of hanging primal rounds and ribs and loins.

"We lost him," he said. "He was all signed up to play right field for the Yankees, on the Columbus Clippers farm team. He hit twenty homers in Double A ball the year before, and they were talking another Rusty Staub. But he drowned. Jones Beach, the Forth of July, 1976. Freakin' Bicentennial day.

"That was the same week that Pilgrim Provisions put the key in the door and moved to Florida to get away from the union."

As Joe talked, I noticed that he could project emotion, as well as sound, with his back turned. Watching the broad surface of his tall, slightly humped back, I felt as if I could read the despair and weariness through his white butcher's coat. The only other person I've ever seen who could project with his back was George C. Scott in the movie *The Hospital,* in which he has the back of his suit jacket to the camera through most of the movie, yet still projects the despair of a troubled hospital administrator.

"We shouldn't have brought him," Joe was saying, the flesh beneath his chin all loose and ropy. "He didn't know how to swim. He was fooling around in the surf and got knocked over by a wave or something, and next thing we know they're pulling his body out of the water."

"That's a shame," I said.

"She's never been the same. She can't go to work no more, she can't even clean the house. She had a good job too, part-time for the city. But now she just sits around the house all day, and the doctor gives her pills, but when she forgets to take them I can't even get her to look up from the television when I come home from work. Sometimes she says she can't look at me because I remind her too much of him.

85

"And then I came here to this freakin' place, and everybody I talked to said, 'Don't work for this guy, he's a fuckin' snake,' but I figured what I've gone through I could put up with anything. I could have gone with them down to Florida and been foreman down there, but she couldn't leave New York and her sisters, and especially with Tommy — that was our boy — so we stayed here."

He stopped talking and went on fastening the plastic straps around new boxes printed with the futuristic Denny Packing cow-skull logo, filled with boneless ribs for the Breakers. Now I understood why he looked as if he'd lost weight fast. In two weeks he'd gone from being a foreman, with a son on the Columbus Clippers, to being an order assembler with a twenty-two-year-old supervisor and a dead son and a mentally ill wife.

"That's it on both these Miami orders," Joe said to Chris, who checked something off on the pink tissue-paper invoice, and charged, almost running, out the green canvas flap-door saying, "Thought I was gonna piss my pants that time!"

Herman and Wilfredo bought me lunch that day, in the Market Café, among all the other white coats. A few salesmen were eating lunch, carefully leaning forward with each forkful so as not to stain their sport jackets. It was nice to think that soon I'd have a decent suit of my own, not that stupid-looking European plaid. In the steam of our three open-faced sandwiches, Wilfredo started talking.

"I want to ask you something, Chuckie, because I speak to a lady who tell me to ask the luckiest man I know, and I couldn't think of nobody. I know a few guys who win maybe a hundred dollar, but then when I see you in that dream, it say in the Book for Dreams if you see somebody get out of a car, it means he's a strong man. So maybe you can tell me something, yes?"

"I'll try."

"My cousin have a hot dog truck that he drive to the beach and to block parties, and he want me to go in the business with him. I said I'd think about it. But he say hurry the fuck up and say yes or no. And I don't know what to do, to quit from the *carnicero* business, or stay where I'm at. And now I got this money, I can go in with him if I want to. What you think?"

I told him to speak to Tom Chambers, the union representative, and find out what the chances would be of getting his old job back should the hot-dog business not work out; and I told him to be very specific about asking his cousin just how much money he could expect to make.

"Ask to see his tax forms," I told him. "If he doesn't want to show them to you, he's hiding something."

Herman wanted to know if I thought he and his wife and baby should move in with his wife's mother for a few years and save up money to buy a house. I told him to think about getting a second job instead of sacrificing so much privacy.

It was strange to have people asking my advice. I should have been asking them. They were the ones who had played the number, not me. Even Jill was asking my advice. The hotel she was going to be staying in in Philadelphia had two all-night restaurants and a Baskin Robbins, and she was worried about midnight episodes.

My problem was that I didn't mind her being fat nearly as much as she minded it. That's why she wouldn't marry me, in fact—not because I was so crazy but because she was so fat. She had told me about the "Fat Is a Feminist Issue" support group she had dropped out of, where burly-armed diesels from the West Village had talked for hours about masturbation techniques. She told me about an ad she'd seen in *Weight Watchers' Magazine* for outsize bridal gowns, a picture of a lovely fat blushing June bride and her fat husband.

"That picture made me so sick," she said, "that I decided that moment I wouldn't even think about marriage or a family until I got this weight issue settled once and for all."

The transit strike had traffic gridlocked all around the market, and as I walked up 13th Street to the Kinney lot, I could hear the horns, even angrier than usual, like dogs waking each other up in the middle of the night, far away in farm country where everybody had dogs. I like dogs. For some reason, most people in the meat business, Slavs in particular, hate dogs. Competition for food, I suppose. I've heard Slavs brag about how many dogs they had killed in the Old Country. Men were yelling from doorways on 14th Street as I struggled through the traffic toward Twelfth Avenue.

"Fuck you and your fuckin' horn!" I heard a man say. "Give my fucking ulcer a fucking break, for Christ fucking sake!"

Suddenly, two things became absolutely clear to me. First: I didn't want to work in the City anymore. Second: I didn't want to speak a word of Fuckinese. I decided to get 14th Street out of my career, and I decided to get the lower-class adjective out of my vocabulary.

I stopped on my way home at the Hillsdale Service Center, off the Garden State Parkway, and bought the *Rockland County Journal News*. I found a classified ad for "Butcher/Truck Driver" at a company called Suburban Wholesale. I called the number and talked to a young man who said that the job was probably filled. If I wanted to, he said, I could come in and fill out an application.

Sometimes when I'm tired I get more done, because I'm too tired to be afraid, or too tired to think of all the reasons I shouldn't do something. I found Suburban Wholesale Meats, in Congers, New York, the same town where my first private school had been located. The company was hidden in the rear of a big cinderblock building, the rest of which was deserted. A thin young man with a wispy blond beard looked up from his ashtray and introduced himself as John Crikki, a part-owner of the company.

"How many marks on your license?" he said, his fleshless lips hardly moving.

"None. It's clean."

"That's a point in your favor," he said, handing me a tablet of application forms. "Let me tell you one thing right off. The main thing I'll need from you is hours. That's what this place is about. We don't fuck around with time clocks here. We do our work and we get paid, but we don't have the fuckin' *time* to count minutes on a fuckin' piece of paper."

Then I was back home. The job was probably filled, the kid had said. It looked as if I would have to keep working in the City for a while. If only I could be sure that my voice would not be corrupted. I decided that I would make a pledge, even if I had to work in that environment, a pledge that at least I would never again, as long as I lived, use the lower-class adjective, except to describe coital penetration. In the dark, I watched a dollar bill burn in a Pyrex salad bowl. Again I smelled the clean driftwood smoke, again I thought about the Vineyard, the lights of illegal beach fires, wrapped in the night. If you look long enough into the fire, you can see out the other side, into another time, in which people strummed guitars decades ago, in the night, the three-dimensional geometry of the solid night, which hangs like an umbrella over my Hotchkiss classmates as they walk hand in hand with their wives into the dunes to lie on blankets beneath the mottlings of the Milky Way, while on the beach the nylon-stringed chords ring softly, and the firelight glints off golden cans of Naragansett beer, like the light on 14th Street flickering in perforated garbage cans, the holes in the sheet metal glowing like the windows of office buildings where account executives are working overtime; and around the garbage fires every morning stand groups of black butchers and butcher's helpers, drinking tea from Styrofoam cups, staring with a gaunt, silent, shamanlike wisdom into the ancient magic of the fire.

10

Dog Crescendo

As I walked up the metal stairs to the locker room, I could hear the butchers' voices ringing through the early morning air. It was the usual Terror-Talk, but even louder and shriller than usual.

". . . fuckin' get killed for shit-ass general make mistake!"

"They *NEVER* get out now! Fokkeen' shit country this America can't even fly a fokkeen' helli-*HOP*ter! Just like a goddamn shit American car break down all the time . . ." They were waving their arms, making whirlwinds in the cigarette smoke. Sitting at the end of the bench, outside the gallery of white-sleeved opinions, Sergie, the grinder operator, held open the *New York Post*, whose headline read:

IRAN RESCUE FLOPS
8 YANKS DEAD.

"Fuckin' peanut-butter farmer president . . . somebody oughta *kill* that stupid asshole!"

"So what the fuck you want him to do? Bow down and kiss the fuckin' ayatollah on the assaholah and tell him, 'salami salami baloney, we won't lift a fuckin' finger!' That's what you want him to say?"

As I listened to the Slavic voices, I felt again that same frantic anger I had felt when I almost ran that old black man over, in response to the triumphant Islamic intonation of voices on the radio. All at once I understood why Balkan butchers were so vocal about American helplessness in the face of the Crisis. Balkan Slavs are a conquered people. Their thousand-year-old conquered-peoples' mentality melds with the mentality of a conquered America. The voices of Slavic butchers in despair are an essential part of an enemy's psychological warfare program; and the butchers' mood seeps into the meat, and the mood spreads around, until the whole country is turning to All-News Radio 88 every time they wake from drunken sleep. On the way to work this morning, I had wondered if there was some new development in the Crisis. As I waited at the light at 39th Street, I had heard, on the radios of cars stopped beside me, the modulated tones of an announcer's voice, the audio signal having been processed through a graphic equalizer, all the high frequencies lopped off.

"Yo, Chuckie!" said Al, rosy behind stubble. "Hey, lucky Chuckie, what you think about you peanut-butter president today, yes? Them fokkeen' eight soldier die for you fokkeen' hero, what you think, ha ha?"

"What can I tell you?" I said. I was hurrying to change my clothes as the voices rang in my ears. I was wondering what it would be like on the floor today. Perhaps Sandy would be worse than ever.

"Hey, Chuckie, maybe you tell Jimmy Carter what number to play in the lottery, yes? You peanut-butter president need the money to buy some new fokkeen' heli-*HOP*ter!"

Sandy and Chris and Joe G were standing around Chris's lectern. They, too, were talking about the Crisis, but in quiet, almost inaudible tones.

"He went on the radio and apologized to the American people," Sandy was saying. "He said he'd take full responsibility. I guess I can't fault him on that. He did what he thought he had to."

They didn't seem to be in any hurry to get started on the orders.

"It's a damn shame, you know," Chris was saying. "That guy loses whatever he does. I think he'd fuck up a nigger picnic." It was strange how quiet their voices were, these men who could shout as loud as any but who knew there was a time for quiet, a concept unheard of by the butchers, who would be loud at a funeral, who at that moment, like a long chugging string of white locomotives, came puffing and Crisis-shouting through the main cooler.

"Fuckin' country defeated, and that fuckin' asshole president ought to admit it and give the ayatollah what the fuck he wants, 'cause that's who's running the world now!"

"President fucking Carter, kiss my *GAS!*"

"Vill be var soon, you see. Big bomb they shoot everywhere. I go today buy food in the can to last one year."

After the butchers had passed through the cooler, the sounds of the day settled into their morning hum, the conveyor belts, the buzz of the finned cooling evaporators hanging from the ceiling.

"Well, men," Sandy finally said. "I guess we'd better get on those orders. Those hotel guests are still going to get hungry today."

Soon we were bustling around putting up the morning orders, and we moved like well-drilled soccer team, turning and charging back and forth across the cement floor from scale to conveyor to strapping machine to bacon rack to morning flat, nobody bumping into anybody else.

"City Squire!" Chris shouted, "Six boxes Uni-bacon" Sandy was already over by the bacon boxes.

"Yo! Deckle! Catch 'em!" Sandy shouted, and started throwing the fifteen-pound boxes at me, and I caught every one and slammed each one down onto the flat.

"Good catching there!" Sandy said. "We got another Roy Campanella here, right, Joe?" Joe didn't say anything, just stared, rheumy-eyed, at something far away, across the partition that separated the order room from the storage cooler.

We rushed around in a sort of frantic harmony, all the anger and despair of living in a defeated country channeled into our work rather than our mouths; and I realized at that moment that I was management material. Perhaps my job here was not so bad after all. Perhaps it was a mistake to be looking for another job now. It was just a matter of stepping back from the yelling. If I could learn not to take the yelling personally, I could float to the top like a cork in a storm, and could keep a good pair of slacks and a good wool sport jacket in my locker to put on at the end of the day, and maybe finance a new car—nothing fancy: a Plymouth Horizon or some such, in which to be well dressed, in which to listen, on the tape player, to the music of my choice instead of the endless melodious bulletins, a financed car in which Jill and I might ride of a summer night through the mild exhausts and the sweet vapors of charcoal lighting fluid, past the yellow lights of the Carvel Ice Cream stand, with posters of ice-cream sandwiches and chocolate shakes taped on the inside of the windows, the colors dull and distorted in the insect-proof lights.

All day the Crisis symphonied in the butcher voices. I was alone in the locker room, with my cheese-product sandwich. Suddenly the room was filled with butchers.

"Fokkeen' America go down the fokkeen' drain you see. Every fokkeen' country in the world gonna turn against this America can't build a fokkeen' heli-*hop*ter no good to fight against a picnic in the Sunday school!"

"Fucking oil companies started this whole thing anyway. They're the ones should be the hostages. All they want is gas to go to two dollars a gallon. It's all fucking *money*, the whole fucking thing!"

"President Carter, kiss my *GAS!*"

"I heard about this guy invent a new carburetor to make a motor get a hundred miles to the gallon, right? Day before he brings the copyright papers to Washington, they find him dead in a fuckin' car-crash! You think that's a fuckin' *coincidence?*"

"Fuckin' *ASSHOLES*! Fuckin' money-grubbing Jew bastards, and now they got American boys getting killed to make those pigs get richer. Somebody oughta *shoot* that shit-ass president!"

Twice I opened my mouth, about to say something to the effect that sometimes economic and geopolitical forces work in ways that even educated people don't understand, but their voices were too quick to fill a pause. That was just as well. Anything I said would have sounded stupid.

Perhaps they were right anyway. Perhaps believing in conspiracy makes the conspiracy real. That is the direction in which quantum physics is moving, according to a *Scientific American* article I read once in the dentist's office. At the wildest frontiers of theoretical physics lies a land of ghosts, in which the universe is shaped by our apperception of it. Perhaps reality is fluid, a quantum function of whatever people want to believe. Perhaps a quorum of instant credulity makes *National Enquirer* stories come true. Perhaps the ghost of Elvis Presley does indeed haunt the studios at Capitol Records, padding through the darkness, nibbling a phantom Fluffernutter, intoning secret messages backward onto master tapes. Rest, perturbed spirit! Perhaps this quorum of perception makes legitimate all the churches of faith built around conspiracy theories concerning John F. Kennedy. Perhaps parallel realities exist, thousands of them, in which the belief in it has brought into physical being the reality of a paralyzed president, lying in a secret room of Parkland Hospital in Dallas, which free-lance stringers for the *Enquirer* have seen Jackie and Caroline and Ted come out of, red-eyed, each Christmas. Like the wave-particle duality; what is real depends on the questions you ask, depends on what you already believe, and the word spreads around, from butcher to butcher, in the councils of heavy television viewers, until at last the universe is ringed with conspiracy.

I was checking off the weights on a load of boxed shells as the butchers were going home, their voices tired from the long forum, as they filed through the shipping platform, to the street, to the subway, to the Bronx.

". . . fuckin' oil companies . . . Jew bastards run the whole freakin' . . . carry dead soldier in the street . . . fuckin' peanut-butter farmer . . . fuckin' country gonna crawl over and die . . ."

After work, Herman and Wilfredo and I rode in a taxi to Barney's clothing store on Seventh Avenue at 17th Street. It felt strange to wander among the racks of banker's gray worsteds and commanding pinstripes wearing my not-very-clean brown corduroy jeans and a yellow flannel shirt. It's the kind of store where most men put on a suit to go shopping.

The salesman, a short, stocky Puerto Rican in a three-piece gray herringbone, talked with Herman and Wilfredo in rapid Spanish as he showed me through the racks until I found one in just the right shade of blue, and another man stood me in the three-mirrored nook and made chalk marks around the shoulders and crotch. It would be ready in five days. Wilfredo counted the money out of a blue-and-white bank envelope, and the three of us rode by taxi back to 14th Street where they dropped me off at the Kinney parking lot, and we shook hands, and the taxi pulled away into the traffic with a whooshing of hydromatic drive, and I watched the Checker's boxy yellow dome blend with all the other yellow vehicles, and the traffic was yellow, and my car was yellow, and sad little yellow curtains flapped from a curtain rod in the open third floor window of one of those fifty-thousand-dollar artist's lofts above Spectranome Electroplating Laboratories.

I drove home softly, as tabloid headlines shrieked from inside laminated acrylic vending boxes, and the Crisis was everywhere, or so it seemed, even in Waldbaum's, where I stopped for groceries. Ladies with shopping carts were not stopping to chat. The checkout girls would make fleeting eye contact with shoppers, then look away, embarrassed. Prices were going up every day; even Mary Tyler Moore, in the opening sequence of her show, shuddered in helpless disgust at the price of steak. Defeated. I felt that I could see the hyperinflation in the eyes of tightly coiffed housewives as they hurried to get the canned goods to the register before prices went up again. From countersunk speakers set flush with the ceiling, the vibrato of electric guitars and pizzicato strings of E-Z-Listening WPAT gave way to the soft female voice of a news reader.

"Waves of religious joy are sweeping across Iran today in the wake of the failed rescue mission," intoned the processed voice.

As I took a walk around my neighborhood, I could see the hugeness of the Crisis, or so I thought, in the very façades of the houses all up and down Get High Street, something toothless and humiliated and empty in the vacant stares of windows and doors, and dogs were barking, but their voices seemed drained of all fierceness, and other dogs would hear them and start their own spiritless barking, and kids were riding bicycles around and around at the spot in Brookview Estates where Plantation Road and Shirley Street came together in a T, the kids not saying much, just circling silently, and more dogs started to bark, until every dog in the neighborhood was barking, and somebody's homework papers were blowing around in a little whirl-wind, and here and there a car would slowly wind through the streets, trying to conserve gas.

I could still hear the butcher voices in my ears. For a moment I wished I knew either much less or much more. If I were an unemployed bulldozer operator, if I were a carpenter and my friend Jill a receptionist, perhaps we could understand issues in their iron simplicity. Or if I knew more, I could understand all five sides of every question, and such understanding would bring with it a kind of tranquility. Doubtless President Carter understood all the reasons why the rescue mission had failed, knew the economic, organizational, command- and-control reasons that lay behind the failure, understood them all as thoroughly as he understood the physiology of his own intractable hemmorhoids, and perhaps all that knowledge gave him the comfort he needed while apologizing to the American people.

My problem was that, by virtue of three years at Quinnipiac, I knew that there was such a concept as complexity, but I wasn't well enough informed to expound on the actual issues. If I were to read every week the lead articles in *The New Yorker,* I could have made progress in understanding the World Situation. But as I have said, I never read *The New Yorker,* even though it is my favorite magazine.

Charcoal fires were starting up around the neighborhood as I went inside to my TV Dinner to find that the Bugs Bunny special, "Go West Young Rabbit" had been preempted by CBS for a special report, "America: The Agony of Defeat." My next-door neighbors were trying to train their cats not to go "Up There," wherever "Up There" was.

"NOOOOOOOOOOO!" my neighbor Ralph roared above the stereo. I could hear the slap of hand against fur. "I've told you *THREE TIMES!* Do you fucking *understand me?*"

My living-room wall rang with music and angry voices. Outside the open window, the Cresent Drive Spelled Wrong evening settled down, with smells of steaks on hibachis, and I could hear dogs barking, and other dogs barking, could hear the traffic, the cars and motorcycles of those who still lived with their parents roaring and screeching up and down Get High Street, everybody else driving very slowly to conserve gas for the long war to come; and then the Hillcrest fire siren started up again, blanketing the hills and the bare trees and the roofs of houses with its one long howl.

11

Lounge Rivets

Later that evening the phone rang, and a man introduced himself as Carl Miller, the owner of Suburban Wholesale Meats, where I had applied for a job on the day Sandy yelled at me so ferociously in the dry-aging room. The semiretired policeman whom they had offered the job to had turned it down. It was now down to me and one other applicant.

"I'll tell you right now, Chuck," the full and hearty voice said, "your application looks very good. Most of the kids that applied for this job have a list of tickets on their license a mile long. Do you know how much each ticket costs me in insurance?"

"How much?"

"About fifty fucking dollars, that's how much. And there's something else that my partner John was impressed with when he interviewed you the other day, and I listen to him even though he's only twenty years old, because he works his ass off in this business and he's a good judge of character. John was impressed that you didn't come off like all the other applicants and start asking right away about money money money. That's *all* some guys want to know about, and I end up wondering if they're going to have time to do any work after they've finished thinking about money all day.

"Now, here's the situation. It's down to you and this other guy, and frankly, we'd rather have you. But the other guy has already said he'll take the job if we offer it to him. So we need to work fast here and come to a decision."

"This is kind of sudden, Mr. Miller," I said. "We really haven't talked about any specifics."

"Let me tell you this, Chuck. We'll take care of you, and you won't be disappointed; you can hold me to that. Just remember, this is a new company, and you're coming in on the ground floor. As soon as things really get moving, I expect to lease a car for each one of my employees. And if you want to really help build the business, all you have to do is take some of your own time and start walking into delis and restaurants and see if you can pick up some new customers. You want to go that route—I can see you being sales manager within a few months.

"But I'm going to need some hours from you, especially at the beginning. We don't fuck around with time clocks and counting the minutes it takes for you to go to the bathroom, I can promise you that. So let's not beat around the bush. I want to offer you the job right now. Will you take it? Will you go in with us?"

I sat there with the receiver pressed against my ear. I could hear faint voices on the overloaded lines. It was tough to be put on the spot, but then again, that's what being successful is all about: being put on the spot all the time, making split-second decisions dozens of times a day. I thought about Denny Packing, the bustling, snarling, pressure-cooker mornings when nobody has time to go to the bathroom, about Joe G's white-coated back, sullen with grief, taking whatever Sandy chose to dish out, about Sandy's face, ruddy with cold and rage, screaming into my face so close that I could smell the coffee on his breath. I told Mr. Miller that I would take the job. "All *right,* Chuck!" he said. "You'll be glad you made this decision. And you won't have to worry about any fucking union sticking its nose into your business." After he hung up, I sat there, still listening to the phone, and suddenly realized that I still hadn't asked how much he was going to pay me.

I've always liked the expression "ground floor," and I've always dreamed of getting in on a ground-floor opportunity. Perhaps, if I brought in some new customers, I could start wearing my new Barney's suit to work. I could stop at the supermarket, wearing a suit, and pretty girls would know I had been to college, and perhaps our shopping carts would almost collide, and I would apologize in a soft voice, my silk tie loosened at the end of the day, and we would stand there yielding the disputed space to each other, so unlike the drivers on 14th Street with their territorial imperatives, shaking their fists out of their van windows at each other. Perhaps it would develop into a flirtation. Perhaps it would be someting I would have to apologize to Jill about, and perhaps we would have a fight. Men who go to Waldbaum's in a suit can afford to have a fight with their girlfriends, and everything turns out all right in the end. Perhaps at the moment that our voices became raised, she would say, "Are we having our first fight?" and I would say, "Yes, I guess we are; isn't it *cute?*"

I could understand her being uncomfortable with what I did for a living. She probably had to lie to her friends at the hospital. But now that could all change, and she would be impressed that I had taken things into my own hands. It's still a tough business, and people still get yelled at, but when a man in a suit gets yelled at, the words don't ring so loudly in his ears, and he can be cold and materialistic about things; although there are some things I could never be cold about, some things I have no choice about loving so much that I see the lights of it whirling in the night. I thought about the lights of a Holiday Inn rippling off the surface of a swimming pool of a summer evening in the airport glide path, with silver planes full of salesmen and stewardesses coming in on final approach, so close you can see the rivets in the sheet metal. How did airplanes become so beautiful? How did motels become so magical, full of salesmen and cocktail waitresses, the soft red light of a Holiday Inn cocktail lounge making all the faces soft and pretty beneath the lead margin-work of Tiffany lamps, the stools mounted on shiny brass armatures studded with brass rivets, and boat-shaped baskets of peanuts strewn about the bar; while in the pool, a young girl's hair waves underwater like seaweed. I realized that I was still holding the receiver in my hand, listening to the long hoot of the dial tone.

When I gave notice the next morning, Sandy's face was calm and thoughtful, without anger. He mused through a stack of invoices on his desk, while outside the luggers were loading trucks, grabbing the boxes with loud slaps of their gloved hands on the cardboard.

"Sit down," he said, pulling a wheeled chair from under the desk next to his. It was the first time I had sat down in the office. "I'm surprised, Chuck. I had you figured for management material here. But thirty miles is a long commute, and I guess it's pretty expensive."

"Anyway," I said, "I hope I retain at least some of what you've taught me. I really appreciate it. You probably think I'm leaving because I got mad at you for yelling at me, but I'm not. I've got no regrets, none at all." That was true. In five months I had learned about yield grades, about pressing open the "eyes" on a loin of lamb to make them look bigger, about reweighing every case of ice-packed chickens that came into the plant (because poultry distributors are notorious for making their customers pay for ice), how to prevent freezer burn, how to recognize overaged meat when it gets sort of waxy and heavy like proscuitto, how to use recycled boxes from other companies, how to tell by the smell of calves' livers which one should be sold first, how to judge which customers will accept wasty meat and which won't.

"Let me tell you something about yelling," he said. "The reason people yell in this business is to stay alive. Everybody in this whole market, from Freddie out there loading the truck to me and Marty Cohen; we're all under a hell of a lot of pressure. It's everywhere. Hell, I know I'm a son-of-a-bitch here, and I know that most people here hate me; but I also know that if I tried to be a nice guy the deadlines just wouldn't be met, and a piece of meat would go sour and we'd lose a customer. Shit, you know the kind of profit margin we work with. Most companies mark up three percent; I keep ahead of my competition by marking up no more than two and a half. That doesn't leave any room for mistakes. And on top of that we have all this time pressure. Our customers can't eat excuses.

"You know what would happen if I lost a major customer? You'd see every fucking banker on 14th Street come swooping in here like a fucking vulture and pick this place apart so fast that you wouldn't have time to take your Thermos bottle out of your locker before they took it away and sold the coffee out of it. That's what happened to Royal Boxed Meats across the street. Word gets around. Fucking vultures can smell a shop in trouble like a shark can smell blood.

"That's why I'm a son-of-a-bitch here. The only part of this business where you can get away with being a nice guy is in the frozen portion-control line, because you just don't have the same time factor. That's why I envy your old boss Jack Packard, because he can get away with being a nice guy and I can't. With us it's 'Sell it or smell it.'"

Outside on the loading dock both truck doors were slammed shut, and both trucks pulled out with a roar.

"So let me tell you something, Deckle. I know you're a nice guy, but if you *really* want to be a nice guy, the best way you can do that is to do something to make jobs for people. That's what people need in this screwed-up Carter-flation disaster area of a country — jobs, not slogans, not a Mr. Nice Guy President who feels sorry for everybody and reads a dozen books a day about how terrible it is to be poor, and sends letters of sympathy to people who lose their jobs. You want to know about poverty, just ask Herman and Wilfredo how much good Carter did when he went to the South Bronx and went on television weeping and wailing about how terrible it was.

"It all boils down to one thing. People need jobs. And people's jobs need other people to be mean sons-of-bitches."

He looked me straight in the eye, his cold, pigment-deficient blue eyes unblinking.

"Be a bastard," he said. "I'm serious. Be a mean son-of-a-bitch, and most of the people you work with are going to hate your guts, just like they hate mine. They curse me all the way to the bank, and I'm a happy man. I love them for it. They hate my guts every time they write out their mortgage check. They drive out of the Chevy dealer in their new car, hating my guts."

He shook my hand, and looked me in the eye. "Go for it, Chuck," he said. "Do something to help get this country working again, and you'll be a happy man."

All that afternoon, the sounds of Denny Packing seemed muffled, all the high frequencies lopped off as if by a graphic equalizer, like the modulated voices of the woman Crisis announcers on the E-Z-Listening radio stations.

"I can't say I blame you," said Joe G. "That fucking pipsqueak Sandy would insult a snake."

"Shit man, we gonna miss you," said Wilfredo. "You a fuckin' wise man. You pick the number to win money. You help me think about the hot-dog business. Last week I ask my cousin some questions about the money he makes in the hot-dog wagon, and you know what I find out? He don't make *shit,* and he wants me to run the wagon in the slow times, and he gets Saturday and holiday. I ask him about the wintertime, he say in the winter he has to drive a fuckin' gypsy cab to pay off the loan on the hot-dog wagon. I almost quit my job here for a piece of shit!"

Chris wanted to know if I had any chance to go in as a partner at my new job. "It makes all the difference in the world," he said. "Even if you have to sell everything you own. Just so you can have your name down that you're a partner and an officer. That's what I did here, and

I'm up to my ass in bankers, and I work fourteen hours a day, but it's worth it. It's the only way to go. "

The drive to the city seemed shorter every day, streets and ramps deserted, streetlights shining down on nothing. The days were getting warmer. There was a softness in the air, a mildness to the fatigued afternoons. After work I would grill lamb chops or chicken wings on the hibachi, sweet and vaporous in the leafy breeze. It would have been nice to have Jill over to celebrate my last few days at Denny Packing, but she was on vacation, at her parents' summer home on Block Island. She said she liked the off season, when there was nobody on the beach to see how fat she was.

Then it was my last day. In the locker room, I noticed that nobody was talking about the Crisis. Even crises have to have slow days, I suppose. Sometimes I regretted leaving, but I had thought the whole thing through, and it was too late not to.

"Chuckie, please!" said Herman. "Find us one more number before you leave from Denny Pack!"

As I was eating my last lunch in the locker room, Red came in and began loosening his system of trusses while gazing at the drugged girl's enormous labia, and for the last time he told me about his house and his car.

"Fuckin' thing giving me trouble . . . *psshhhhh!* Got a howling sound from the rear axle, and I don't think that thing gonna last . . . *kkkssshhhhh . . . ghsssshhhhh . . .* And I gotta use it this weekend to carry roofing paper from Perth Amboy so's I can re-roof the garage . . . *sspphhhhhssssshh . . .* "

I stared out the dust-mottled skylight at a rainless white sky, and I could almost feel the iron armature of Denny Packing sinking, like the motion of a plane landing, when you stop worrying about whether it's going to crash or not and just let yourself sink with the long luffing descent, and I was seasick and homesick, in the sad old locker room where sad old men whom I would never see again would return on Monday, back to work, back to discussions of the World Situation, from which the world takes a break, poor working stiff, every week-end, the Sundays given over to panel discussions with the earnest and the frightened and the well-informed and the recently briefed, and even Walter Cronkite was working seven days a week, trying desper-ately to update his knowledge. I was reminded, feeling the soft motion of the old building, of something I had known since the day Nixon resigned: that good-byes are sad even when you are saying good-bye to something you don't like; and the first time I realized that fact had turned out to be the very first politically incorrect thought I ever had, back at the old farmhouse, watching Nixon, whom I hated as fero-ciously as I was supposed to; watching my old enemy saying good-bye to his staff, tears running down a blond secretary's face, saying his mother was a saint, giving for the last time, in the doorway of the air-force helicopter, that two-armed salute that we hated so, my old enemy for whose death I had thirsted so many nights; and I was sad to say good-bye to all that hate, and it was a sad day for America, and it was sad later to see the tape of the moments before his resignation speech, trying to make jokes about how he'd better not pick his nose; and my friends were outside setting off M-80s in celebration; and now it was good-bye to everything, to the shrill voices, to labia shining on glossy paper like sliced calves' liver, and the truss exhalations; and then I was shaking hands with Joe G and Chris and Wilfredo and Herman, and in the narrow office I was shaking hands with Sandy and looking him straight in the eye, and he told me good luck and to use him for a reference anytime, and I was walking down 13th Street, and voices shouted in fluent Fuckinese through the doorways of meat companies, and chunky figures waddled through the streets with short puffy steps, and the warm sweet gassy winy yeasty flatulence was rising again up from somewhere among the saturated catacombs beneath the pave-ment, the yeast smell mixing with the thin sharp fumes of hundreds of diesel engines; and I drove very carefully so I wouldn't have an accident, all the way to the Grand Atrium mall and bought another suit, in Sears, a gray pinstripe from the Johnny Carson Collection, and bells were ringing as I stood, being pinned and chalked, in the three-mirrored nook, and I walked along the upper level walkway to the circle of fast-food shops overlooking the water and the greenery, and rills and waterfalls hissed and sparkled beneath the skylight among the waxy leaves, the mall almost deserted today, with children in school, a few old people navigating in pairs along the concourse, some Japanese tourists clunking around in the paddle boats, laughing and chattering; and between the main escalator and the eating terrace with stand-up tables bolted to the linoleum, stood a cylindrical birdcage, as tall as the birdcages in the Bronx Zoo, and bright green parrots screeched and screeched, and yellow-and-black finches flashed around in the caged air, and the skylight shone down above us all, cool and bright, and the pennies in the water glowed with a round bronzy warmth, good-luck pennies saying good luck to me, and good-bye to the old men and the old roaring voices, and I could see the copper kettles and skillet bottoms glowing in the window of the Well-Tempered Kitchen, and I could hear the thin hush of cascading water and the escalator humming and bells ringing in Lord & Taylor's linen light, and soft Muzak without bulletins, and Japanese laughter and paddle boats clunking, the air, the ventilation fans, the escalator machinery, and the water and the light and the wheels and the bells and the birds.

PART
TWO

12

Cherokee Volcano

As they scooted on short legs across the Red Hill Road shortcut, the eyes of skunks and racoons gleamed cold and bright, retinae reflecting my headlights, which pointed an hour o'clock to the left of where the car was going. I was hurrying down Red Hill Road to my first day on my new job at Suburban Wholesale Meats. Rockland County was in the middle of a drought; perhaps the animals were looking for water; perhaps they had rabies. Pascack Brook had dried up. The school of chubs that I used to feed, in a pool behind Building B, had died, landlocked in the airless puddle.

Here and there beside the road lay bags of leather and fur and bone, road-kills from before the winter, which the sanitation department hadn't gotten around to cleaning up yet. I had seen on Sunday, in front of the Caldor Plaza shopping center, the skeleton of a large dog, bones clean and neatly aranged, as if in the Museum of Natural History.

This morning I saw a German shepherd, alive, lying wounded by the side of the road. He looked up into my lights, imploring, and his eyes glowed. I wanted to stop and help him. But it's a bad time of day to be lying by the side of the road; everybody is either drunk or behind schedule or a criminal.

All around, in this subdivision in which most of the trees had been left standing, the branches bridging over the sidewalkless road, the houses stood silent, wrought-iron lamps illuminating the walkway, and all the doorbells were bright with a soft internal ivory-cool fluorescence. A skunk scuttled along beside the raised cement curb, glancing over his shoulder at me as if he knew I didn't live in this neighborhood.

When I saw in the dark the building where Suburban Wholesale Meats was located, the building where I had been interviewed by day three weeks ago, I remembered instantly what it used to be, from the nights at Rockland Country Day School, when we would pass that building while being driven home from Wednesday night madrigal practice, the *fa-la-la*s still ringing in our ears in the dark station wagon. It was Bubbles' Lounge, the topless capital of Rockland County.

At the side of Route 9W, a sign had stood—and the shell of it still stood with the insides broken out of it and backward swastikas spray-painted on the sheet-metal sides—a sign showing a girl outlined in fluorescent tubing, the amber curves of her body lithe and perfect, hair traced in flowing electric yellow, eyes outlined in argon blue; and I remembered how much I had desired that sign, as much as I desired the girls who sat next to me in class; those flowing lines in the night. Set back from the road, the building itself had been outlined in a cool Tinkertoy armature of light, the parking lot full of low-slung waxed cars; and I felt for a moment a twinge of desire, like the memory of an odor from fifteen years ago, like a song on WABC that I hadn't heard for years, which station had rung over the car radios in the parking lot where little clutches of over-eighteen boys and girls had stood next to the cars, Cousin Brucie's voice ringing with a slight reverberation.

I remembered those nights, the harmonies, and a taste at the back of the throat, and I remembered what it felt like to be sixteen and to desire something in a way that a thirty-year-old man might forget if he does not sometimes see things in the night to make him remember that one night is connected to all the other nights in a heritage of night, a geometry of night. I remembered the standard joke of a Wednesday madrigal night as we would pass the lines of that curving sign: "Mrs. Blake, we're really thirsty from all that singing; can't we *please* stop for a Coke here?"

Bubbles' had closed down while I was away in college, after a robbery left three employees dead. The building lay dark in the night, with only the green-and-gold lights of the Green Villa Motel across Route 9W to light the empty parking lot that sparkled with broken glass. The windows had been boarded up and the plywood painted brown, and on the cinderblock walls, among backward swastikas, the words CONGERS SUCKS! had been crossed out and replaced with

CLARKSTOWN SUCKS DONKEY DICK!

CONGERS #1   NOW AND FOREVER!

It was strange to be working outside of the City, among lakes and fields and trees, in the fertilizer smell of a newly planted cornfield separated from the parking lot by a row of trees. I could smell the soft algae of Congers Lake, and the exhaust from the trucks that went booming through the dark over the cracked pavement of Route 9W, whose broken sections of dried and friable concrete were patched with a bead of tar. Above the building I could see a few nighthawks swooping and diving, with a white patch at the crook of their thin jetlike wings. A driver passing by couldn't have guessed that there was a meat company doing business here. There was no sign, no lights, and the delivery trucks were hidden behind the square bulk of the building. I walked in the door into cement-floored loading area lit by the purple light of a bug-zapper with no catching pan beneath it. A haze of dead bugs had gathered on the floor.

In the bright-lit office, two men sat at their desks, both talking on square modernistic telephones. John Crikki, the youngster who had interviewed me for the job, bent over a large ashtray and talked. Carl Miller, whom I hadn't met in person, was shouting into his mouthpiece.

". . . up to my *neck* in accounts receivable and you're giving me this bullshit about . . ." His voice was tense with flutish anger and fear. He seemed to be talking to a creditor. "It just don't make no sense to try and beat my head against . . . Solly . . . SOLLY! *SOLLY, for Chrissake will you listen to me for ONE FUCKING MINUTE?*" Carl was a tall, athletic-looking man in his forties, like a very homely Jerry Lewis, in a white felt Stetson cowboy hat that covered most of his thick black hair. Beneath a clumsily trimmed black mustache his lower lip stuck out like a mantelpiece.

"You'll get paid when I get paid—what the fuck more can I *tell* you, Solly?" He was wearing a soft glove-leather vest, designer jeans, and what looked to be a very expensive pair of shiny yellow cowboy boots. Above his desk, on the wood-grained paneling, was tacked a poster of a yellow kitten hanging from a crossbar, mewing in terror, beneath the caption HANG IN THERE, BABY! Below the kitten, beside some framed photos of children, another sign advised CALM DOWN!" in frantic blurry Parkinsonian boldface.

Finally he got off the phone, and I introduced myself.

"Hey, I'm really glad to meet you, Chuck!" he said, shaking my hand firmly. "I'm glad you're here. This place is gonna go places, and you're in on the ground floor. You could work for ten years on Fourteenth Street before you get the opportunity you're getting here."

"Sounds good to me," I said. He showed me around the plant, first outside, where the motors and compressors for the refrigeration system were protected by a barbed-wire-topped enclosure of chain-link fence. It was just beginning to get light.

The main cooler was a concrete-floored room lined in galvanized iron, shiny and cold, and all the refrigeration motors were rushing and whooshing and turning themselves on and off every half minute. In

112

the far corner of the room, next to a white plastic cutting table, stood a two-chambered Cryovac machine, the insides of the chambers lined with smooth blue Fiberglas, like the inside of a swimming pool. It was the kind of Cryovac machine whose lid may be clamped down over either chamber, leaving the other chamber open so the operator can remove the sealed packages while the sealing machine is at work in the closed chamber.

"The way I figure it," he said, his breath steaming in the cold air, "we'll have you doing the cutting first thing in the morning and then making the Hunt's Point pickups and the Westchester deliveries, and that'll leave me time to do some more selling. There's a hundred places within fifty miles of here that we could be doing business with, but I just can't walk in and introduce myself when I've been working sixteen hours a day without any sleep. So you can take some of this off my hands and we'll all come out ahead."

He showed me the walk-in freezer, all bright and frosty, the air sweet and sharp and garlicky from the bags of Shofar kosher franks that lay in open boxes on the wooden pallets that kept the boxes from freezing against the sheet metal floor. A fringe of frost, like an Amish farmer's beard, had gathered around the rim of the doorway. I could feel my nostrils freezing in the air, like a winter night in Vermont, and for a moment I was homesick for the New England winters, the skiing weekends at Mad River Glen, the indoor months at Hotchkiss and Quinnipiac, the smell of sheepskin coats steaming in the cloakroom in the lobby of the main academic building. I wondered where I'd be by the time winter came around again, if I'd be dressed as well as my old classmates surely were, if I'd have a new car, if I'd have my vest-pocket sales accounts who would call up the company and insist on talking only to me. Perhaps I would stop at service areas on the Garden State Parkway and make phone calls, standing next to all the other salesmen at the row of phones between the men's room and the ladies' room.

It felt good to have a knife in my hands again, after months of working without one. I was cutting and tying deli-trim top rounds, beveling the coat of hard white fat down to half an inch, trimming the slanted face down to bare lean meat and tying it tightly with cotton butchers' twine so that after being roasted the whole top round could be sliced down on a deli slicing machine.

I'd never used a Cryovac machine myself before, but I had watched Herman and Wilfredo at Denny. There it would have been against union regulations for me even to turn the machine off at the end of the day if they had forgotten to. The Cryovac motor whirred and groaned as I clamped the lid over the ends of the bags that I had fitted into the gutter that ran around the inside of each chamber; and by the time I'd gotten chamber A ready, chamber B would have finished sealing and the lid would release with a great sneeze, like air brakes, and then I'd clamp it down over the other chamber and remove the sealed packages, on which the clear plastic wrap followed every contour of meat and fat and gristle and string, without a single air bubble. When it is sealed away from oxygen that way, meat can keep for weeks.

I rode with John Crikki down to Manhattan in the larger of the two trucks, a big sky-blue step van that Carl had bought from a bankrupt dry-cleaning establishment. We were in a hurry. The radio gargled with static from a faulty condensor, picking up the revvings and slowings of the engine. He showed me how to break a little piece out of the plastic lid of a Styrofoam coffee cup so to sip the coffee without spilling. He said it was strange that I'd gone so many years without ever learning how to do that.

"The whole thing about this business is to work fast," John was telling me as he weaved in and out of traffic on Route 9W, his cigarette hanging loosely out of his mouth and seeming to bend with every bouncing of the truck, like the optical illusion where a pencil appears to flex when held by the tip and loosely jiggled. He was a skinny little kid with an almost invisible wispy blond beard and a mouth and chin that seemed to have almost no flesh in them, as if all the flesh had been absorbed into the ever-present cigarette.

"If you can get in and out of these places fast enough and don't let them jerk you around and make you wait," John was saying, "then you can get home at a decent hour and have a normal life like anybody else. But you gotta push, push every day, or else you're looking at sixteen-hour days every day. It's all up to you. We don't fool around with time cards here; you're gonna be responsible for your own schedule." We were in Fort Lee, boxed in on all sides by carpool cars, whose mosaic of colors were reflected by the walls of glass office buildings, and I could smell the sweet morning exhaust, with a slight tang of sulfuric acid from the catalytic converters.

At 14th Street John sent me into Meilman Brothers for an order of extra-lean bull meat, which I locked in the truck and then met John at Colonial. He introduced me to Jimmy-the-Colonial, the shipping foreman, a powerfully built young man with neatly combed receding hair and a certain European precision to his features. I shook hands with him, and his grip was extremely tight. He grinned and looked me in the eye and wouldn't let go.

"Okay, okay!" I said, wincing. "That's enough! You're stronger than me, I admit it," but he just gripped harder until my hand was doubled over and I was jumping up and down like a man caught by a joy buzzer. People turned around and stared at me.

"Come on, *please, let go,* for Christ's sake! You've proven your point, whatever the hell it is!" Finally he released my hand, his eyes twinkling.

"Very good to meet you, my friend," he said with a broad smile. "You stronger than most, but not stronger than me, yes?" Then we were scooting with our high-piled handtrucks across 14th Street to where the truck was angle parked.

"He's quite a guy, that Jimmy, huh?" said John as we piled the boxes of Colonial hamburger patties into the truck.

"Oh yeah, sure," I said. "With a sophisticated sense of humor like that he should go on the 'Dick Cavett Show.'"

"How about 'Real People'?"

"YO! Johnny Quick!" a voice rang out from inside the narrow door of a meat company as we hurried down Gansevoort toward Quality Veal. John waved and smiled, his cigarette bouncing on his thin lips.

"Hey, Quick-Draw McGraw!" said another voice. "You got a minute to lend me, Speedy Gonzalez? Fuckin' time is money, man. I'll pay interest!"

John just grinned as we hurried up the street. "They always make fun of me because I say 'Time is money,' but I don't give a shit. I laugh all the way to the bank, just like Liberace." He was starting to talk so fast that I could barely understand him.

"You probably think I take speed or something," John said. "I've never touched any of that shit in my life. If I took speed I'd move so fast that I'd be clear into next week before my friends even got out of bed in the morning."

"YO! Chuckie!" I heard a voice say. It was Wilfredo the helper from Denny Packing, on coffee break. He hurried across the street and I introduced him to John.

"You Chuckie's new boss?" Wilfredo said. "You treat him good. He a fuckin' lucky man. He find me the number to win five thousand dollar. I don't stay in this *carnicero* job too long. Soon as I find a business to go in, I gonna quit this meat market shit."

John told me to head down 12th Street to Downtown Lamb Packers where we had an order waiting. As I pushed the empty handtruck ahead of me I could hear John and Wilfredo trying to talk, but they were both trying to talk so fast that they could barely understand each other.

"We might have a new partner," John said as we drove uptown. "That Wilfredo's coming up and talk to Carl tomorrow afternoon about investing in the company." As we headed up Tenth Avenue to the 125th Street market, where we would meet up with Carl, who was making the Hunt's Point pickups today, John started telling me about his baseball career.

"I was All-County for three years," he said in a rapid mumble, "and I hold a stolen-base record that still stands today. I turned more double plays than any shortstop in New York State for two straight years. Arizona and Florida State both wanted me on a full baseball scholarship."

"What happened?" I asked.

"My girlfriend got pregnant, so we got married. Got a job in Burger King—assistant manager. I was Employee of the Month three times. That's when Carl started coming in to eat dinner every night because he wasn't getting along with his wife, and he saw how fast I liked to do things, so he asked me if I wanted to go into the business with him. I didn't have any money of my own, so I sold my van for five thousand dollars—it was a beauty, all plush and carpeted with professional paintings of this beautiful naked Cherokee Indian girl standing next to an erupting volcano—and I sold it on the condition that I could always have the use of the small delivery van."

"I put it all into the business, which makes me the youngest corporate officer in Rockland County, unless you count those Junior Achievement deals where kids take out a business certificate for their own lawn mowing corporations. I've been written up in the *Journal News* as Rockland County's youngest businessman, and I even came and gave a talk to an economics class at Mercy College. That was fun, except I had a hundred-and-three fever and had to go back and work that night until midnight."

"You ever think about going back into baseball?" I asked him. "You could make a million dollars if you're lucky."

"I don't know," he said, and the smoke swirled around his tiny yellow teeth. "I can run, and I can field, and I can draw a base on balls like nobody you ever saw, but I just don't think I could hit major-league pitching. I guess I'd rather stay in this business, where I know I'm a star."

We scooted past the blank rear walls of Lincoln Center, pushed through the crush of traffic at Lincoln Square, where Tenth Avenue and Broadway intersect in a long acute angle and the whole square opens up for blocks on both sides of 72nd Street, the streets full of intellectuals in long blowing black coats, teenagers in groups of three on patrol shoulder to shoulder among the pigeons and the pale geriatrics who sit all day on the benchwork that runs around the edge of a skinny triangle formed by the coming together of the two almost-parallel avenues. Crossing 72nd Street, beside the tomblike sooty stone of an aboveground subway entrance, I could see to our right all the way east on 72nd Street to the edge of Central Park, could see the oxide-green trim of the famous Dakota Apartments, the setting of *Rosemary's Baby* and the home of John Lennon.

"Keep your eyes open," said John. "Maybe we'll see Yoni Oko."

"You mean Yoko Ono, don't you?"

"Whatever. Those names all sound the same to me."

13

Cellophane Merchandise

The 125th Street market, where meat companies clustered against the Hudson River, was a great sunless and airy space beneath the steel arches holding up the Henry Hudson Parkway and the even higher Riverside Drive. John and I had been waiting for an hour for Carl to get back from his pickups in the Hunt's Point market so we could exchange whatever items we needed for our deliveries without having to travel back to the plant in Congers. As we waited I took a walk around the market, across the pavilion of cement and cobblestones where small two-story meat companies faced each other across a wide plaza of rocks worn smooth from years of truck tires, with highway stanchions and butresses rising out of the ground.

There was something about the light down here, with traffic hissing overhead, and the general hum of the city all around, and the river to the west, steel-gray water with steel gray palisades rising on the other side, topped with towering high-rise apartment buildings. Pigeons flashed and fluttered through the haze, a thin haze over everything, a thinness of light and sound, with the weight of the roadways overhead, somber, supported by green copper oxide arches, and the smell of the brackish water, purging, dead fish, pale and inflated like bleached footballs floating downstream; and outside the Market Diner, whose tables overlooked a little parking lot against the water, six middle-aged black men, with what appeared to be good rods and reels, fished. Nobody was catching anything.

When I heard Carl pull in to the market with much rhythmic honking of the horn and much waving of his white cowboy hat, I hurried across the shadowy plaza, toward Miller Meats, the company owned by Carl's cousin Randy Miller. The procedure was that we would use Randy's company as sort of a base of operations, where we could exchange whatever we needed for our own deliveries; and then we would go upstairs into Randy's office and add up the items on our customer invoices and then call up Lena, Carl's bookkeeper in Congers, and read the numbers off to her.

"You'll ride with me in Big Blue on the Westchester run today," Carl said as we were transferring cases of tenderloins from the small brown van to the big blue van. "We might as well get you broken in on your regular route right away."

We climbed the stairs in the little Miller Meats building, down a dusty hall and into the office, a small room, thick with the smell of Lysol, windows painted shut. Behind a desk, Randy's secretary, a thin, birdlike, middle-aged woman with tightly coiffed black hair, was writing numbers in a book as she bent close to All-News Radio 88.

"There's another *hostage drama!*" she said loudly as we walked into the room. A man in the Bronx was holed up in his apartment, threatening to kill his wife and daughter. The secretary was trying to pretend to sound as if she thought it was funny. "Isn't this a *great country?*"

It was strange to think that the term *hostage drama* was entering people's working vocabulary. Carl and John and I sat down at the table by the window, overlooking the cobbled pavilion.

"Guess what he's saying now?" she said, pretending to laugh. I was trying to add up a column of figures for the Goody Shop's invoice, but I kept losing my place and having to clear the calculator to zero and start again. "He's giving an *ultimatum!* He says he's going to kill his wife in five minutes if they don't give him a plane out of the country!" I could hear the modulated tones of the news-voice, but I couldn't make out the words. The secretary had her ear next to the little digital clock radio and was cocking her head like the dog in the RCA trademark. "I ask you! I *ask you!*" she shrilled and quavered and twittered with ersatz laughter. "What is this world coming to?" She looked me straight in the eye, intense and desperate. "I want to *know!* What is it *coming to?*"

"I don't know," I told her, and cleared the calculator to zero once again. Outside, a single-unit poultry truck, loaded with hundreds of chicken crates packed in ice, snarled and boomed over the cobblestones. John was making little snare drum noises with his mouth as he riffled through the invoice snap-sheets for the New Jersey customers.

"*Tshh, tchh, tch-tsshhhh . . . Tsshhh, tchh, tt-tsshhhh . . .*"

"Now he says he's got a *bomb!*" chirped the small voice. The thick and homey smell of Lysol spray seemed to be getting stronger. "He's going to *blow his whole family up!* Isn't this a great country? Where a man can get *away* with that?"

All I could think of was how glad I was that I didn't have to listen to this lady's news commentary all day. Soon we were finished with the invoices, and I said, "Have a nice day," as we gently closed the door and left her alone with her hostage drama.

I rode with Carl in the big van, through the streets of Harlem, full of wobbly-wheeled baby carriages, across the Third Avenue Bridge into the Bronx, and up the Major Deegan Expressway, past the towering roundness of Yankee Stadium, where the marquee announced, FRIDAY 8 PM—MILWAUKEE.

"You know my partner John played baseball," Carl said as we passed through the stadium's shadow. "He had a baseball scholarship to Arizona University, but he got married instead."

We drove through a gray and empty forest, with the abandoned shells of cars lying here and there like dead cockroaches, past the low-slung brick buliding of the Stella D'Oro Baking Company, its yard full of delivery vans; and I could smell the cookies, warm and fresh in the midmorning air. There were little buildings that hunched against the expressway; there were trees with fresh yellow gashes in their trunks. In Yonkers Raceway a few sulkies trotted around the track beneath the empty grandstands. Just north of the raceway, the expressway ran below ground level with high concrete retaining walls on both sides of the eight lanes. On one section of wall, carefully painted words in giant green and black and red letters proclaimed: STOP BRITISH TORTURE IN NORTHERN IRELAND!!!! and BOYCOTT ALL BRITISH IMPERIALIST MERCHANDISE!!!

Carl began to tell me about the meat business, how he had been a partner with his father until the Daitch chopmeat scandal had bankrupted Mort Silver Meats and sent Carl's father to prison for a year.

"Him and Moe Felder stiffed my cousin Randy and I for seventy-five thousand dollars," Carl said, his mustache drooping sadly beneath his big felt cowboy hat. He told me how hard he had worked to get back on his feet again, about working sixteen hour days with a 103-degree fever, how he had to borrow on daily accounts receivable to meet operating expenses. He told me about how he had given up his only hobby, hydroplane racing, because of the anti-Semitism rampant in the sport.

He told me about his hopes for the business if he could ever get out from being undercapitalized. "That's the one thing I want to stress to you, if nothing else," he said as I guided the truck around a roadblock where the state police had an accident scene cordoned off with flares. "If you can raise a few thousand dollars somehow, beg borrow or steal; if you can make yourself a partner instead of just an employee, it'll make all the difference in the world."

I liked Carl. He had the sort of energy and determination that I admire. And he was right about being a partner. I made a decision, there in the truck, with the suburbs humming and rolling around us; I decided that this would be the place where I finally succeeded. I had the energy, I had the desire, I knew the meat business, and I had two good suits. All I had to do was to plunge into the work and raise a few thousand dollars to become a partner.

Carl introduced me to all his Westchester customers, to Hans, the chef of the Bedford Hills Country Club, to a wild-eyed little chef named Chaz who looked just like Charles Manson, but who apparently was the most brilliant chef in all of Westchester. We drove from restaurant to restaurant, and rotated stock in damp wooden-walled walk-in coolers and I shook hands with people and we drove some more, past immaculate clapboard farmhouses, on bridges across half-empty reservoirs, and we walked in the backs of restaurants where the rusted-out cars of kitchen help were backed against the cinderblock walls, and dishwashers drank beer and smoked joints, leaning against the humming blue finned boxes of the refrigeration units.

Then we were back at the plant. I was tired, but I felt strong. I bustled into the main cooler to clean things up, and I took out the garbage, dumping the wet Cryovac bags into an outside dumpster filled with a churning froth of maggots.

"You're doing *super!*" Carl said, shaking my hand, and roared off in his black Porsche.

I could hear the cars and trucks going by on Route 9W, the same old sound, of my home of my career, of cloverleafs and cul-de-sacs; and I thought of all the restaurants and all the kitchens around me, all getting ready for another night, knives chopping celery, frantically fast, the air all warm and fragrant with sweet sizzling onions, all the white coats of cooks and chefs and dishwashers, white tablecloths, happy customers, smiling managers and quick waitresses, the soft, nervous buzzing of a moderately busy night of electronic cash registers. There was money to be made in this business.

The next morning I rode with Carl into the Bronx, to the Hunt's Point market, where all the new companies and anybody successful enough to be able to afford it had moved. Instead of being crowded together higgledy-piggledy in the chopped up streets or huddled beneath the stanchions of the elevated highways, the companies here were neatly arranged in rows of brick buildings. There was one complex for the produce market, and another completely separate facility for the meat market, both with their own police forces and maintenance departments; and there was always someplace to park, and all the loading docks were lined up side by side, at truck-tail level against an empty turning-around space.

Hunt's Point Avenue, which ran from the Bruckner Expressway exit to the intersection of Market Road, was lined with dozens of used-auto-parts emporiums, closed diners, storefront churches, and a few dark-windowed tenements not yet torched. Even the poor people had moved out, most of them, leaving the streets to the roaring food trucks and the few wispy figures who shambled through the weeds and pavement.

Dust flew from the tires as we went booming over the dry potholes. Carl began telling me about the drought.

"This thing is going to get worse, you better believe it. Have you ever read a book called *Nostradamus: Prophet of Death?*

"No, I guess I missed that one."

"That guy, five hundred years ago, he predicted everything that's happened in this century: Hitler, the atom bomb, the freaking hostage crisis. And there's a big prophecy in that book about the 'Years of Dust,' about how the whole ecology of the world is going to be disrupted by acid rain from the nuclear power plants. And I personally think that's what's happening right now." I was driving fast, up the long slope of Hunt's Point Avenue, and as we came over the crest at the top we could see over the junkyards, across Flushing Bay to where the flat landfill of LaGuardia Airport jutted out into the water. I could see little silver planes, like toys, lined up for departure.

124

"Maybe what this guy predicted already happened fifty years ago," I said. "Maybe he was talking about the Dust Bowl in the thirties."

"No way! The chronometry is very exact: first Hitler, then World War Two, then the atom bomb, then he even predicted that Kennedy would be shot by Marilyn Monroe's ex-husband, and that he would be a vegetable hidden away in a hospital for the rest of his life. So I'm afraid that this is the real thing, just like Press Secretary Jody Powell says, worse than the Great Depression. He says we should all stockpile a year's supply of canned food."

Carl's voice was getting louder and louder, ringing through the cab of the light blue step van. We bumped over another dry pothole and his white felt Stetson cowboy hat crumpled against the cab ceiling.

But perhaps he was right. It was a serious drought, the worst in years. Civil Defense was preparing emergency distribution procedures should the water supply fail completely, and the dust was everywhere, above and below, and the drought was all over the headlines and on everybody's lips, dust all over everybody's mouth, under the smoke, laughing, dust on the brown-and-yellow umbrella of the Sabrett hot-dog wagon that stood at the corner of Hunt's Point Avenue and Market Road.

At the T formed by the two roads, in a forest of tall dusty weeds, a few prostitutes were standing and talking to the hot-dog man. They were the sorriest looking hookers I had ever seen, with stiff metallic wigs and oversized dentures, black-and-blue marks all over their drug-addicted arms. I could see foot paths worn into the weed field: escape routes, probably, for when the police came. As I turned the corner, one girl extended her tongue to us, making a small beckoning motion with the tip.

"Step on the gas, Chuck," Carl said. "You can get a disease just from looking at those broads."

I could hear above us a long hissing whine, like shapeless thunder, and a Delta jet passed overhead, on final approach into LaGuardia, all rounded shapes and shining painted metal, wobbling gently in the airs of the Bronx morning. The hookers and the hot-dog man stood still and watched the huge form go luffing down across the sky. We passed a Monfort tractor trailer stopped by the side of the road, and through the tractor's open door I could see, for an instant, a cellophane-shiny blond head bouncing up and down on the shaking pot belly of a cowboy-hatted driver.

We picked up pork loins and Shattuck hams at Stoll Packing Company, blocks of Swiss cheese and boxes of top rounds at P&L, some boneless portion-control chicken thighs at Poultry Specialties; then we headed into Manhattan to meet up with John at Miller Meats on 125th Street. John had only a few New Jersey deliveries that day, so Carl was going to ride with him in order to be back at the plant by the time Wilfredo got there to talk about buying into the business. I had my Westchester map, and I was ready to start making deliveries on my own.

Upstairs, the airless and disinfected office was quiet, E-Z-Listening music on the radio today. The little secretary didn't even look up from her desk as Carl and John and I walked in the door to add up our figures. I was wondering how yesterday's hostage drama had turned out, but I decided against asking.

Then I was heading north, alone in the big truck. All afternoon I made the Westchester deliveries, from restaurant to country club to catering house, in and out the loose and banging screen doors of kitchens full of oily warmth, rock and roll rasping from cheap radios, lovely waitresses gathered around communal ashtrays. "Where's Johnny Quick?" the dishwashers asked.

For hours I drove and delivered and tucked signed invoices inside the aluminum invoice box I had been given, and between deliveries I thought about the business, about the pledge I had made that this would be the place I would finally succeed. Somehow I would have to raise the money to become a partner. If I could do that, it wouldn't matter if I had to work sixteen-hour days for a few months.

I got back to the plant and parked the truck as they had shown me how, hard against the wall of the building so that kids couldn't get to the gas tank. In the office, Carl and John and Wilfredo were sitting around drinking Andre Champagne from the conical coffee containers that snap into a permanent plastic holder. Wilfredo jumped from his chair and shook my hand heartily.

"Well, Chuck, we got a new partner!" Carl said. "Have a drink!"

We stood around drinking champagne and talking and laughing and making plans about how we would arrange things as soon as Wilfredo's two-weeks notice at Denny was up. Although Wilfredo had only been a helper at Denny, he was an experienced butcher, and he had been assistant manager of a retail store in Ponce. He would be based in the plant, taking over the cutting duties from me. I would now be doing both the Westchester and Rockland deliveries, plus whatever canvassing I could manage on my own time. We toasted the future, brushing the soft plastic containers together, toasted the company, the meat business; then we closed the office and the four of us drove, each in our separate cars, to Howard's Calico Kitchen in the Grand Union shopping plaza in West Nyack. Carl bought us a prime rib dinner and drinks. Under the arc lights in the parking lot, we all shook hands again.

I was driving home, slightly drunk, in my crooked, crabwise car, and every time I passed a restaurant or a delicatessen or a catering house, I pledged to myself that I would visit that place in one of my two good suits and bring them into our company as a new customer. Perhaps I could negotiate some way to make myself a partner that way, through what is known as a "contingency investment."

I remembered a book I had read about selling, by Joe Girard, the world's most successful car salesman. He told about how, when he talked to a prospective customer, he didn't see the guy's face, but saw instead a bag of groceries balanced on the client's shoulders, and as long as he could visualize that bag of groceries and think about his wife and children waiting for him at home, he never ran out of motivation, never ran out of things to say.

And as I passed all the restaurants on Route 59, their lights twinkling in the darkness—Hong Luck, Athenian Balcony, The Terrace, The Hofbrau Haus, Pepe's Taco Garden—I tried to imagine them as enormous bags of groceries, with the tail ends of cars sticking out of them, great Santa Claus bundles of electronics and textiles, all waiting for me, for me to string words and smiles, and strategy and shoeshine and handshake, together in just the right order. I could see it all, the slowly turning interlocked platforms of a carousel-system of prizes, like the prizes in the opening sequences of game shows, all-expense-paid trips to the Bahamas, Christmas in April, gold nest eggs on a bed of straw; and I could feel the car's worn wheel bearings hum and shimmy as I passed furniture stores and light-fixture stores and windowless toy stores floodlit from above and below in yellow and red and blue and green, fabulous and exciting merchandise, the vagaries of fortune, oval-cut diamonds in a breathtaking setting from Van Cleef and Arpels, and the thousands of little transactions that make such things possible, vagrant breezes above the golden arches, eggs over easy, the pale and pimply skin of an ice-packed stewing fowl, the clatter and clink of a thousand fragrant kitchens, the voices of cooks in a hurry, vowels for sale, Thuringer, mortadella, sweet sagey scrapple, the kidney business, the liver business, diaphragm steaks, a world where once you buy a prize it's yours to keep, and all the beautiful waitresses standing around, millions of dollars just waiting to be earned in the brokerage of offal, little oval patties of minced and spiced by-products, minted rack of lamb, the awful offices of industrial dismissal, the 500 Club, the "21" Club, the country club, money on account or in a gift certificate, lights and wind and crabwise wheels over the rolling hills among the lawns without sprinklers, the children's hour, the cocktail hour, the hours of economic destiny falling like a bright blanket over my green-and-gray gravy-scented sidewalk of dust and bicycles O Vanna!

14

Walnut Abbreviation

On Wednesday night Jill called me from Block Island to say that she was in ice-cream trouble.

"I'm really sick of this, Chuck," she said, and I could hear the high trembling note in her voice, wavering over the underwater communications cable. "I purposely got maple walnut, which I don't even *like,* so I wouldn't go crazy with it, but I've already eaten a whole quart."

For some reason I knew exactly what to tell her. I asked her what was the most expensive take-out restaurant on the island. She said that the Harbor Light sold take-out lobster for twenty-five dollars.

"Here's what you do, Jill," I said, without having to think. "Go outside right now and throw the rest of the ice cream into the water, and then call the Harbor Light and order the lobster dinner, and get on your bicycle and ride over there and pick it up. Bring it back home and put on a record and eat at least half of it, and preferably the whole thing. That way, if you have to feel guilty, you can feel guilty about money instead of food. Okay?"

Jill said my idea was perfect, and that she felt stronger already. She said she loved me. She would be flying back home on Thursday, and we arranged to have dinner together on Friday night.

When Friday came around, I was already in a state of mild shock. My first paycheck was less money than I had ever made since I'd been in the meat business. But Carl and John were very straightforward about it. They admitted that my pay was low, but they both pulled out their personal calculators and started factoring in gas and tolls and wear-and-tear and the time I had been spending on the road driving to Denny Packing, both arriving, simultaneously, at an almost identical figure. All in all, I wasn't really much worse off than before, and I had to agree with them. Plus, they assured me, it could only get better. All I had to do was buckle down for a few months, and all would be well, as soon as my driving days were over and I was sales manager.

They encouraged me to get started with the canvassing on Saturday, and I agreed. I was glad that I already had my two suits. All I needed now would be some new shirts, ties, and shoes, which I would get at the mall after Jill and I had dinner together at her house.

When she answered her door, Jill looked better than I had ever seen her, tanned and trim and smiling.

"That little maple-walnut crisis was just a momentary glitch in a very well-behaved vacation," she said as we sat down to a crouton salad and white wine. "I ran for an hour on the beach every day, I didn't even bring my portable television with me, I read my Spanish books every night, and I lost a total of eight pounds."

"You can read Spanish? You never told me that."

"Oh, sure. I speak it fluently. I even dream in it sometimes. We lived in Puerto Rico for three years when my father was director of the Firestone plant in Ponce."

I sat across from Jill at the Formica dining nook and watched her carefully spooning up the vinegary croutons and ragged kale, and I saw, especially in the low dining light, that she had lost a good deal of weight, especially around the soft curves between her ear and her jaw; but instead of being happy for her, I was aware that all I felt was a dull nagging fear, as if watching her drift out to sea, getting smaller and smaller, like a bright beachball in the wind.

I told her about my new job, about long hours in the wilds of Westchester among half-empty reservoirs, the thrill of being paged on the plant intercom for the first time, how John insisted on spelling Idaho *IDAO* on the order sheets for the steak fries we distributed, and how he would not be instructed in the proper spelling. I told her about my sales plans for tomorrow, about how someday I was determined to raise enough money to buy into the company, about coming home half drunk down the Route 59 Miracle Mile, how all the restaurants had glittered like bundles of shiny cargo in the night, how I promised myself that I would land those accounts. I like the expression "land that account."

The gronky, droning barrelhouse guitar of Boomer Williams filled the living-room speakers. A frail canary jumped and fluttered in a hanging cage beside the window. Neon tetras drifted, wormlike, around the perimeter of the fish tank. I was remembering how I had held her and protected her in my arms that crazy day when she was throwing up, how soft her red-rimmed eyes had been. But now I saw something stronger, a woman who could rattle off a language I knew nothing of beyond memorizing the warnings about not riding between cars in the subway, a woman whose thighs were firming week by week, who earned twice as much as I did.

Suddenly it came to me, as clearly as the points of light in my glass of Almaden Chablis: I wanted her to stay fat. As long as she was fat we were safe together. I could protect her against ice-cream crises, and she could comfort me when my job got too crazy. I just wanted to relax. I wanted for us to be able to sit around and commiserate for years and years as the wild seasons blew around us, leaves and sun and fog and smoke, and we would be a constant, a pair of twin compasses, anchored, whose firmness draws one another's circles just, a plump and peaceable binary star around which the galaxy wheeled its astonishing carousel.

We drove in the dark, to the mall, in the moist and dusty rainless night. From the upper parking lot we could see the red taillights queued up for a hundred yards at the Hess Gaseteria, beyond that the gelled fountains of the Kabuki Garden Japanese restaurant, and the lights of Waldbaum's. She took my hand as we walked toward the north entrance. I wanted to ask her again to marry me, but I knew she never would. As long as she was fat she would never marry me, and as soon as she stopped being fat she would end up marrying one of her brother's stockbroker friends, and I would never see her again. I wanted to pretend we were teenagers, among the snarling boom boxes, wanted us to be able to sit on the benches beside the sand-barrel ashtrays and kiss each other on the lips the way some of the kids were doing. But it would have looked ridiculous, the two of us, who looked so torpidly married already, a little too old, a little too fat.

We walked slowly from store to store, past the pinstripe suits standing at trim and headless attention on the carpeted terracing of Wallach's display window. Babies in strollers gurgled. Shiny brown wing tips, with pairs of argyle socks neatly draped over the heels, glowed in Florsheim's diffuse light, the leather all warm and bronzy, like the pennies underwater downstairs among the rills and fountains. Kids were hanging out, buying nothing, a few of them clunking around in the paddle boats, others smoking cigarettes. Boys holding imaginary electric guitars pantomimed long skids close to the linoleum.

Jill bought a butter-pecan cone from Ice Cream Emperor and threw it in the garbage. This, she said, was her new method for controlling ice-cream crises, as inspired by my suggestion to her the night she called from Block Island.

"This way I feel a little guilty about wasting money," she said, "but

I still get the satisfaction of throwing the I.C. away." She always called ice cream "I.C."

"That night when I threw the rest of that half gallon in the ocean, I felt so good I wanted to run twice around the whole island. The moon was full, it was a beautiful warm night, and I just stood there for five minutes watching that lump of maple walnut float out to sea like a little iceberg."

It was nice to have a shopping companion with taste as conservative as my own. Jill helped me pick out ties and shirts, and she encouraged me to go for the good shoes, the ones I really wanted instead of the cheap ones, and the Visa trolley went *chunk-a-chunk,* and we walked out the north entrance into the darkness, the moist and rainless lukewarm air full of sweet mild exhausts, and I could see the hazy brightness of the Miracle Mile, and the headlights and taillights, and the chalky brightness inside the local buses onto which kids crowded with their boom boxes. I could hear the six lanes of Route 59, a long uninterrupted breath of airy traffic, the suburban hum of a thousand soft voices, soft motors, kids on the curb laughing and trying to knock each other's hats off, shiny Corvettes and Trans-Ams, with sonorous Glas-Pak mufflers, woofing down the long space between the parked cars; and I could feel below us the beginning of summer coming up from under the ground, a softness underfoot, an elasticity in the tarry macadam, and I thought about the soft loam beneath, all the worms and centipedes and roly-poly bugs, and I could feel, through the soles of my new eighty-five dollar Florsheim wing tips, the first Florsheims I had ever owned, that the ground was warm under my feet, that the long traffic song of the night was mine, that Rockland County was mine to be explored and shaken hands with, a place to do business, to take people to lunch and be taken to lunch, to wake up at a reasonable hour and put on a clean shirt and drive to work in a waxed and financed car; and I knew I was on my own, starting tomorrow, a salesman with a vision. Salesmen are all dreamers, and their wives are all beautiful.

The same white Camaro was going round and round the parking

lot, and each time he went woofing past, the Bee Gees Doppler-shifted down a half tone. The Conrail train came clattering along a ridge at the south end of the upper parking lot, the line of bright windows snaking through the dark. We walked and walked, holding hands. I couldn't remember where the car was.

The next day I put on my suit and shirt and shoes and tie, and drove all day from restaurant to restaurant, walking in the back doors of restaurants tucked into miniature shoppping centers, parking my yellow Volkswagen beside the rusted-out clunkers of kitchen help. Dishwashers without green cards eyed me nervously. Most of the owners weren't there, but I shook as many hands as I could and left my business card.

At lunch in McDonald's, among the jeans and football jerseys, I was the only person in a suit. Everybody must have thought I was a Jehovah's Witness.

Late in the day, I walked into a place called Mr. Kold Kuts, a narrow little delicatessen squeezed between a discount beverage outlet and an Allstate office, and introduced myself to the owner, a man named Frank. He had just had a fight with the local Boar's Head Provisions distributor.

"Sure, I'll give you a try," Frank said, taking a quick inventory of his walk-in. "Can you get me a dozen deli-trims and six boiled hams early Monday?"

"Yes sir, I sure can!" I said, my ears buzzing. We agreed on the standard one-week credit for new customers, shook hands, and I was out the door.

Every salesman remembers his first sale. I was dizzy with it, everything buzzed and tingled; the barrel-shaped transformers atop the telephone poles hummed; and the traffic seemed to be going faster and faster. I could feel the warmth of the earth beneath my tires, the rolling and solid ground, just a ball of dust and money and business lunches spinning through the formatted emptiness of Einstein's curved space. The traffic was an enormous smooth machine through which I could have drifted without touching the controls. Lights winked on and off, automatic transmissions wheezed and whooshed, like platelets marshaled through capillaries, and it was all mine, all the warp and woof of cross streets, the whole municipal fabric.

In Shop-Rite, I could feel the smoothness of the linoleum through shopping-cart casters as I taxied down the aisles, and colors blazed under the white tubes of light that ran along the ceiling, wild and bright, Froot Loops, Count Chocula, Fab, Alpo, Skippy, a bin of thick-skinned oranges, the vitamins, the Band-Aids, bright cosmetics, cheese product, each slice wrapped, and all the shades of meat, first-cut shoulder steaks marbled with flecks of white, thick wedges of bone-in New York sirloin, the porosity of the saw-cut bones pink and young, the white fat cover of portly shoulder roasts standing high above the surrounding meat like the arched tops of old-fashioned cars in a modern parking lot, the deep brown of loin lamb chops, six to a tray, tails overlapping, tarry brown slabs of beef liver, the ochre-amber glow of calves' liver, the mild pink of center-cut pork chops, the white bloodless beige of milk-fed veal, and all the chickens, yellow as a taxi in the rain. Kids with Bugs Bunny balloons were running up and down the aisles. A toddler, his face swollen with tears, shambled behind his mother's cart and howled with despair. A trapped English sparrow flew around fast and frantic in the space between the lights and the tops of shelves, and the checkout girls were all pretty.

On Monday, Carl was busy on the phone with creditors. I was hoping he would get off the phone before I left for Hunt's Point so I could tell him about my first sale, but he just sat there and gripped the phone, so tightly that the veins in his hand bulged.

"Solly . . . SOLLY!"

"Heavydaytoday . . ." said John, percussing with his mouth as he handed me the list of the morning's pickups. "*Tshh, tshhh . . . tt-tcchhhh!*" It was warm outside. Insects were hatching in the muddy flats of Congers Lake. In the darkness of the loading dock, the bug zapper buzzed and crackled. Oriental swastikas, arms pointing counterclockwise, had bloomed over the weekend, like angry red flowers on the white cinderblock of the south wall of the building, and one had been daubed on the rear door of the blue truck.

Cars were bumper to bumper on the Tappan Zee Bridge above the angry gray water, and all the trucks had American flags lashed to their radio antennas. IRAN SUCKS said the bumper stickers in handsome rainbow letters against a black background. Many of the cars had in their rear windows a plastic hand on a stick that waved slowly back and forth with the motion of the car.

At Hunt's Point, in the jets' glide path, the herpetic horse-toothed hookers were out again, among the weeds, as trucks boomed over the potholes of dust and jets came whistling down the flyway, voices singing high and sensuous above the low and pressed-down Bronxscape. The loading dock at P&L Packing was a jumble of angry voices. The order department there was running late, and six of us were waiting around for our orders. Beefy-armed young men chugged up and down the little stairway. At Stoll Packing I had to wait in line behind the other white coats in a side office where a grim-faced fat man with the mangled end of a cigar in his mouth tallied up the invoices on an old-fashioned Burroughs mechanical analogue adding machine that went *chunk-a-chunk-a-chunk,* counting decimals on its metal fingers.

All week I drove, picking up and delivering, trading items with John at 125th Street, loading ribs for the Bedford Hills Country Club, Prime shells for the Overlook in Mt. Kisco, skirt steaks and frozen five-pound lumps of gray chopmeat for the Goody Shop. The hours were long, it was getting warm, and I would be sweating beneath my paper hat by noon. Frank at Mr. Kold Kuts repeated his order for next week.

"You're doing great!" Carl told me on Friday, handing me a twenty-dollar bonus with my check.

On Saturday I put on my other suit and drove from restaurant to restaurant, walking past finned outdoor compressors that turned on and off with a shuddering clunk, into the warm kitchens fragrant with chives and onions and hot oil, steamy garlic, marinated lamb-kebabs, dilled stewing fowl. I soon learned to give up on Italian restaurants. They all had cousins in the business. The owner of Hong Luck jabbered at me in Chinese, pretending not to speak English. The Village Tea Room liked our chopmeat prices and wanted to see a sample on Monday; and I took that as a positive sign, driving home in a dream through the lights and merchandise.

15

Lysol Trail

It was Monday morning. Carl and John were bent close to the crackling bulletins of All-News 88. A volcano had erupted in the state of Washington.

"We have lost radio contact with a large area of central Washington," intoned the bulletin voice, "and speculation is increasing that at least a quarter of the state has been destroyed by this, the worst natural disaster in the history of the United States."

"You know, I really think this is the beginninng of the end!" said Carl, his eyes wide and darting beneath the long brow of his cowboy hat, his voice gathering volume in the office light. "A freaking *volcano!* This is just the kind of thing that's in *Nostradamus: Prophet of Death!*"

"They're saying that so much dust is coming out of that thing," John said, rushing the words out, his cigarette bouncing up and down with the motion of his lips, "that it's going to block out all the sunlight and start another ice age, just like the one that killed the dinosaurs."

Wilfredo was on the phone, droning in rapid Spanish.

"He's trying to call his brother in Oregon," said Carl. ". . . if there *is* an Oregon."

There was still an Oregon, as it turned out. Wilfredo's brother wasn't home, but he had managed to get through to one of his brother's neighbors. That area had been upwind of the eruption anyway.

"They didn't see nothing," Wilfredo said.

The toll gates were frantic, the clerks grim-faced, radios rasping in the tiny glass booths, even the Crisis preempted today, with the rolling gray water shaking beneath the mile of backed-up traffic on the Tappan Zee Bridge. At Hunt's Point the girls were there as usual, in the forest of weeds, and the silver-white jets came hissing down the same trajectory, with the same overwhelming sweet and sexual whisper of sky being torn apart, moving with the streamlined grace of the very large, and I saw the shadow of one flash dark across Market Road in front of me. It was a beautiful day. The sun was round and gold in the rainless haze. In the distance I could just make out the soft blue shapes of the Manhattan skyline. Horns honked, motors snarled, refrigerator motors clattered idly on trailers queued up outside the Daitch Central Commissary. A Dodge Window-Van, weighted down with boxes of meat, bore on its radio antenna a large American flag topped with a plastic skull.

Over the course of the day, and over the subsequent days, it became clear that the world was not ending any faster than usual, and the voices went back to normal, and the drought hung stalled over the air. The Village Tea Room said the chopmeat sample that I brought them was too gristly. One morning as I sat waiting in line for gas, it rained for two minutes, and the large drops kicked up little puffs of dust between the gas pumps.

The sun shone through days of gray dust; Congers Lake purged and stank sweet and flatulent. Nighthawks screeched in the darkness above Suburban Wholesale Meats, where long ago those bright bars of light had made the night wild and the liquid lines of a girl's hair and eyes traced in argon blue had been set off against the cold nights of traffic and the echoing reverb of WABC. Trees were green, with the white rags of tent caterpillars everywhere. We worked and worked.

I came in at five every morning, to an office full of coffee and soft music. John would be making snare-drum sounds with his mouth as he shuffled papers around. I usually spent the first hour helping Wilfredo get the morning orders ready, then I would drive the blue van to Hunt's Point, in the dawn light, with the land stretched all around, open, with pieces of horizon visible in spots. The gouged hillside of the U.S. Gypsum Company's Haverstraw quarry grinned in the distance, like a mouth full of bad teeth. Blue Hill Tower, Rockland County's only skyscraper, stood blue and hazy in the distance.

I usually took my coffee break in the middle of the Tappan Zee Bridge, and I often had lunch on my way from Hunt's Point to 125th Street, on the Third Avenue Bridge, hard by the edge of the Harlem River, where the fleet of Marino Concrete trucks stands huddled against the bank, jolly red and blue balloons painted on the white hulls of the mixers, like the balloons on a Wonder Bread wrapper.

I would usually get to 125th Street before John did, and I would park the truck and walk around, in the ringing space, sunless and bright beneath the arches of the Henry Hudson Parkway and Riverside Drive, while huge white single-unit poultry trucks jerked and braked and snarled and honked, jockeying themselves tail-end against crabbed loading docks. It was warm now. The sweet air of dumpsters and fat barrels rolled through the hazy space, stirred and blown by wind-displacing square hulls of trucks. Little pieces of spleen, or *melts* as they are called in the meat business, lay here and there on the rounded stones, a deep paintlike red. Dusty-coated dogs licked slowly, as if without hunger, at the blood. Black men fished, staring across the gray slick bending downstream from the 155th Street Sanitation Facility, staring at the Galaxy Towers, rising from the palisades in the town of Guttenburg.

As soon as John had picked up everything he needed from 14th

Street, he would drive uptown, pulling into the 125th Street market with horn tooting in a shave-and-a-haircut rhythm, and we would trade items for our respective deliveries, then hurry upstairs to the airless lysol-scented office and add up our figures, while John percussed and the secretary bent her ear to the bulletins. John would call Lena, the bookkeeper in Congers, and read the figures off to her, and then we would be off, in the heat of noon. I drove and drove for hours, in the furnacelike box of the van, sometimes so hot that I could feel the outer capillaries around my brain working hard to protect my cortex from becoming thermally compromised. No matter how carefully I read the map, no matter how many shortcuts I discovered, I still couldn't seem to save time. My days got longer and longer. I never got back to the office before six in the evening.

I drove fast, gunning the strong motor in the unrefrigerated blue truck, cutting people off when I had to, leaning on my horn constantly. Sometimes I could hear the tires squealing on the exit ramps.

One day, running late, I was doing sixty-five down the Crow Hill Road shortcut near Mt. Kisco when a state trooper pulled me over for speeding. By the time I got back to the office that night, John already knew about the ticket. Great Eastern, Suburban's insurer, had an information-sharing agreement with the State of New York whereby any change in the status of an insured driver would be fed immediately into the Great Eastern computer.

"You just cost me a hundred dollars in insurance," John said as I walked in the door.

During this time I didn't see much of Carl, except in the mornings when he would be on the phone with creditors. Then he would roar off in his leased black Porsche. One day I managed to speak to him just as he was leaving. I asked what we could do about these long hours. A glaze went over his eyes, and his voice got very loud.

"Don't worry, Chuck," he said. "You're doing super! Just *super!* We're all going to be breaking our asses for a few months, but I promise you'll thank me in the end. I'm trying to work out a deal where I can merge with All-County Produce Distributors and we can be a full-service house. This whole county's going to be eating out of our hand. Literally!" And we both laughed at the joke.

On Saturdays I went out selling, drifting off-line in my bent car, but most people didn't even want to talk to me. Something would go blank in their faces.

"What are you selling?" deli owners would say with immense weariness. Too tired to interrupt, they would hear me out, then sadly shake their heads. "Sorry."

One hot Sunday we had our first company picnic at Carl's house, in a green wooded subdivision full of droning insects. Jill wasn't sure if she could make it; she was working Emergency that day, but I gave her directions in case she got out in time. Carl's wife and two teenage sons flipped big porterhouse steaks on the grates of a permanent stone barbecue. Above the pool, set into the chain-link fence, like one of those billboards at the edge of a Little League field, was a sign saying:

WELCOME TO OUR 'OOL.
Notice that there is no *P* in it.
PLEASE KEEP IT THAT WAY!

It was a clever sign, I suppose, but somehow it seemed a little out of place. Sometimes you just have to trust your friends. There's such a thing as being too territorial, like the drivers on 14th Street who shake their fists out the windows of their graffiti-covered vans, who display bumper stickers that say YOU TOUCHA MY TRUCK—I BREAKA YOU FACE!

The sun streamed through the fluttering leaves, bounced off the surface of the urine-free water, sparkled on the ice in the galvanized washtub full of beer. Lena and her husband sat silent on lawn chairs, holding ashtrays in their laps.

Over the picnic table, Wilfredo told me about his last week at Denny, how I had been replaced with a big fat Yugoslav who could

142

barely speak English, how Herman had already lost all his lottery money in Atlantic City.

It was just beginning to get dark. Carl and John and Wilfredo and I were sitting around the redwood table with beer and pencils and paper trying to figure out how we could divide the deliveries so that we could cover more ground without having to hire anybody else.

Just then I heard the small burring *tockety-tock* of Jill's Chevette diesel pulling into the driveway. Jill appeared around the side of the house where the flagstone walkway led from the driveway to the back yard. She still had on her nurse's uniform.

"*Mira,*" said Wilfredo. "We don't call for no ambulance!" and we all laughed loudly in the dusky light of beer and water. I introduced Jill and she shook hands with everybody. The barbecue coals were still glowing, but she wouldn't let Carl put on a steak for her.

"I already ate at work," she said, but I knew she was lying. She had told me earlier about her current self-discipline project, in which she would put herself in what she called "pigging-out situations" and eat nothing at all.

We sat around the table and talked of work and meat and money and gasoline. It turned out that Wilfredo's father used to work in the Firestone plant in Ponce where Jill's father was the manager. They talked and talked in rapid Spanish. Carl was belching, and John was making snare-drum noises. The mosquitoes were starting to bite, so we moved the picnic inside to the leather furniture of the den.

Then it was time to go home. Carl's driveway was filled with smoky exhaust and handshakes. "*Muy gusto!*" Wilfredo said to Jill, kissing her hand through the window of her car, and we all left together, Lena and her husband in their LTD, John and his wife in the small Suburban van, me in my crabwise Volkswagen, Wilfredo in his old Camaro, Jill in her boxy little diesel; and we toodled along through the soft curves of the Sylvan Acres subdivision, to the stoplight at Little Tor Road; and we all turned left together, like a little train, past the Dairy Queen, an island of mothless yellow light. Over the tops of trees I could see the screen of the Rockland Drive-In, giant faces arguing, the wheels of a jet landing.

I like summer, the way the air hangs like a fishbowl over the night, over the yipping voices of children playing tag, or whatever they play these days. The air hangs over everything, and the time becomes as thick as clotted milk, and a man working fourteen hours a day can lose track of time, and things can happen in the warm secret places where things have been known to happen; things can happen so quietly that hearing about them will feel like a slap in the face. In McDonald's, two weeks later, Jill told me that Wilfredo had invited her to come to Atlantic City with him that weekend, and that she was going. My Big Mac lay cold and half-eaten in its hinged plastic container.

"It just doesn't make sense, Jill," I said. "What the hell are you going to have in common to talk about once the novelty of speaking Spanish wears off? *No entiendo!*"

"I don't know what to tell you, Chuck," she said. "It just happened, that's all. I don't want to hurt you, but shit, I don't want to hurt myself either. And I can't ignore how I feel, the chemistry he and I have together. You're right; it doesn't make sense. But things aren't always *supposed* to make sense. And if anybody can understand that, you should be able to, because you were the one who taught it to me. That's what I've always loved about you; you don't have all these standards and logical frameworks for the world to fit into."

"But for Christ's sake, Jill, couldn't it have been somebody else? Number one—I gotta work with this guy. Number two—it looks *terrible.* Couldn't it have been a doctor at the hospital, or one of your brother's stockbroker friends? Somebody with a six-figure salary and a three-piece suit? If I have to lose you, couldn't I lose you to somebody more respectable? What am I going to tell people when I'm crying in my beer? They're going to laugh at me."

"I'm sorry," she said. She touched my hand, on the clean Formica tabletop. This was the first I had known that they had even been seeing each other.

144

Later, as we drifted in my car, through the dust and Dairy Queen lights, I could feel through the tanned skin of her shoulder how much weight she'd lost.

We were busy every day. I drove into the dust plumes of road construction projects, gunning the motor, spinning the tires on dry packed earth, from kitchen to hot kitchen, little musical ovens full of sizzling oil and onions and rock and roll.

Then one day the drought broke. It rained and rained, and dishwashers stared, hangdog, out the screen doors of kitchens. The wide space of the 125th Street market became a sea of brown water, knee deep, across which white-coated figures slogged. Once I drove up the Major Degan with my pants off, my feet bare, clothes drying out in the breeze from the heater. I drove very carefully, so that I wouldn't get pulled over with no pants on.

Isis was back on television on Saturday mornings, beautiful Isis, glossed lips shining, coal-black hair blowing in the wind as the Egyptian gods appeared in response to her touching the magic amulet. I love Isis, and I love Chrissie Evert at Wimbledon and I love the pencilled eyes of all the beautiful girls in cartoons. The whining whispering singing jets glided low over my head each Bronx morning, and the old-fashioned Burroughs adding machine of the Grim Tabulator at Stoll Packing went *chunk-a-chunk-a-chunk*. Every day in the Congers office I would say "Good morning," as I have always believed in saying whether it be a good morning or not; and Carl would be belching, and John would say, "Heavydaytoday," and resume his percussing, and the bug-zapper would be zapping bugs in the anteroom.

"BUUURRRRPPP!. . . . Bzzzzttt!. . . . Tshhh, tshhh, tt-tschhhh!"

On Sunday nights my favorite show came on: "Chobin, the Star Prince," a Japanese cartoon about a little neckless imp who lived with a father and son in a forest. For the first fifteen minutes of the show, nothing much would happen. Chobin and the boy and the old man would bump into things and laugh and squabble in rapid Japanese.

Then a squeaking bat-winged shape would appear in the corner of the screen, a robot spy for the villain, and everything would get all convoluted, and the fabric of space would turn inside out, to the sound of hollow gangrenous laughter; and the villain, whose name I never learned, would appear, seated on an undulating throne, barking malevolent Japanese commands.

Every time the show came to this point, I would think about Monday morning, my job lying in wait for me like a troll beneath a bridge—long hours, low pay, with no improvement in sight, unless I could come up with the money to become a partner. That would make all the difference in the world. People would respect me. Perhaps Jill would even get tired of Wilfredo, but not neccesarily. He was a smarter man than I had thought, a mathematical wizard who instantly understood Carl's abstruse inventory system.

The unrefrigerated blue van that I drove began to take on a sweet and cloying stink from the chicken juice that leaked from ice-packed Perdue cases and festered and fermented under the wet rubber floor mats, a thick and steamy bubbling stench, like hot soup. Every day I would spray Lysol and drift for hours in its homey, friendly, safe, and round-edged floral cleanliness, trailing a long and fragrant wake of sweet vapor. I drove through long days of rain and sunshine, perched high in the van, and all the heavy fragrances stewed and boiled in the sun as I passed construction flag-bearers and kids on bicycles going to play baseball. My paper hat, which said IT'S OUR PLEASURE TO SERVE YOU, was soaked with sweat by the time I got to my first Westchester delivery. Waitresses were blond and cool-fleshed and beautiful, but until I could become a partner in Suburban, I was too ashamed of myself to talk to them.

All the trucks flew flags, and the bumper stickers flashed in the sunlight. Traffic ran for days like a tired and voiceless machine; flags charged across the Tappan Zee Bridge, among the whitecaps.

On the Fourth of July, my father stopped at my apartment on his way from Florida to New Hampshire. His brother, my Uncle Charles,

146

had died in Florida, and my father had been there to close up his apartment and take care of his final affairs. He pulled up in my driveway in Uncle Charles's Oldsmobile Vista-Cruiser, while all over the neighborhood, for miles and miles, the streets and hills sputtered with thousands and thousands of firecrackers.

Over dinner at the Roman Steer, which I had chosen because they were one of our best customers, my father told me about Charlie's final hours in the cancer ward, but the restaurant's P. A. system was playing so loud, with quotes from Carter's Fourth of July speech, that I could hardly pay attention.

He said he'd seen the will. Each of Charles's six nephews and nieces would get a small share of his money, probably four or five thousand dollars, but only if they could meet certain requirements.

"The money has to be used either for educational expenses, or for investment in a legitimate business operation," my father said. Outside in the parking lot, we could see crowds of people streaming across the lower parking lot of the Grand Atrium Mall, toward the American Legion baseball fields. The fireworks were about to begin.

"There's a time limit on this money too," my father continued. "If it's not invested within one month after probate, that money will revert back to his estate. It's a crazy stipulation, but you know how he was, and Tom Foster says it's legal. That's the sad thing about his life. With all his success, and all his money, he never learned to have confidence in other people."

We heard the first explosion of the municipal fireworks, a loud echoing single blast. I told my father about my own situation, how I had been looking for a way to buy into the company I was working for. He said it sounded like a good idea. All I needed to do would be to have Mr. Foster, Uncle Charlie's lawyer and executor, check out the company and give his approval.

We finished our desserts, and then went out to Uncle Charlie's car just in time to see in the distance the last of the fireworks going off in a not-very-grand finale of sputtering air-bursts and catherine wheels.

Strung between one of the Little League foul poles and the raised ladder of a hook-and-ladder truck, an array of blazing letters formed the words LET OUR PEOPLE GO! and all around we could hear the throaty choir of a thousand car horns, gathering strength in the summer night; and then with a soft spreading roar of exhaust, the engines were starting up.

We were marooned in a sea of family station wagons, all trying to get back onto Route 59. People were tooting their horns in rhythm. Children were holding napkins around the base of their ice cream cones. There was a terrible smell in the car, like scorched saliva. My father said that it was Charlie's ashes, packed tightly in a five-pound box.

On soft Vista-Cruiser springs we drove through the hot night of traffic. My father wanted to stop and visit one of his old colleagues from Prudential, but we couldn't find Hillside Terrace. We drove through subdivisions full of smoke and sparklers and bottle rockets streaking skyward, like meteors going the wrong way. We asked some kids for directions. They didn't know where Hillside Terrace was. They had been setting off so many firecrackers that the scraps of shredded paper covered the pavement like the duff of dead leaves on a forest floor.

16

Phosphorus Hatbands

Two weeks after the Fourth of July, a memorial service for Uncle Charles was held at my parents' summer house in White Lake, New Hampshire. I made a coach reservation for Friday night on Amtrak's "Montrealer," which would get me to White River Junction, Vermont, early Saturday morning.

After work I took the local Red and Tan bus down to the City, getting on the southbound local just as the commuters were getting off the northbound express, jackets slung over their shoulders, ties loosened. All around us the evening thunderheads gathered. The air was thick, with a whiff of ozone, as I leaned back in the bus seat and watched all the shapes pass by, trees and houses and Dairy Queen stores, firehouses with flags at half mast. For some reason the flags at firehouses are always at half mast, and there is always a black-and-purple commemorative plaque hanging above the garage doors.

I thought of Uncle Charlie's last days. It was remarkable how little sadness I felt. All I could feel was the pleasure of taking a trip to the country for a weekend. The person I was most interested in seeing was Mr. Foster, Uncle Charlie's executor, who would be there to discuss the probate situation with all of us. I had already told my father about my plans to use my inheritance to buy into Suburban. Perhaps Mr. Foster was already in the process of approving the project. I drifted off to sleep.

When I woke up we were almost there, the bus held up in traffic at the ramp that inclines down from the Union City cliffs and around under itself into the three bright mouths of the Lincoln Tunnel. I could see the skyline, lights everywhere, whole floors of tall buildings lit up in the towering gray dusk. The weekend is a quality of light, a change in the register of horns and voices, and I could feel the quickening pulse of Friday night in the city, as red taillights winked on and off, lined up for the tunnel, going to a Broadway show, and I could feel the heaviness of the meat business beginning to lift as we whizzed through the yellow tiles of the tunnel.

The train had not even left Baltimore yet, the lady at the Amtrak ticket counter said. Thunderstorms had knocked out the power north of Washington. People in designer jeans, carrying fancy leather suitcases, were scowling, cursing under their breath. I checked my bag at the baggage window and walked out into the air of the night.

I was tired, but I walked and walked, up 34th Street, through a little tunnel of an arcade full of egg-roll shops and beauty parlors, past the three-story McDonald's Town House, past the long brightness of Macy's window, where it was already fall, wrinkled construction-paper leaves around the feet of mannequins in tweed. I could smell the metallic ozone air that exhaled from a subway entrance, and in the smoky light of a plywood newsstand the *New York Post* was stacked high as a man's waist: KHOMEINI'S U.S. HIT LIST. Girls with Macy's shopping bags stood at the curb, raising their hands to hail the low-slung yellow taxis that went whiffing through the streets.

I walked up Broadway to 42d Street, where movie marquees lit the night, and the pavement was a wilderness of milling figures, and disco music throbbed into the street from the open doors of peep-show emporiums. Behind the window of Tad's Steaks, beneath the sign that advertised New York Sirloin steaks for $2.89, potato and salad included, a cook flipped the wet, marinated meat on the powdery white bars of the grill, and little puffs of flame shot up from below, lighting his oily complexion.

I walked uptown in the humming of light, hearing the quickness of city shoes scuffling on dry pavement, and I could feel the heaviness of the night hanging over us like the hulking shapes of the buildings, full of ionized moisture, and all the lights were cool, and the air was warm. I sat in a Roy Rogers on the second floor, and watched the taxis surge like stampeded cattle down the long space of street where Seventh Avenue and Broadway, both one-way running downtown, intersect in a long oblique angle.

There was music and light and air and sirens and laughter, fried-potato smells, beef kebabs on wooden skewers grilling over charcoal, and the sweet lampblack of bus exhaust. I could smell the warmth of greasy marinated lamb wrapped in pita bread, vented from the door of a Souvlaki-Stop, with sour cream and onions and hot sauce. In the chalky light of an adult bookstore, the faces of men without ties stared, expressionless, at the glossy flesh of magazine pages; and on 48th Street young men peered through steel bars at the racy shapes of electric guitars.

Peddlers stood on almost every corner, youngsters selling butane lighters and cigarette-rolling papers, holy men in white fezzes and jackets selling incense. Some peddlers sold electric yo-yos that blazed and sparked in the dark. Others sold bands of phosphorescent plastic in the form of glowing bracelets, belts, and hatbands. One peddler had dozens of the bright bands around one forearm, and he made half of them whirl in one direction and half in the other. Kids were walking around wearing the cool and moonish cyaluminescent plastic around their hats.

I walked through a green glass tunnel under a floodlit waterfall, beneath the dance of foaming water. I walked all the way up Seventh Avenue to Central Park South, where the large and serious shapes of the New York Athletic Club and Marriot's Essex House stand watching over the darkness of Central Park, where nobody goes. People in light pastel shirts and summer dresses strolled along the sidewalk on the park side of Central Park South, through the thick and windless embrace of thermally inverted air, lit from within by its own internal urban diffusion, beneath the overhang of trees, everybody making sure not to walk too close to the wall that marked the edge of the empty park.

Columbus Circle was a carousel of buses and taxis going around and around beneath the bright façade of the New York Coliseum; and wispy figures, children, stood alert between the granite columns of the entrance to the park, and whispered hoarsely, "*Smoke! Cocaine! Joints and bags—check it out!*" All around I could see the bright moony greenness moving in the dark, swinging at the end of people's arms.

I sat at a table by the outdoor bar beside the lobby of Alice Tully Hall, sipping on a gin and tonic, watching the taxis flash by. I had walked all the way to Lincoln Center. My feet ached. I watched the fountain in the middle of the open-ended quadrangle formed by the New York State Theater, the Metropolitan Opera House, and Alice Tully Hall, watched the dance of white water in the lights.

I wondered about all the people I had been talking to and working with this morning, whose chugging walk and labored breathing seemed so absent from the city tonight. Where do the serious ones hide when the night blows in with its breath of light and children? How can a place so opposite to itself remain one city? Where were all the shrill-voiced butchers? Where was the Grim Tabulator with his mangled cigar, the birdlike secretary with her hostage-drama updates?

Perhaps their part in this picture of the night was hidden; perhaps the light of their televisions flickering blue tonight and every night would add to the city's brightness. Still it was sad to think of so many people sequestered in the dark family rooms of the Bronx, all the houses old, the streets old. Everybody was old, and they all hated the City, hated it with their whole lives, but without rage, dull, faces like gray putty. Even young people in the meat business, and other Bronx-related businesses, were old. My twenty-year-old boss John, except for driving through it between the downtown and uptown meat markets, had never been in the City, never ridden a subway or flagged down a taxi, never even been curious about it.

I could hear the breath of summer traffic, could feel the embrace of the City, all the food and money and motion and sex, thousands of tires scuffing soft across an intersection; and I felt sad for all those who had fallen out of friendship with New York, who had chosen to hate it for its smells and strangeness, who dare not stroll down Fifth Avenue on a Saturday afternoon, who spend evening after cholesterol-saturated evening around the backyard barbecue with the same old neighbors, not even drunk, talking about nothing.

At 1 A.M. the train finally left Penn Station, the seats rustling with the motion of people settling down for the night in the hissing of scrubbed and air-conditioned air. We glided over the Bronx, past floodlit playgrounds where strings of amber streetlights stretched off into the dark, the glare of tenement street after street. The air blew cool from vents around my window, and the shapes of light and darkness blended into a formless motion of night.

We were going fast now, into Westchester and Connecticut. I watched the platforms of commuter stations flash past, too fast to read the names. As we passed the sooty Gothic walls of the Mianus power plant, I knew that we were going through Riverside, where my Uncle Charles had lived most of his life. I wondered how many mornings he had waited, briefcase full of Young and Rubicam storyboards, on the very platform that now flashed past and disappeared.

While we were stopped at Bridgeport, the power went off. All the motors fell silent. The doors of the train were open and people were getting off and walking around on the elevated wooden platform in the heart of the summer, in the middle of Bridgeport. It was too hot in the train to sleep. I stood at the edge of the platform, looking through chain-link fence down at the Pequonnock River, where it rolled in lazy dimples through the cement caissons of a low bridge.

I was exhausted. I'd been up since four in the morning, and now it was almost two the next morning. My ears were buzzing from the busywork of a long day. I could smell the river, and the steamy exhaust of traffic. In the distance I could hear the Connecticut Turnpike, where nighttime cars and trucks, wide awake, went singing over an arched bridge strung with light.

It was the middle of the night, the depth of summer, the middle of Connecticut, and the whole state seemed to breathe and snore with one secret respiration. In the harbor's hazy brightness, even the most ordinary things had a secret middle-of-the-night look to them, the dark wood of a rotten piling at the water's edge, the dusty bark of trees on the street beneath us. A police car prowled by, slow and silent.

There is a place that stays up all night, somewhere, everywhere, a land where clocks don't stop, and nothing disappears. Some lights, in factory stairwells, hospital storerooms, have no off switch; somewhere in the thin blue hospital night, a psychiatric nurse is all alone in a dispensary, counting green capsules into a pleated paper cup. I thought about Jill, busy in the blue light of the late shift, how clean her uniform in the hours when most people are asleep, but I didn't even know if she was working this weekend. Maybe Wilfredo was over at her house right now, the two of them luxuriantly air-conditioned together; and the more I thought about that possibility, like thinking about the man whose sad death I was on this wild excursion because of; the more I thought, the less it hurt; and it occurred to me at last that I was a spiritual athlete, a marathoner of limbic invulnerability, batting a thousand, that all I had to do was fix my gaze on the land around me, on the textures and the undulations and the haze of bright smoke in the shape of the night; if I looked at such things, then other things would fail to hurt.

154

There are people on the graveyard shift, night dispatchers, night editors, and there are people who drive around all night in shiny station wagons from hospital to hospital, delivering blood. There is a sound the night makes, not a collection of sounds, but one long and tired and endless sound, the sound of a living city smothered with sleep, where beneath amber steeetlights the cars lie dreaming, domed with all-night summer dust, and the old river drifts, dirty, and somewhere a nurse looks out a tiny blue-lit window and catches a moment of light on the slumbering surface.

I love a dirty river. A dirty river is a river where things are happening, a functioning conduit in a living municipality. I would like to walk beside the dirtiest river in the world, on slippery flat rocks, in the sweet steamy smell of summer. There are rivers that were meant to be dirty, brown slime of the Thames, algae-choked Liffey, the mighty Hackensack. There are rivers who carry that dirtiness without shame, who wear a texture of trash and decomposed lawn-stuff like a slum child with a dirty face. I love the way oil puddles and foils out into coppery rainbows, and I love the way the motion of brown water raises little dimpled roils in the surface, like cellulite in a fat girl's legs.

A state is a single thing, with its own wholeness, its own blood and magnetism, its own breath; and it is divided by rivers, some filthy, some merely dirty, with dangerous sooty straight-necked whistling swans waddling up onto people's lawns; and it's difficult to say where the Pequonnock ends and Long Island Sound begins, and you can't see the boundaries between the townships and counties, and the trains and trucks and sleepless cars go whiffing all night from zone to zone, and the old river rolls, and butchers get up early, in the steamy sweet darkness of Connecticut, and they report to work in the hard light, amid the somnolence of Hartford, where my father was an actuarial intern at Prudential the night I was born to the buzzing light of hospitals, close by a warm and fetid channel, where little pieces of rotten wood, then as now, float beneath low bridges, and splinters cling, like magnetized dust to a dry pencil, around the broken spot in the water where a snag gathers slime.

Down below in the dark, a pickup truck poked through gravel pathways, nosed itself against the land-retaining pilings at the edge of the water, and lowered its headlights. Nobody got out. I could hear the loose and easy thrumming of the engine, mixed in with all the summer sounds, the long Turnpike song, the hum of barrel-shaped electrical transformers, and the wavering skittish note of tires on the metal grating of a drawbridge. I could smell the river's soft mucky brackishness, and the haze of all-night car exhausts, the old salty New England smell of a comatose harbor, where fresh and salt water blend and stew in a tract of cattails, a flat marsh out into which is built the cinder landfill where stands the American Shakespeare Festival's replica of the Globe Theater, the boxy theater and the parking lot of a hundred buses all surrounded by the spongy earth, the brackish wash of mud and papery reed stalks creeping up into the parking lot where years ago, let it be known, I have stepped onto Hotchkiss buses after seeing a play that we had studied beforehand.

I was happy. The hugeness of the night hung over the little Amtrak station. Something important flew in the night, on invisible white wings, and all was calm and bright, the secret hours when chimes are turned off and clock towers glow like hazy moon faces, and insects whistle and sing, and nobody in the world is angry about anything, even the delayed passengers in no great hurry, off on a Montreal weekend, lounging around the platform, chatting with the conductor, leaning against the silvery ribbed steel of the train. White moths fluttered in the light of a Seagram's billboard overlooking the street below the station. A bat flew back and forth, papery gray in the floodlight, just another shift worker with an all night job, systematically harvesting the cloud of insects.

The power came back on with a bright whinnying shudder, and the train lit up, like the bars of light on a Ferris wheel. Everybody hurried back aboard. We slid away into the New England night.

The funeral the next day was a simple outdoor memorial service, on the lawn of my parents' house, cooled by a breeze blowing off White Lake. We sat in folding metal chairs whose feet dug holes in the grass. On the porch a string quartet played. As we listened to the eulogy, we could hear the faint strains of amplified fiddle music. This was the weekend of the annual White Lake Summer Festival. The village was filled with tourists. At the other end of town, a flatbed truck was being used as the stage for a country fiddling contest.

After the service, Mr. Foster called all the nephews and nieces together and we all walked across town to meet with the town clerk, who was also officiating at the horse-pulling contests. We sat down at a table that the town clerk had set up in back of the barbecued-chicken concession. Mr. Foster, a precise little man in plaid slacks and a maroon Izod polo shirt, who looked as if he were not at all used to doing business in anything but a suit, explained that this was not actually a legal proceeding, but rather an exchange of information made necessary by the demanding but altogether legal stipulations of the late Mr. Deckle's will. Most of the projects outlined by the beneficiaries were quite straightforward, he explained, although he would need to see all the proposals on paper before he could give any final decision.

"Charles, I'll need to speak to you in private," he said to me as the meeting adjourned. We walked together back to my parents' house, between the concession tables of the Summer Festival. Kids were running around holding corn-on-the-cob on wooden skewers.

"I've taken the liberty of checking into the company you were proposing to buy into," he said, "and I'm sorry to tell you this, but Suburban Wholesale Meats doesn't meet any of your uncle's specifications as to what is a permissible investment."

"It's just a small company, Mr. Foster. What's wrong with that, besides not being listed with Dun and Bradstreet?"

"I'm not worried about their D and B rating. But I did check into their credit rating and into the background of the CEO—what's his name, Miller?"

"That's right. Carl Miller."

"It turns out that Mr. Miller has already declared bankruptcy twice before in other companies. He's got four lawsuits pending against him, and most suppliers refuse to do business with him at all. I suggest you don't either, Charles. The guy doesn't pay his bills.

"Your uncle was very specific in his will about what he thought was a sound investment and what was not. I personally thought, when he and I went over the document, that he erred on the side of conservatism, and I anticipated having mixed feelings about being required to veto some basically sound proposals. But I'll be frank with you, Charles: I have no mixed feelings about vetoing this plan. Your boss is a crook."

On Sunday I sat and looked out the airplane window, watching the curves of the Connecticut River pass below, watching how the twin roadways of Interstate 91 would follow the river for a few miles, then wander off to do business with cloverleafs and factory complexes. A haze hung over the land, my head throbbed, my ears popped. I had spent most of Saturday night in the Landing, White Lake's only bar, with my cousins Harrison, Stuart, and Franklin. It was the first time in years that I'd closed a bar.

Route 91 was busy with cars coming home from vacation, getting ready to go back to work. I thought about other people's jobs, all those offices where people said "Good morning" instead of just "Heavydaytoday," thought about the open sprawl of subdivisions where people owned their own houses and drove to and from work in shiny financed cars; and I thought about my own job, lying in wait for me, in the darkness of the morning, like the monster in "Chobin, the Star Prince."

I understood at last why we had to buy from suppliers in all three markets and spend so many hours shuttling betweeen them; it was because only a few companies would do business with Carl. Now I understood why there was no time clock. Only by getting free work out of people could Carl Miller undercut the prices of union shops; only by manipulating his investors could he keep his creditors off his back. Now I understood why he didn't have any partners his own age. And now I couldn't even get back in the union, since I had voluntarily accepted a nonunion job; that was the rule.

Below us the land was becoming more populated, full of meandering subdivision streets, factory parking lots, empty high schools, the bright crescent of a baseball diamond, and all the pools, little blue drops set into the hazy green. As we passed over Hartford, I could make out the sleek glass Prudential office building where my father had supervised so many training seminars. The Connecticut Turnpike was bumper to bumper, a Sunday haze of a million family station wagons.

The sun glinted on a patch of windshields. We were beginning our descent. I thought about the weeks ahead, about the vacation I wasn't allowed to have. My parents had the Menemsha house for two weeks at the end of August, but I couldn't get time off.

"A vacation the first year is out of the question," Carl had said, loud and serious, his lower lip jutting out beneath the brim of his white Stetson cowboy hat. "We have to make sacrifices in this business."

I could feel the soft motion of the plane as it came whiffing down through blankets of air, for a moment I thought I would be sick, last night's scotch still heavy around my temples, but then I sat back and surrendered to the motion, and everything waltzed and buzzed and tingled, the large and airy motion of the USAir DC-9, the hard sunlight glittering off polished metal surfaces below. I didn't care if we crashed. I wasn't the pilot; I couldn't do anything about it except surrender, let the soft luffing lullabye motion carry me wherever we were going, down over a hundred cloverleafs all choked with cars, through the Sunday haze of the inner suburbs, over a thousand swimming pools, the red clay of tennis courts, all the golf courses with their little yellow sand traps and the blue puddles of water hazards, parking lots full of thousands of boxy yellow school buses, the saddest sight in the world, yellow as cheese, yellow as the sun riding low in the afternoon, the flat shapes of supermarkets with roofs cluttered with refrigeration machinery, and all the houses, thousands of sad little houses going on forever.

We were coming in over the Bronx. I could see the tall blocky shapes of Co-op City, and off beyond the green forest of Pelham Bay Park, City Island jutted out into Long Island Sound, as if hanging by the thread of its only bridge. Out-of-business factories and vacant gravel-fields drifted beneath the plane. We passed over Hunt's Point market, sliding down the same glide path as the planes I watched every morning as I made the Bronx pickups.

How square and orderly the two markets looked from the air; the produce market and the meat market, each surrounded by a wall, amid weed fields and automobile junkyards whose broken windshields glittered in the sun, the rectangular buildings ranged in military precision, like the cellblocks of a state-of-the-art prison from which no man has ever escaped alive.

I took the Carey Transportation bus from LaGuardia into Manhattan. The driver was angry about something. At each airline terminal he would shout through the bus's open door, *"Rotten apple!"* or *"Crime city express!"* After he had stopped at all the terminals, he roared out into the Sunday traffic of the Grand Central Expressway, into a world of green trees between the inbound and outbound roadways, grinding the bus's gears through the long rolling green of cemeteries.

17

Chlorine Puddles

I washed the outside of the blue van with a mop. With a can of turpentine I erased the backward swastika on the van's rear door. I rinsed under the rubber floor mats as well as I could, and poured Pine-Sol around the places where the mats were glued down. For a few days the smell disappeared.

Then the chicken juice began dripping down again and running under the mats, which baked all day in the sun. The decay began again, rich and full-bodied, a soft-edged, round sweetish, earthy, soupy bubbling smothered fragrance of chicken rot, all the fat-soluble proteins decomposing in the warm darkness under the wet black rubber pads, and with every application of the brakes the smell would drift forward and fill the cab with its warmth and softness, everything sweet and stinking, complex amino acid molecules breaking apart into a hundred primordial compounds, a hot ooze of hydrogen sulfide, like overcooked lamb, too sweet to be sour, too rich and close and dark and

161

fecal to be sweet, an overpowering cloud of gassy barnyard complex-
ities steaming in the air around me, as all day long the van's crackling
AM radio updated the latest developments in the Hostage Crisis. I had
gotten in the habit of leaving All-News Radio 88 on all day, and every
day I could feel the old anger boiling up inside me like the sulfur soup
that boiled and bubbled beneath the rubber mats of the van. I thought
of President Carter's ruined and exhausted face, he who could do
nothing; I thought of my own ruined career, and the loud-voiced ones
who benefited from it.

And the old van smell came rolling back like a river of weighted air.
Below the wet-intestine smell of chicken juice was the friendly reassur-
ing smell of Lysol, which I sprayed daily, a soft flowery fragrance, safe
and homey, clean and pure, and the fragrances blended and steamed
and stewed like a warm chicken stock in a cast-iron pot, and every day
it got sweeter as the days got hotter. The smell had its up days and
down days, depending on the heat and the humidity and the calendar
of its own fermentation, some days with a sour cucumberish note,
sometimes with a putrescent edge, like the smell of dogs and cats
decomposing by the side of Route 59, sometimes a sharp and maggoty
edge to its bouquet; and sometimes I had to stop between deliveries to
spray more Lysol, and it would be all soft and pink and floral, and the
blue van would drift in a deodorized cloud through the summer
suburbs, through days of green and shade, among swimming pools in
the same shade of blue as the boxy unrefrigerated Dodge where I sat all
day and breathed the strange and private chicken smells. Sometimes,
through the side window, I would catch a whiff of chlorine from
somebody's swimming pool.

Some streets are bridged by a canopy of leaves under which the road
surface is mottled with sun and shadow. Kids in bathing suits would
be riding bicycles, their swim fins in the carrying basket, kids going
fishing, going to play baseball, fielder's gloves hanging folded from a
handlebar, families going on vacation in big overloaded shiny station
wagons; and as the blue van passed through this neighborhood of

narrow Tudor stone houses, on a shortcut between Howard's Tavern and the Jumping Jalopy, among the stone facing and the trimmed hedges and the steady whining trill of insects in the windless heat of the afternoon, it would leave a trail of its sweet chicken fragrance, sulfur and Lysol, fermenting molecules and gardenia nectar, and I would imagine the kids on bicycles wrinkling their noses as they crossed through the vapor trail, knowing somebody had passed through their neighborhood who didn't belong there.

One of my regular deliveries was the Nyack Swim and Tennis Club, whose kitchen entrance was just across the fence from the pool, where the voices of children rang off the hard poolside surfaces, the splashing, the short sharp cries, the timeless sounds of summer, immune to the Crisis. I could smell the clean chlorine, little puddles of sanitized water evaporating on the walkway of fiberglassed concrete that ringed the pool. Sometimes I could hear the dry thumping tight rattle of the burlap-covered diving board, and the plosh of kids doing cannonballs.

"Mommeeeee! Lookit *meeeeee!* Mommeeeee! Watch!" In the light air I could smell the cigarettes of the women who sat around the pool in painted wooden chairs in the hard sunlight, reading mystery novels, could smell the coconut oil of suntan lotion and the steaming puddles on the walkway; and each time I heard thoses voices and smelled the chlorine and soft smoke and coconut oil, and saw from beside the kitchen dumpster how the pool's surface threw wavering patterns of light onto the side of the building; when I heard and saw and smelled those things, I would think about all the things that I was denied by virtue of poor career planning and a dozen split-second decisions gone sour (or was it luck, or demons, or the Welfare State, or the will of an angry God?).

I hadn't been swimming in a year, hadn't played tennis in two. I hated to let myself be seen here, a man in the meat business, in my dirty white butcher's gown and my paper hat saying IT'S OUR PLEA-SURE TO SERVE YOU. The hat was a lie. It was not my pleasure to serve anybody.

I used to be one of those kids, splashing around in a pool that smelled and echoed the same as this one. This was my life, in which I jumped up and down to shake the chlorinated water out of my ears. These were my people, and this was my town, the green and residential buzz of Nyack in its leafy August languor. How did we lose each other?

We go back a long way, chlorine pools and I, the green canvas sheets around the tennis courts with little half-moon grommets to let the wind through. We spent summers in Bethesda, Maryland, at my grandparents' house. I took swimming lessons at the Edgemoor Club, and we splashed and yipped in the pool, and my mother sat in a chaise longue, which she *never* called a "chase lounge," and the town drifted in a green summer trance, and yardmen were trimming hedges, and six lanes of traffic whispered through downtown Bethesda, and the hard sun beat down on the orange tin shingles of the roof of the Hot Shoppes restaurant.

I hadn't seen Jill in a few weeks, although I had talked to her on the phone. She seemed to be going out with Wilfredo regularly. I was surprised how little pain I felt on the morning that I was replaying the tape machine for the day's orders and suddenly heard her voice telling Wilfredo to call her at the hospital. It was as if my feelings toward her were at last independent of any issue of fulfillment or consummation. It was enough just that she was around, part of the suburban landscape. The times I loved her most were the times I had to make a delivery to the Chicken Pit, which was in the Grand Atrium Mall, and I would remember the times we had spent there, drifting through light and music.

Carl owed eighteen thousand dollars to P&L Packing, one of our main Hunt's Point suppliers. One day they cut us off. Rich managed to find a supplier in the middle of the South Bronx who would still give us credit.

The bonuses stopped. The "good mornings" stopped. Suburban ground down to its grim business. Wilfredo started calling in sick a few times a week. One Friday the drive-in bank refused to cash my paycheck. When I called Carl's house his wife told me that he wasn't living there anymore. On Monday he covered my bounced check with cash, then looked away, saying, "Let's get to work."

Every day as I drove through green streets in the stench of the van, my long-hours thoughts, and my News Radio 88 Crisis thoughts, would come roiling up, confused and feverish in the van's heat. Sometimes I would get so angry that I would start driving crazily, slamming on the brakes when nobody was around to see, leaving a smoking black trail of rubber behind me. Sometimes when I thought about long hours I would put the van into neutral and gun the motor mercilessly. Once the fan belt broke, and the van overheated in the middle of Yonkers. I hated to do things like that. I had nothing against the blue van. It was a good vehicle, except for the smell.

I was driving crazy sometimes in my own car too. On the way home, when I passed the Empire National Bank time display and saw that I had worked fourteen hours that day, I would fly into a rage and go roaring up New Hempstead Road, the flag that I had lashed onto the antenna fluttering, the tires screeching around the turn onto West Clarkstown Road. I got a ticket for running a red light in the van. This time Carl made me pay the fine myself, a hundred dollars. Another day somebody saw me slamming on the van's brakes, and had called the company to report my dangerous driving.

One day when the blue van was being tuned up, I had to drive my own car down to 14th Street to pick up some boxed top rounds at Meilman. As I was stopped for a light on my way uptown to 125th Street where I was to meet up with John, a man with a brown paper bag in his hand started yelling at me.

"*Mira!*" he said, making large motions toward my flag with his middle finger. "Fokkeen' *peeg!* Fokkeen' fascist *PEEG!*"

I tossed a quarter on the street in front of him and said, "Here you go, Fidel. Buy yourself some nice *vino.*"

As I was pulling away, the man threw a brick through my rear window, spraying chunks of diced safety-glass all over the inside of the car. I pulled over to call the police. As I got out of the car, I could see the man running toward me, shouting, "You insult me with fokkeen' quarter, you fokkeen' *peeg!*" He reached into a dumpster in front of a burned-out storefront, and pulled out a long metal pipe. I ran away up Tenth Avenue to the next corner. As I called 911 I could see the man attacking my car with the pipe, pounding on it furiously. Nobody tried to stop him. Ladies with baby carriages turned around and strolled the other way. He knocked the engine cover off and jabbed at the engine as if with a harpoon, then threw down the pipe and walked away.

The Volkswagen was totaled. The man had broken all the windows, crushed the roof, torn the flag off the antenna, and smashed the alternator and the carburetor. The police told me that there wasn't much they could do.

"What're you gonna do, sue him?" the cop said. "Garnishee his income?"

I called John at 125th Street and told him what had happened. He said he would be down with the other van to pick up the meat.

"You provoked him with that flag," he said, and hung up.

As I waited for John to show up, I tried to pick the chunks of glass out of the boxes of top rounds. I took the license plates off the car, and I picked up the flag from the ground, folded it into a little triangle the way you're supposed to, and stuffed it into my pocket.

I'd had some good times in that old car, shimmies through the world. Now it was just another junker, like all the other abandoned cars that lie dead all over the City. By tomorrow it would be picked clean of every usable part, and after a few weeks the bare skeleton would be winched onto the back of a sanitation truck.

Finally John showed up, and we put the boxes of top rounds into his van and drove up to 125th Street.

"I already told Carl what happened," he said. "We've decided that you can use Big Blue to get back and forth from home to work until

166

you get back on your feet." As we started up Tenth Avenue I could see, in the convex safety mirror on the passenger side, the yellow Volkswagen, getting smaller and smaller, until it disappeared completely.

18

Trix Kettles

It was a lovely hot, green, and lush summer morning in the Bronx. I was tired. I hadn't slept well, lying in bed thinking about long hours, about how whenever I complained to Carl about unpaid overtime hours he referred me to John, who was now the official personnel manager. Since everybody else at Suburban was a part-owner, that made me the only personnel for John to manage. Quick on the draw, he pulled out his calculator from its leatherette holster and started figuring in car rental charges now that I was using the blue van to commute.

I had taken my usual coffee break in the middle of the Tappan Zee Bridge, stuck in traffic, above the bristling battleship gray of the river, looking north across ten miles of water, across patches of blue and traveling shadows, toward the Indian Point nuclear power plant, its twin kettles half buried, seething with hard energy.

In a sense, that power plant had gotten me kicked out of one of my houses, the farmhouse that I was sharing with my friends when I first got into the meat business. Judy had come home one day from a meeting of the Survival Alliance with CLOSE INDIAN POINT bumper stickers for each of us to put on our cars. I didn't put mine on. I had found that day in a box of Trix two bumper stickers, part of a national referendum about whether the Rabbit should be allowed to have Trix. One said, YES! LET THE RABBIT HAVE TRIX! The other said, NO! TRIX ARE FOR KIDS! I was staunchly pro-Rabbit, and I put the *Yes* sticker on my Volkswagen. My house-mates took this display as a personal insult. Disputes arose about the restocking of ice trays. Michael complained that my food was encroaching on his space in the community refrigerator. During one of his encroachment communiques, I suggested that the police be brought in. Soon I was living alone.

I had a similar problem with my parents about the movie *On the Beach*. To them it was the Word of God. We had all seen it once, but when I declined to join them for a second viewing, saying it was completely unscientific, voices were raised.

Across from Yonkers Raceway, the slogans had been freshly re-painted: DEATH TO BRITISH IMPERIALISM! ENGLAND OUT OF IRE-LAND! and I thought about the time at Jak-Pak meats when I had made an enemy of an Irish butcher by suggesting that perhaps Ireland should get out of Britain.

The air above Hunt's Point sighed with the soft thunder of jets whispering down through the thick air, planes full of people who didn't work in the meat business, people who didn't work overtime for free. Strange to think what a different world those passengers moved in, a world of suits and tailors and green lawns and vacations. There are people who don't have to get up at four in the morning. There are people who are allowed to stay up for Johnny Carson, people whose Holiday Inn bills are paid through their company credit cards. There exist people who don't know what a dumpster *is*.

At Stoll Packing I had to wait in line with a dozen other truck drivers while the Grim Tabulator humped over his invoices and chewed on a mangled cigar butt.

In Harlem, as I crossed Madison Avenue, I thought about how this was the same avenue where I had once applied for advertising jobs, downtown, in the clean silver buildings. It was hard to make the connection between the Madison Avenue of the advertising-agency business and the Madison Avenue I crossed every day, where men drank from brown paper bags and crowds of people in short-sleeved shirts perched on the stairways like flocks of chickens.

"We're making good time today," John said as we double-checked our loads in front of Miller Meats.

As I drove through Westchester I thought and thought, as usual, about time and money and the world around me, so close that I could smell its chlorine and coconut oil and the sweet cow-stomach smell of freshly cut grass, yet it all seemed a thousand miles away. I was driving faster and faster. I threw my sunglasses out the window. Soon I was slamming on the brakes, as usual. I could see smoking black trails of rubber in the rearview mirror. I knew it was dangerous, and I knew it was stupid, especially now that the blue van was my only transportation to and from work, but I didn't care. I knew that I might just as well be stupid as be smart for all the good being smart ever did me. I speeded up to seventy and slammed the brakes on again, and the van went fishtailing and screeching through the green and leafy sleepiness of the summer afternoon. I could smell the scorched odor of overheated brake linings. A station wagon honked loudly at me as it passed.

I wheeled my handtruck beside the tennis courts, and I was sad. I could smell the soft cigarettes and the suntan lotion. I might have married one of those women, in a modest Protestant ceremony devoid of powder-blue tuxedos, at the bride's home, under the trees.

What would they think of me—these pool-lounging Protestants, my own people—those who could never see the thoughts beneath my adjustable paper hat, Chuck Deckle, Diaspora of One? Would they think I'm the kind of person who goes bowling? I haven't been bowling in years, even though I am rather good at it. Would they think I come home to a wife who fills me in on the plot of all four of her soap operas? Let it be known that I come home to nobody, to luxurious clutter and the world's greatest privacy, and that I regret nothing. I never ran for student council, nor sang for my father, nor was promised a garden of roses in this, the business of meat, nor did I win the hand of the girl I loved, and I don't care. I love her anyway, and forever. I see her face, calm above the traffic, part of the air, part of the land, the background. I did not choose to go to the college of my choice. I went instead to Quinnipiac, once named by Allen Ginsberg as the spiritual center of the Universe, whose most famous graduate now plays trombone in Doc Severinson's orchestra on the "Johnny Carson Show."

And I've got relatives here and there, in small Protestant families, and our voices are soft when we get together at funerals. We celebrate Thanksgiving sometimes. There was a separate children's table, with candles in the shape of headless Pilgrims. We set the tablecloth on fire. I remember everything, Thanksgiving tweeds, Uncle John, drunk on his polio crutches, who fell down in the middle of saying Grace, like a great oak in a forest, and all the voices were hush-hush around the table as we helped him up, and he finished the prayer. And make us mindful of the needs of others, through Jesus Christ our Lord. And I've known rivers, meandering along the edge of the sloped lawn where we are playing touch football with neckties on. With brown leaves drifting like tiny boats, rivers older than time, where people's dogs drowned. Quiet, dirty rivers, with long Iroquois names, Ompompanusuc, the lordly Housatonic, Pequonnock, Naragansett, Amagansett, Merrimack, Hackensack. O pool loungers, tennis-lesson groups, my secret family, this is my last press conference. You won't have Chuck Deckle to kick around anymore. My analogues, my siblings, keep this dog far hence, that's friend to nobody and loves everybody, because he digs up graves, trying to find his old schoolmates.

Why couldn't I have gone truly insane? Why was I not made of stone like thee? Why was I just sort of Mickey Mouse crazy? Why could I not have wrestled with intergalactic conspiracies? Decoded cruel and mocking cryptograms against me, imbedded in the *New York Post* headlines?

I would have liked to have some intergalactic conspiracies, cold eyes in the clouds, anything but this life among the ethnic voices, throaty, mush-mouthed. I knew it was stupid to be prejudiced. Bigotry is the small beer of the downwardly mobile. Money makes the world go round.

I was trying to blow up the engine in the van, stomping on the gas and letting it off again, and the truck lurched forward and lagged back, shifting in and out of overdrive as I crossed the Tappan Zee again and drove the last few miles back to Suburban, where I had to drop off some bacon that the Overlook had ordered by mistake, and from there I would take the blue van home as usual.

John was waiting for me when I got there. "We have a problem," he said, "and I think you know what it is." His voice was low and expressionless, and a cigarette dangled from his lips.

"I got a call today from a gentleman who was driving on the Thruway at noon today, and he saw you slamming on the brakes and skidding all over the road. He said you left a rubber mark two hundred feet long. I need to know what your problem is."

"No problem at all," I said. "I'm very happy. I love to work overtime for free. In fact I love it so much that sometimes my high spirits get the best of me."

"This is the third complaint I've had about you, not to mention the tickets, and all the extra insurance money you've been costing me." I noticed for the first time that John's lower lip was beginning to stick out just like Carl's, and that the cigarette wiggled like a little baton.

"Maybe you should balance those extra premiums against all the unpaid overtime you weaseled out of me." I could feel blood drumming in my ears, could see the letters of the CALM DOWN poster vibrating.

172

"If you had a problem you could have come to me," he said. "My office is always open."

"I did that. I did that several times, and you just pulled out your damn calculator and pushed a few buttons to prove how much of a favor you were doing me by letting me work for free. So thanks for all the favors."

He took a deep drag of his cigarette and let it out slowly through his small teeth. "This is a full week's pay," he said, handing me an envelope. "I'm sorry you were unhappy, but that's not my problem. No hard feelings I hope."

"You really suck, do you know that?" I could feel my voice trembling.

"And one more thing. I think you could benefit from some professional help."

"That very well might be true," I said, trying to talk as slowly and quietly as I could. "But I would like to call to your attention the fact that the type of help you're referring to does not happen to be covered in the package of medical benefits available in this filthy little sweatshop."

"Give me the keys," he said. I took the three truck keys and the two office keys off my key ring, threw them on the floor, and walked out through the cement-floored loading area.

"YOU *SUCK!*" I yelled at the top of my lungs, and walked out into the bright light.

I walked along the side of Route 9W toward where the Congers Mini-Trans bus was supposed to stop. I could take the bus to the Grand Atrium Mall and walk the rest of the way home from there. Refrigerator trucks roared past. I could smell hamburgers grilling in the Welcome Inn. It was hot. I could feel the temperature pressing in on me from all sides, in a still, airless blast of heat. It felt strange to have so few keys in my pocket.

I was thinking about meat, all the meat everywhere, sizzling in restaurants, hanging cold from the rails of refrigerated trucks, a whole world full of meat, and I wanted to destroy it all. I wanted to go into Waldbaum's meat department and slip dead cockroaches into the family-size hamburger packages. I thought about all the cholesterol and the salt and the hormones and the nitrites, pulsing through the arteries of all the meat managers and meat salesmen and meat buyers, and I was glad. I wanted them all to have strokes and myocardial infarctions, wanted them all to get cancer. I wanted to see Route 9W bumper to bumper with ambulances in the meat-scented air of nursing homes.

It was a beautiful day and I walked. I passed the skeleton of a cat, a mud-soaked Betty Crocker cookbook, the cleft hoofprints of a deer, beer cans, soda cans, half-pint bottles of Popov vodka.

It would be nice to walk by the side of the road someday when I had nowhere to go and nothing to worry about when I got there. I have a dream of what I'll do someday. Someday, when the meat-laden air has lifted and thinned like the blood of a man ordered onto a strict vegetarian diet, someday, free from the meat business at last, great God Almighty, I'll have so much free time and so much free money that I'll buy a little sailing canoe and a tent and an aluminum cooking kit, and I'll travel by water, starting from the Nyack Yacht Club, down to New York City, through Hell's Gate, up the Long Island Sound, to Block Island, all the way to Martha's Vineyard. All the meat people will have to get up at four in the morning on the day I set sail.

I'll stop for a day in Stonington, Connecticut. Perhaps I'll get stoned in Stonington. I'll walk all over town with nowhere to go and nothing to do. I'll go to a movie. The ground will be all lush and green and covered with garbage, but it won't be ugly, because the garbage will be half absorbed back into the ground, and the sweet earth will open its soft surfaces. Cars will be rushing everywhere, of course, and they'll think I'm crazy or a vagrant. I'll show them my driver's license and my MasterCard and tell them I'm a yachtsman on shore leave, and it will be the truth.

I like summer. Someday I'd like to be part of it, those lazy crazy hazy days when ordinary people have to go to work as usual, but still have time to grill chicken on the hibachi in the softness of dusk. On the first day of the trip I will dock my sailing canoe in Manhattan, at the 79th Street Boat Basin, and take a walk around the City and have lunch in a Chinese restaurant. Anyplace that a person visits is informed by how one gets there and how one leaves; thus New York that day will be a different city, a city I've never been to. The ground will feel different under my feet, weeds growing from cracks in the sidewalk. I'll take a cab and it will be air-conditioned.

And then I'll putter around in my sailing canoe in Long Island Sound, and I'll have a little outboard motor, and I'll be able to explore any cove that I see, the shores of Port Washington, where we lived for two years when I was in the first and second grades.

The whole landsape, the whole Soundscape, trees with leaves thick as cotton, will stand still in the August afternoon, and I will be looking through my binoculars. They will be Bausch & Lomb, and extremely expensive. I'll be able to see into the windows of brick apartment buildings full of old ladies and hanging plants and bric-a-brac. I'll watch cars going by, men hanging their arms out the windows.

I will be all alone upon the glassy wavering water, wonderfully, luxuriously alone, sailing up Manhasset Bay, which separates Great Neck From Port Washington. It was on one of those banks that Gatsby stood in the night like a ghost, gazing across the water. I don't remember if Gatsby lived on West Egg and Daisy on East Egg or vice versa; but I do know that West Egg is supposed to be Port Washington and East Egg is Great Neck. I know that the mansions are gone, or converted into residential drug-rehabilitation centers.

I will be all alone, looking at Long Island and all its serious structures in a way I never have before. With single-minded serious-ness, the Long Island Rail Road train clatters across a steel trestle at the narrow end of Douglaston Inlet. Somewhere at the northern end of Port Washington stands a house with a porch facing the sound, and the yard is full of trees that form a canopy above the slanted lawn, and inside the screened porch Tanqueray and tonic is being served. Maybe the husband had a grim day at the office. Maybe the City was like an oven. Maybe the whole Financial District is a den of thieves. This will be on the hottest day of the year, lime and juniper in the light airs, between the day and the twilight, when the night is beginning to flower, a pause in the day's occupations, the cocktail hour, voices of children among the tree trunks, the intermittent rushing of commuter trains, the drumming of rolling steel on an iron trestle that one living near it begins not to notice, like the breath of a sleeping spouse, and the children are drinking soda, and they have been warned not to leave their soda bottles on the lawn, because they will get broken by the lawn mower.

The sky will be filled with airplanes, of course, silver shapes bellying down their long trajectory, a whining whispering whistle singing in their smokeless trails. White-hulled Chris-Craft hurry past, in quest of serious bluefish, and water skiers are serious about their sport, cutting tall and serious rooster tails in the water. The August world is a paradise of weeds and smoldering flowers, and cars kick up the dust that gathers beside the road. Through my Bausch & Lombs I can stare at people sitting on porches and they don't even see me. I can see a cove where boys are straining to throw into the water the biggest rocks they can lift, lofting them shotput-style into the sound, and the splash comes seconds later, first the impact, then the plosh of water rushing back on itself. One boy holds a horseshoe crab by the tail and wings it, trilobite pincers waving and fiddling, into the cove.

Somewhere, half a mile inland, is a Carvel Ice Cream stand where children with no problems mouth the smooth sweet coldness. The upper stories of cubic red-brick prewar apartment buildings rise out of the lush canopy of leaves, and beneath that canopy is a world of August at ground level, soda fountains serving Coke in paper cones that snap into plastic stands, beauty-parlor smells blowing out into the street, dry-cleaner smells, McDonald's, men with briefcases asking each other if it's hot enough for them, people with easy jobs, people with air conditioners, people whose color TVs will play late into the night as the moon rises late above the sprawl of township blending into township, each with its name on a water tower.

There is to be found, somewhere where weeds sprout from the joint of old macadam and mold-mottled white-painted cinderblock at the rear of a row of small stores attached to a Grand Union, where green cultures of algae luxuriate in the drippings of a central-air-conditioning unit, among dumpsters caked with restaurant sludge, among the walleyed fenders of big old cars belonging to kitchen help, where black starlings scrabble and squabble over scraps of hard black fat, where dishwashers lounge at coffee break, leaning against the outside refrigeration units that go on and off at random and make the dishwashers jump as they smoke their coffee-break joints, and their friends come by in beat-up cars riding low on broken springs, with drugs for sale, and sometimes there are old pairs of sneakers hanging from the wires, dozens of pairs looped over the low-hanging lines that run from a black Tinkertoy spaghetti structure of tape-wrapped electrical connections and reach across the rear parking lot to telephone poles with extra crossbars and extra transformers; there is to be found, among the Italian restaurant smells of clams and garlic, the beauty-parlor smells, the butcher-shop smells, the excelsior and shredded-paper smell of a china shop's discarded shipping cases, some with a dunnage of white Styrofoam vermicelli for cushioning the glass, which arrives broken anyway; there is to be found among all these wild and worn-out surfaces, with red rivulets of rust; there is to be found a place that can be called a point of rest, a place a man can dream about, that I see in the watery moments before sleep, a place that hides within its own configurations if a traveler tries to budget his time to see it, a place I see out of the corner of my eye but don't have time to stop, a place that disappears if you look at it wrong, a country, a land, something that lives and breathes, the one thing I myself can be serious about, that could have been mine, with better vocational planning. Of thee I sing, off key, not feeling well; but let none forget how I love thee, how I see thee wrapped in August green all warm and lush and dusty in the moments before I drift off to sleep among the beauty of your electric signs.

How did we lose each other? Have I lied, or sinned, or loved too well, or not well enough? And is there time enough left for it to matter? Perhaps we're goners anyway, the angry world turned against us in a rictus of hate, fists in the air, faces lined with rage in the firelight of our flag burning, flesh of our flesh, fabric of our fabric, from the humming, lung-destroying mills of the South, I and thou, the textiles of our adrift lives, and all we have is each other, a chance to walk together after being fired, going down the road feeling bad.

I didn't know the bus schedules, so I just walked and walked, as the cars roared by, whizzing, hissing, woofing. Walking you see more, patches in people's roofs, trash in their front yards, scraps of bright gravel-surfaced roofing paper half swallowed by the ground, and you can hear the voices of insects, their many voices blending into one voice, a high and low trilling background to all the traffic noises, flags lashed to radio antennae, the burr and flutter of printed fabric in the wind, the noises of dogs barking, straining at their chains, a symphony of dogs, some with voices all blunt and foggy from barking all day long, and family squabbles inside the houses, while outside the insects sing, the chirp of a billion agitated mandibles, more insects in Rockland County alone than there are people in the world living and dead, grasshoppers hopping around my feet.

Where New Hempstead Road crossed King's Highway, I could look south and see the sign for the main entrance to Rockland Country Day School, the private school I attended for two years as a stopgap between the end of elementary school and the beginning of Hotchkiss. I walked across the Lake DeForest causeway, the same causeway I used to cross twice a day in the little ten-passenger school vans that took us back and forth from RCDS. A few fish were breaking the surface in lazy boils.

High on a wooded bluff above the lake, I could see the main building of RCDS, gray stucco, empty for the summer; RCDS, where we were all Ivy League bound, the cream of the whole county, all madras jacketed, and the children of every celebrity in the county went there: Burgess Meredith's son and daughter, Neil Simon's three daughters, Mitch Miller's son, everybody who was anybody, and we were all rich, and everybody's parents were divorced or getting divorced, and everybody had been to Europe.

I remembered how I would lie awake at night and dream of Glynn Daly, the daughter of actor James Daly, and sister of the now-famous actress and leftist spokesperson Tyne Daly. I loved her. When I went skiing I wished that Glynn could see me go over the ski jump my father and I had built out of packed snow. She would have seen my courage, and my MacGregor sweater, and everything would have turned out differently. I was a well-dressed kid. I wore Rooster ties with pictures of musical notes or sports cars on them, and brown Bass Weejuns. My mother and I would drive from Gimbel's to Bamberger's to Altman's, and I had leather patches at the elbows of my sport jackets, and I could play the chords to Leslie Gore's "It's My Party" on the piano, and I dreamed of Glynn's small clear voice and her pale eyes and the way she tapped her cigarette with a small stiff finger once when I saw her with her older friends at a summer stock performance of Thornton Wilder's *Our Town*.

I walked up South Mountain Road, past houses set back from the road, the houses of writers and actors. I started remembering school parties I'd been to at this house or that, the rust-red water snakes in Kristine Kidd's pond, the Christmas party at the Fellers' where we got into the gin and topped it off with water, the tennis party at the home of the playwright Maxwell Anderson, where I aced the final point, all those people, all the houses, all the parties, all that gold. I wonder if rich people know what to do with their gold, there on the winding and ramshackle narrowness of South Mountain Road, always in shadow from the leaning trees, all my friends far-flung from this old forest, in oil and arbitrage, theater and textiles. I noted the chipped paint on people's mailboxes, the leatherized mummy of a run-over woodchuck, and all the birds, twittering in the steaming shadiness, rufous-sided towhees, rose-breasted grosbeaks, a dozen species of sparrows, the wiry note of red-winged blackbirds, a million voices all tuneless and perfect, and the closer I got to home the louder the birds sang, until with ears ringing I was home in time for "The Partridge Family."

It was my favorite episode. Laurie Partridge, beautiful Laurie, played by Susan Dey, had been wrongly accused of cheating on a history test. Even with a mouthful of orthodontia she was spectacular. Her brother Danny defended her before a school tribunal, hooking his thumbs into his suspenders Clarence Darrow–style. At the end of the tribunal, the actual culprit, the principal's daughter, whom Laurie had been protecting, confessed in tears, as I knew she would, and they cried in each other's arms, and I caressed Laurie's smooth cheek with the backs of my fingers through the television screen, and everything was all ionized, or deionized—I don't know which—so that the hair on my fingers bristled and crackled in the screen's magnetic field.

PART THREE

19

Rennet Perch

Every morning I had breakfast with the cartoons: Heckle and Jeckle, Yogi Bear, the Three Robonic Stooges. I took long walks along roads with no sidewalks, in the heat of the day, bird-voices everywhere, grasshoppers flipping and flying around my feet with each step. Dogs would bark at me from the edge of their property. Every day I would see this beautiful young girl driving around in her mother's Oldsmobile, wearing heavy black eye makeup, and a blouse with the elastic neck pulled over one bare shoulder. She was so beautiful that I never left my house without shaving and putting on a clean shirt.

As I walked I could feel the old anger leaching out of me, through the lazy days, could hear a change in the long note of traffic, as the sunlight flickered through the leaves and the air was thick with the creosote smell of oil being sprinkled over fresh gravel. Sometimes the wind carried the smell of chlorinated swimming pools, or the smell of hot dogs cooking, or burned marshmallows.

In the State Employment Service office I rolled the control knob of the microfiche machine past hundreds of listings, for experienced high-school Italian teachers, experienced lathe operators, experienced nuclear technicians. There were several butcher jobs listed, but they were all union. As I walked home, with cars whizzing past me and that same beautiful young girl with one bare shoulder, slightly overweight, her eyes outlined in kohl black . . . as I walked I could feel how light I had become, so light that I might blow away in the draft of a speeding Datsun. Labor Day weekend came, and the whole county was fragrant with the smells of meat grilling on a thousand hibachis. Somebody had sold that meat, had made eight dollars an hour cutting it into steaks, somebody was making good money in the meat business, driving a financed car, while I trod among the insects, poor Chuck Deckle, in whose neighborhood so few people fail to have cars that there is no sidewalk.

I applied for all sorts of jobs. I answered ads for dishwashers and waiters/waitresses. I applied for a job as night watchman at a retirement community, as a chemical technician, a kennel assistant, a landscape laborer. I visited the Armed Forces Recruiting Office, but they told me I was a year too old. I applied at McDonald's, across from the mall, and remembered the times that Jill and I had sat at those tables, with the steam from our sandwiches rising between us. I applied for school-bus driver jobs, but you had to be married. I answered an ad for substitute teachers in Suffern Junior High School, even though I knew that my three years of college would hardly qualify me. I found myself talking to a very friendly lady named Mrs. Piccolo who needed substitute teachers desperately. She took my address and number and said she'd send me an application form.

The next morning at six o'clock, three hours after I had gone to bed, the phone rang. It was Mrs. Piccolo. She didn't have time to bother with application forms. Could I come in this morning in place of a general science teacher who had been called away for a funeral?

Exhausted, in a wrinkled suit and unshined shoes, I caught the seven o'clock bus on Route 59 and rode with maids and Haitian factory workers to Hemion Road, where I got off and walked the half mile to Suffern Junior High School. An hour after being woken up by the phone, I was in the academic profession.

It was an old school, formerly the junior and senior high school combined, but now just for seventh and eighth graders, a boxy brick building with wavy linoleum floors and dazed gray custodians and a lingering egg-and-catsup smell of a hundred years of lunches, with a slight sweet undertone of chewing gum.

The homeroom class began to arrive, sugar-charged on their breakfast cereals, the boys miming electric guitar riffs. We saluted the flag. The bell rang, and they rushed out as the first period class rushed in. All I was supposed to do was take attendance and keep them quiet for forty minutes.

Everybody had to go to the bathroom, everybody needed a pass for something. Kids were fighting. It was ridiculous. They threw paper airplanes out the window. They yelled down to their friends playing volleyball in gym class. I talked at the top of my lungs, like a meat supervisor, my voice ringing loud and strong above their many voices. I had nothing to say to them anyway, except to be quiet and sit down. Every class was the same. As I took attendance they would laugh, and I got the feeling that certain individuals were answering to more than one name. At lunch I was a line monitor. The queue of youngsters pushed from the hall into the food line, making mooing noises like herded cattle.

After the last class of the afternoon, I walked toward the Route 59 bus stop, as the school buses roared along Hemion Road, and I could hear the children's voices ringing out the open windows as they passed. It felt strange to be walking along the side of the road wearing a suit and tie.

Every morning Mrs. Piccolo called with a new assignment. Every day it was the same, the bells, the voices, the paper airplanes, the guitar-mimes, then home on the bus, with Haitians and geriatrics.

There were times I missed the meat business, missed the smells and the hard surfaces, the privacy of pulling my hard hat down over my eyes and dreaming about Laurie Partridge and her wax-perfect face and delicate philtrum. Still it was nice to be a teacher, to be in the academic profession, to eat lunch in the teachers' lounge in a jacket and tie. The only other people on the bus wearing ties would be the old men from the Senior Security Village going shopping, gray and frail in their plaid sport jackets and pastel-blue old-man shirts.

After two weeks, my first paycheck came in the mail. I was shocked to find that I was making less money than I could make collecting unemployment. Now I couldn't quit, because then I would be ineligible to collect anything at all. As I typed a letter to my landlord explaining why I could only pay half my rent, it occurred to me that the academic profession was not working out.

One day I saw an ad for general helpers at Hoboken Packing Company, which I knew was within walking distance of the Hoboken Conrail terminal, so I could get there without a car. I spoke on the phone to a man named Mr. Fox, and told him about my experience in various jobs in the wholesale meat business.

"The job is on the kill floor," Mr. Fox said, "and most people who start here don't come back after the first day. If you're squeamish about watching the cows get killed and cut up, don't waste your time. If you think you've got a strong stomach, come in at eight o'clock Monday morning, and we'll see how you work out."

I took the early train from Spring Valley down to Hoboken. I was the only man on the train who wasn't wearing a suit, but I didn't care. I was a working man again. I sat back in my seat and watched the leafy little towns go by, watched the car fill with summer suits and the *New York Times*.

Mr. Rossi, the foreman, assigned me a locker and gave me a white coat and a heavy rubber apron, and led me to the kill floor, where work was just beginning. Today they were killing a shipment of veal calves. I could hear their bellowing voices and the clanking of hoist chains.

My job, Mr. Rossi explained, was to stand in front of a rolling two-tiered tub of guts and sort them out, hanging the liver on a rack of hooks behind me, removing the green bubble of the gall bladder and throwing it into the gall-bladder jar that hung over the side of the gut tub. Then I would take the heart, fat-caked and still fibrillating, and throw it into a white plastic tub with the other hearts. After I removed the heart, I would search around the large intestine for the gray and mucousy pancreas, which would be saved and sold to a pharmaceutical company. Then I would dump the tray, containing the lungs, the bronchii, the large and small intestines, and the bladder, into a large wheelbarrow.

Hoboken Packing was a kosher operation, but not all the meat produced there would be kosher. Only the front half of the animal, anterior to the next-to-last rib, can be kosher. Down the line from where they were killed and eviscerated, the sides of beef or veal would be cut in half, and the hindquarters would disappear through one set of canvas flaps and the kosher forequarters through another.

Kosher law requires that the animal be killed by a rabbi, with one stroke of a knife, and that the knife be washed and sharpened with every animal killed. The cattle may not be electrically stunned or brained with a mallet, as they are in most western slaughterhouses, but must be hoisted, fully conscious, by their rear legs, and their throats cut.

From where I stood at my gut-tub I could see the killing area, like a shower stall with a tiled floor slanted toward a drain in the middle. I could hear the shapeless lowing of cattle, as if in a western movie. It seemed strange to be hearing that sound in the middle of Hoboken, half a mile from the spot where at this moment the Hoboken Terminal was filled with the scuffling of a thousand Florsheims crowding into the blue Fiberglas PATH train entrance, on their way into lower Manhattan, to their offices and secretaries.

Separated from the killing stall by a low double door, like the double doors in a western saloon, was the waiting stall, where I could see the next calf in line. A man was shackling the calf's rear legs. Then, with a clank of chains and a howling bellow, the hoisted calf came swinging through the double doors into the rabbi's killing stall.

When I think of rabbis, I usually picture large, avuncular gentlemen, like the rabbi who said the blessing each morning on Channel 5, or the man who gave a sermon about love and community at the bar mitzvah of my old friend Neil Horowitz. But there is a whole class of rabbis who work in the kosher meat business and never see a congregation, never perform a wedding or a *bris*. The *schecter* here at Hoboken was a wiry little man with thick glasses, a pale face, and a long scraggly nineteenth-century beard hanging down over his orange rubber apron. After dipping the shiny scimitar-shaped knife in a tub of soapy water and honing it a few times with long flamboyant motions on the sharpening stone, he would turn to the hanging calf, grab its head by a tuft of hair, and slash its throat with one smooth motion.

Most of the calves we were killing today were jerseys, tan-coated animals with soft eyes edged in black. After the animal's throat was cut, I would hear the plosh of blood streaming to the tiled floor, and the calf would arch its back and twist and turn with a frantic strength, gyrating and dancing as blood gushed and eddied around the drain. Soon the animal's struggling would lose energy. It is hard, though, to pinpoint the exact instant of death, since it seems to be a gradual process.

After most of the blood had drained from the calf's cut throat, it would be pushed along the rail to hang next to the other freshly killed calves waiting to be gutted and skinned and split and separated into kosher and *treif*. Sometimes one of the hanging carcasses would suddenly begin struggling again, as if awakened from a dream, and the calves next to it would be roused by the first, and on the rail in front of me they would begin a silent and clumsy little dance.

I was not the least bit disgusted. I was fascinated. My hands swam like fish through the warm slipperiness of lungs and intestines and bladders half full of warm urine, where most people's hands had never been. A USDA inspector strolled around the kill floor, from work station to work station. "Make sure this stays like this," he said to me, pointing out how the anus, cut away at the end of the large intestine, with a fringe of hair around it, must stay draped over the edge of the tub, so as not to drop feces into the edible entrails.

It seemed like a good place to work. There was a sort of jolliness in the air. Butchers were shouting back and forth, daring each other to bet on the Mets or against the Mets. Every man had his name embroidered on the pocket of his white coat. I was looking forward to seeing CHUCK in a racy script on my own coat.

My spirits were higher than they had been in months. There was something weirdly beautiful about the place, the shrill harmony of sound and smell, the barnyard odor of the holding pens mixing with the sharp and serious ammonia and disinfectant smell of the cement floor, the sweet wet smell of bladders and urine. A calf being lifted by the clanking chain-hoist would groan with a huge and terrified echoing bellow, and workers would answer with a mock bellow, like the answering section in the middle part of the old Ray Charles song, "What I Say?"

Down the line from the killing stall, the breakers would begin gutting the calves, making a long cut from just below the sternum all the way upward to between the hind legs, and the great ruminant stomach would come billowing out, all pink and white in the hard light, like an enormous balloon of bubble gum; then the breaker would reach into the body cavity and detach the stomach and it would flop out into a low stainless-steel wheelbarrow; then he would cut a circle around the anus, reach into the body cavity again and sever the esophagus and the windpipe, and pull the rest of the entrails out into a waist-high rolling cart that a helper would then wheel over to my station. Holding the large intestine by the anus end so that it didn't drop feces into the other entrails, the helper would tilt the cart's holding compartment until the whole mass would slide into my sorting sink. Inspectors would visit my station every few minutes and gently palpate the lungs, looking for tuberculosis.

After the calf had been gutted, a man would cut the head off with an electric chain saw, and place the head with all the other heads on a stainless-steel rack with dozens of upward-pointing spikes on which the cut end of the neck could be impaled. The pink and billowing stomachs would be wheeled over to a rubber conveyor belt divided into sections by rubber baffles, and the stomachs would go sloshing up to a raised area where a piratical looking young man sat poking into the stomachs and picking something out of them.

The process was moving fast now, and people were bustling around in all directions. Cattle groaned and bellowed in the holding pen. I could smell the sweet wet liver and the lime-scented disinfectant, and I could smell the blood, a mild ferrous odor like the taste in my mouth when I had flossed too vigorously.

"Yo! Dump it!" a white-hatted supervisor said to me, pointing to my lower barrow, which was full of lungs and intestines. I wheeled the barrow toward the far end of the floor where I had seen other gut-sorters wheel theirs, past the rack of severed heads. I slowed down and looked closely as I passed. They didn't seem to be completely dead yet. Some hint of sentience remained in their astonished faces. I could see little spots around the pretty black-lined eyes twitching.

I looked at all the heads impaled there on the head rack, mouths open as if joined in song, tongues hanging out the sides of their mouths at a loony, drunken angle; and all at once I was overwhelmed my how beautiful these animals were. At once I understood Jill's vegetarian issues, and I hoped I hadn't corrupted her too much with my own McDonald's issues. I understood why the Hindu religion held cattle in such reverence, but for me it was an intuition without nausea. I knew that tonight, more than any night, I would have a Quarter Pounder. I understood the whole kosher philosophy, understood why these animals must be killed with love, by a man of God. Those faces, those dark-eyed placid faces, all raised to the light, looked like a choir stall, in a beatific transport of love, as motors clanked and hummed.

I wheeled my gut-barrow up a ramp beside the raised area where a piratical-looking snaggle-toothed fellow was surveying his gutscape of rolling stomachs. I had asked the sorter working next to me what that kid was doing up there, and I was told that he was picking rennet from the stomachs, to be used in making cheese, as a food additive, and as a custard-solidifying agent.

I wheeled the warm guts through a canvas flap-door onto a loading dock under which an open trailer bin stood parked. It was full of bright entrails, speckled blue from the disinfectant that another gut-dumper was sprinkling from a jug. In the middle of all the viscera, the stiffened corpse of a calf lay half buried, forelegs sticking straight out into the air, like a plastic toy.

All around, the Hoboken morning hummed. At the end of the side street that led to the loading dock, a school bus was picking up Puerto Rican children, a bright white strobe flashing on its light rack. With a soft sloshing noise, a cascade of pink stomachs came sluicing down a spillway into the trailer, and the whole mass of shining guts shimmered and shook like jelly, and the dead calf sank beneath the mucousy waves.

On my way back to the sorting tray I watched the head-skinning operation, where two men were picking the heads off the rack and cutting the skin off the heads and impaling the skinned heads on another head rack for another man to trim the face flesh and to remove the brains. With the skin cut away, the heads had a futuristic, racy, spaceman, hot-rod look to them, from another planet, the long insectlike mandible exposed, bright eyes bulging, a delicate French spiral in the cartilage of the nostrils. All over the facial mask of muscle and connective tissue, there were tiny twitchings in the flesh, as severed nerve fibers fired their last meaningless bursts of electrochemical code.

All morning the motors shrieked, calves bellowed, stomachs billowed from not-quite-dead animals and flowed up the baffled conveyor to an elevated pan where the sea of pink flesh was surveyed by the nautical-looking rennet picker. His was the best job of all, I decided, perched there above a rolling gastric ruminant horizon, as if in the crow's nest of a sailing ship. . . . Abaft on the peritoneum, me hardies, all helms a'lee to the duodenum. . . . Rennet ho!

It occurred to me that this was the real world, what work is supposed to be; hard, noisy, and dirty, but with a kind of ragged joy to it, the kind of place where people would always say "Good morning," even on the worst day of their lives. I thought about the grim mornings at Suburban, days of heat and chicken-stink and brake-slamming rage. Those days seemed like years ago.

After lunch, there was a commotion in the rabbi's killing stall. A hoisted jersey calf danced and gyrated so feverishly that the Rabbi couldn't get a grip on its head to slit its throat. He stepped out into the main part of the kill floor, waiting for the animal to get tired, stared into the bright windows at the other side of the building, his pale face sullen, dull eyes expressionless, as if waiting for a bus that is always late. Even with its throat cut, this calf was a troublemaker. It jerked and gyrated wildly, splattering blood all over the man's face.

As the day was winding down, and men with yellow aprons had appeared with steam hoses to wash the blood away, Mr. Rossi called me into the office to fill out some papers. Where the employee Statistical Form asked if I had ever been a member of any other UFCWU local, I answered yes, figuring that my past union work would reduce the time I would have to wait for medical benefits to start.

Mr. Rossi's face fell as he read over the form. "You resigned from Local One seventy-four?" he said.

"Yes."

"I'm afraid that means you can't work here," he said.

"But this is a different local, isn't it?"

"That doesn't matter. Our union has a strict rule about this. Anybody who leaves the union to work at a nonunion job is ineligible to work in Local Five."

"But that's not fair," I said. "My last company *made* me resign from the union. I had no *choice*."

"I'm sorry," he said. "You seem like a good worker, but if we break that rule we'll have a strike on our hands."

"But this is crazy. They *made* me do it! I was under duress!"

"I'm just as sorry about it as you are," he said. "But rules are strict. In fact I can't even let them see your name on a check." He took out his wallet and counted five twenty-dollar bills into my hand.

I walked out of Hoboken Packing into the warm evening, and I could feel all my meat-business problems rolling back again like the tide, eternal as the tide. All I had needed to do was to lie. But I hadn't thought quickly enough, just like I had never learned to cut meat quickly enough, and that made all the difference in the world.

I rode the train back to Spring Valley and watched the softness of the evening flash past the train, all the intersections and shopping centers and fall softball-league games, everything wrapped in a green blanket of September. I thought about the times I had ridden these trains with my father, when he would take me with him to his office at Prudential, platforms full of silk ties and leather briefcases, posters on the walls of the station buildings advertising Schafer Beer, Broadway musicals. I still remembered that sound of the morning, as I was getting off in Hoboken, the scuffling of thousands of well-shod feet, flowing toward the PATH trains into Manhattan, past the fluorescent lights of newsstands and orange-juice counters.

It would have been a good place to work, a place to live a normal life, with my name stitched on my pocket, and plenty of stories to tell at parties, and maybe in a few months a good used car.

I was riding in the smoking car, where I thought the smell of blood and urine on my clothes might not be noticed. I felt as if I were riding in a bubble, sequestered from my old schoolmates, and saying good-bye to everything again, good-bye to the beautiful jersey heifers with soft eyes lined in black like mascara, kindly, beatific, even glamorous. I remembered the eyes of one calf looking through the slats of a holding pen as I walked to the lunchroom. For a moment we had looked into each other's eyes, as if across a million years of separate evolutionary pathways, with nothing more in common to see. Where do their voices go, and the flickerings of cow intelligence?

I could feel the pulse of a new season quickening, a new school year. I knew that the great white steamers were pulling out of Vineyard Haven, loaded with cars, loaded with tanned families of students whose colleges didn't start until later in the month. I knew that all the shopping malls were bustling with fall fashions, and the katydids getting louder every night, ratcheting against the downward calendar, against the shortness of their own days, counting with agitated mandibles the days, counting the nights until Orion's three supergiants blaze cold and blue in the night and frost falls like sleep across the land of my desire.

20

Dervish Clarinets

My next job was in a kosher butcher shop called Glatt Mart, tucked into a five-store mini shopping center across from where the old Shop-Rite had closed down. I used to pass it on my way home from substitute teaching, but I had never stopped in to ask for a job because before working at Hoboken Packing I had assumed one had to be Jewish to work in a kosher establishment. The owner was named Howie Shapiro, a tall stoop-shouldered man in his forties, with a tiny yarmulke bobby-pinned to the back of his bristly untrimmed hair. He seemed a friendly fellow, though a bit homely, with a lower lip that stuck out even farther than that of my old boss Carl Miller.

In the mornings I would help Howie and Mack, the old man who worked with him, stock the display case with whatever items — beef, veal, lamb, chicken, or turkey — needed to be replenished. I did all the grinding of chopmeat, and made all the patties. In the middle of the day I would make deliveries in Carl's old brown Pontiac station wagon, to the kitchens of split-level houses, each with the mandatory two refrigerators, one for meat, the other for dairy products.

In the afternoons I would help them break apart and *treibor* the meat. *Treiboring* meant opening up the seams between the major muscles with a dull knife and digging out the buried blood veins, which the kosher law required to be removed. Like most meat-cutting operations, this was a job I was not very good at. I had a hard time remembering which vein was which, and soon Howie would be puffing with impatience.

"You're *not very good,*" he would say. He was right. Then we would continue the koshering process by throwing all the *treibored* ribs and necks of beef, and shoulders of lamb and veal into a stainless-steel tub and soaking it in water for thirty minutes, after which we would take the meat out of the water, carefully sprinkle all surfaces of each piece with coarse kosher salt, let the meat sit with the salt on it for forty-five minutes, then rinse the salt off and hang the meat in the storage cooler to be cut for the store the next day. Less strict classifications of kosher food required that meat be soaked and salted only if it was to be fried. Howie's customers, members of the local Orthodox community, required a stricter observance of the law.

"These Reform Jewish housewives, the ones that shop at places like Herbie's Kosher Meats," Howie told me, "they just want the butcher to go through the motions. But my customers are the *frummies,* and they depend on me to protect the integrity of their kitchens."

At the end of each day, I would sweep the floor of the cutting room, wash all the cutting tables, scoop the bone dust out of the band saw, throw down a fresh coat of salt on the floor to prevent slipping, sweep the floor in the shopping area, and catch the local bus home.

All in all, it wasn't bad. There is a kind of hard cheer in a kosher butcher shop on a busy day, among all the stale and vinegary smells of fat and chicken skin and cigarettes. Israeli music would be rasping from the cutting-room radio, whirling mixolydian dervish dances, or Yiddish folk music of snarling comical clarinets, interrupted every

196

two minutes by a blast of static from a faulty refrigeration compressor. Often I would work on the other side of the cutting tables from the two men, with a shelf full of plastic foam trays that they called "boats" between us at eye level, so that all I could see would be their hands, in a desperate hurry, frantically trimming flanken, or scraping the bone dust off freshly cut lamb chops.

It was strange to watch those hands. They looked like the hands of dead men, Howie's all twisted and stubby, with anvil-shaped thumbs, all the fingers a deep nicotine-yellow. Mack's hands were pale and lifeless and rubbery, like great albino frogs preserved in formaldehyde. As they worked they would talk, their loud voices ringing through the store, mostly about the Bronx, about old times in the kosher meat business.

"You remember that store that Benny Gelker had on Lydig Avenue?" Howie was saying one day during my first week there.

"He died," Mack said.

"I worked there for three years before I got married, before the *schwartzes* took over. Worked with Sonny Fox, should rest in peace, and—"

"He died."

"Oh, I knew that. I went to his funeral. But what I was going to say, that hophead Louie Millstein was working there, and one day he comes in with all this money he won at the track, and announces he's buying the store. The next day he fires me and Sonny Fox, hires a bunch of *schwartzes,* and turns the place into a *treif* store for the nigger trade. Fucking bastard."

"He died."

They talked and talked, and everybody was dead. Sometimes I thought I could feel Howie's eyes watching my slow hands. Sometimes I could hear him muttering, but he didn't usually say anything.

My favorite part of the job was making deliveries in the old brown Pontiac station wagon. It felt good to be driving again, and good to have a steady job. Steady jobs lead to normal lives. The night before my first day at Glatt Mart I had made a pledge, ritualized with the burning of a dollar bill, had pledged at last an end to crises, to negotiations with creditors, an end to being a clown in rags.

"I will live a normal life," I said out loud in the flickering light and the clean driftwood sweetness of the burning dollar. "No matter what happens, I will live a normal life, and I will do a good job."

The Pontiac had a very good FM radio in it. Usually I listened to WNCN, the classical-music station, and I would drift through the midday traffic of housewives and bumper stickers and kindergarten buses, lost in the counterpoint of string quartets and chamber orchestras, in the precise and tragic harmonies of Heifetz and Horowitz, of Stern and Zuckerman, Mendelssohn and Mussorgsky. I would carry the bags of groceries into the cozy and redolent kitchens, full of vinegar and spice fragrances, children's crayon drawings stuck by magnets to the refrigerators, and I would remember that kitchen smell from when I used to go over to the house of my old girlfriend, Cheryl Bergman. We would sit in her mother's kitchen, above where her father had his podiatry office, and look out the window, and the smell was sharp with burned potatoes and pickles and gravy, so different from my mother's sanitized and odorless WASP kitchen.

She was a beautiful girl, Cheryl Bergman, the pride of Pomona, with a smile as warm and generous as her breasts. Sometimes I could see, in the thick features of the children who helped their mothers put the groceries away, a trace of Cheryl's dark and languid beauty.

I remembered a winter Saturday in New York, when Cheryl and David and I, and a few other kids from RCDS, had ridden into the city with our history teacher to do research on our midterm projects.

"I smell *Jews!*" roared a drunk on the steps of the Donnell Library. I could see the hate in his eyes, like barbed wire, could see his jagged yellow teeth bared in a sneer, and his psoriasis-ravaged hand, red and cracked like broiled alligator skin, as he brandished his middle finger. It was strange. Living in Rockland County it was easy to forget that there were people like that.

My first job every morning was to grind the chopmeat into various-sized packages, to be weighed and wrapped either by Howie's son Jerry or his daughter Leslie, whichever didn't have classes that morning at Rockland Community College.

"Good morning," I would say, walking into the cutting room.

"*Fleische* in the machine," Howie would always say, meaning that he had already measured the meat trimmings into the hopper of the grinding machine. He always called meat *fleische*.

Sometimes they would be in a good mood. Howie's belches would resonate through the store. Howie and Mack seemed a single mood-entity. When Howie laughed and joked, Mack would laugh and joke. A few weeks after I had come to work there, we got in a crate of lamb heads with the brains still in them, and as the two men labored feverishly with their dull knives to crack the mandibles off and pull the lemon-sized cerebrae out of the skulls to be blanched and frozen, I remarked that now I knew why sheep were so stupid.

"Think your brains are any bigger?" shrilled Mack's throaty voice, and his bright eyes twinkled among the folds of pouchy, red-veined, exhausted flesh of his face, and the store rang with his mirth, loud and full-voiced, until Howie's laughter migrated from voice to bronchial tubes, and he was hawking up phlegm the color of gray brain matter, which he turned around and blew into the barrel of waste fat behind him.

"HOCCCCCCHHHHH! HOCCCHHHHH! . . . *SNUKKKK!* P-*TOOO*ie!"

Once I asked Howie about the kosher law, if I should avoid eating bacon for breakfast before I came to work.

"I don't give a fuck what you eat in your own house," he said. "You can eat your own *shit* if you want!" and the cutting room echoed with laughter. I tried to join in, but I couldn't work up much of a laugh. It was a stupid question anyway. I don't even like bacon.

Mack told me about growing up in the Bronx after his aunt and uncle had fled from Hungary with him, how he had to fight his way through Irish and Italian neighborhoods on his way to school. He was a small man, only five feet tall, but solidly built; and he moved like a man half his age. His white hair grew in two tufts on either side of his black stocking cap, giving his face a squared-off look, like a miniature Fats Domino in a photo negative.

He told me about the butcher shop he used to own, on Allerton Avenue in the Bronx, about all the *schwartzes* he had fired for stealing.

"That whole neighborhood's gone to shit now," he said, hefting a neck of beef from the tree-hook onto the cutting table. I would try to do the heavy lifting for him, afraid that he would have a heart attack, but he would wave me off, his face red, his breaths coming in gasps.

"Forget about it!" he would say. "When I can't do this no more, should start measuring me for a *box!*"

He told me how he had never eaten nonkosher, or *treif* food in his life. All pork, he said, was riddled with tiny worms.

"That's why I can work twice as hard as any other man," he said, "because I don't drink, I don't smoke, and I don't eat no *chazerai* from McDonald's where they fry the meat in lard. How old do you think I am?" He looked about seventy, so I figured he must be seventy-five.

"Sixty-five?" I said.

"*Seventy*-five!" he crowed, eyes blazing with triumph among the tired folds of pouchy vein-webbed flesh.

He told me about his childhood in Hungary, and about the day he watched from inside a haystack as a gang of army deserters raped his two sisters while their parents watched, then shot them all.

It was hard to imagine that scene, hard to imagine Mack as a child at all. He looked as if he had been an old man all his life. But I knew that his story was the most common in the world, and I knew that all the Jewish kids I went to school with had the same story in their family, and that the tiniest accidents, like being sent to the store for eggs on the day the soldiers came, had allowed certain children to survive, without whom my old girlfriend Cheryl Bergman, and my old friend Neil Horowitz, would never have existed at all.

One day I had a delivery to Cameo Gardens, to an apartment in the same building where Jill and her roommate lived. As I walked out the front door of the building after leaving the meat in the kitchen of two frail old ladies, I saw Jill pull up in her little clattering diesel Chevette, right next to Howie's brown station wagon.

She had lost about ten pounds since the time I saw her last. There was a strength in her face that I hadn't seen before.

"Hi, Jill," I said, and she turned around, startled.

"Chuck! What a surprise. How the hell have you been?"

"Oh, not too bad, working hard. How's everything with you. How's Wilfredo and my old Suburban colleagues?"

"You mean you didn't hear what happened? They're out of business. Miller skipped town, and nobody knows where he is. Wilfredo moved back to Puerto Rico. Federal marshals seized the whole plant and all the trucks, except when they locked the place and turned the electricity off they forgot about all the meat in there. They had to go in there a week later with gas masks to clean it out."

A warm wind came breathing around the corner of Building B, full of leaves and humidity. We stood there in the Cameo Gardens parking lot, between her car and Howie's car. She had been promoted to shift supervisor. I told her about my new job.

"I didn't think they'd let a WASP like you touch their meat," she said.

"They don't mind, as long as I don't have milk on my hands. That's the important thing. The rest of it, they don't care. There isn't even a bar of soap in the bathroom." She laughed. I asked her if she would like to have dinner with me somewhere that weekend to celebrate my raise, but she already had a date with one of the doctors at the hospital.

I'd forgotten how beautiful she was. I wanted to hug her, but I remembered that I hadn't shaved this morning, being late for the bus. My white coat was filthy, and her nurse's whites, a full size smaller than her previous set, were spotless.

And then I was driving again, and the world was bright with school buses, kids yelling out the windows. I thought about how strong Jill looked, how even now her face was fading into the suburban geography. She was gone. She was part of the land now, someone whom I might see going by in her car once in a while, someone to be loved independently of any issue of getting or losing, part of the pattern of schools and streets and seasons; and the world seemed to move gently, like a floating island, and I felt my old love for her blend, painless, with the love I felt for the trees and the stop signs and the orange drain scuppers, and the Golden Arches standing proud above the colored bands of traffic, all the vehicles together forming a great sibilant relentless machine of motion and money and the boxlike, resonating dance of school buses.

21

Torture Garden

Glatt Mart was located in a small one-story commercial building across from the Tallman Volunteer Fire Department, whose firehouse stood at the corner of an abandoned shopping plaza where Shop-Rite used to be. Sharing the row of stores were a Kwik-Chek covenience store, Speedcraft Auto Parts, who owned a wrecked Volkswagen that stood, flat tired, serving as their billboard, on the grass strip between the curb of the parking lot and the edge of Route 59.

Next to Glatt Mart was a gift shop that I thought at first was called the Mange Tree, because of the flighty script painted on the picture window. Actually it was the Mango Tree. At the east end of the building was a Chinese restaurant called the Torture Garden. Actually it was the Fortune Garden, but the stylized pseudo-Chinese lettering looked more like Torture Garden.

On the flat roof above Glatt Mart stood a life-size papier-mâché model of a three-legged Hereford steer, with a Star of David painted in white upon the brown of the animal's chest. One of his front legs had been replaced by a broomstick. Every Halloween, Mack told me, the steer would climb down from his lookout and be found the next morning mounting the Speedcraft Volkswagen. This had been going on for years, he said, and it was during last year's Halloween sally that the old fellow had lost his leg.

The rest of the year he stood silent and dignified, overlooking the little Tallman Mini-Plaza parking lot, staring across Route 59 where traffic flashed all day, stared toward the Mobil station and the firehouse, which was in a perpetual state of mourning, its flag at half staff and a black-and-purple plywood plaque in the shape of a giant Lorna Doone cookie mounted above the double doors saying, WE MOURN OUR LOSS. It was cancer, I knew without asking. Everybody in the entire fire department had cancer. Before the mourning period for one brother was over, another would have succumbed.

On top of the bereaved firehouse stood a tall scaffold that held up a siren. Several times a day the siren would start up with its long howl, so loud that one couldn't speak in the front of Glatt Mart, and the surviving firemen, those in remission or those not too weakened from chemotherapy, would pull up at the station with blue lights flashing on their Toyotas, and the firehouse doors would open and the trucks would pull out with a screeching whinny of horns.

When the siren would blow, the women shopping in the store would stop talking and begin to scowl, and around and around they would wheel their wobbling shopping carts, their ankles edemic above tight black old-lady shoes as crooked as the squeaking and bent casters on the carts. The store would be filled with a confusion of perfumes, sweet and floral, immodest, geriatric soaps and powders.

Since Howie had three dogs, I was curious about whether dog food, since it is kept in people's kitchens, needed to be kosher. One day when he seemed to be in a good mood, I asked him about it, phrasing the question very carefully. He stared at me for a moment, taking a long drag on his cigarette, with an immense weariness that seemed to weigh the flesh down on his face, then blew the smoke out in a burst. "Great country, America!" he said, his eyes cold. "It's *great* to work with intelligent people!" And he stalked into the storage cooler, trailing blue smoke.

"I give the guy a raise," I heard his loud voice say to Mack, "and he *spits in my face!*"

He yelled at me for two days. "What's the point?" he demanded when I arranged boats of chicken legs on the aluminum platter in an awkward and space-wasting configuration. "What's the fucking *point?*"

As I made the morning batch of hamburger patties, the pattie machine ran out of the squares of waxed paper that go between each pattie. When the machine is out of paper, the metal weight that holds the spindled paper-squares makes a distinctive jingling sound, like the bells of an ice-cream truck, and Howie heard it before I did.

"*Chuckieeee!*" he shouted above the radio's blast of static. Before I could turn the machine off, he yelled again, shrieking at the top of his lungs, "Chuck*EEEEEEEEEEEEEEEEEE!*" so loud that my ears rang and the plastic foam boats on the shelf above the pattie machine buzzed with a low harmonic.

Sometimes I would forget to scoop the excess meat out of the pattie machine after I had finished making patties. "It don't make no *sense!*" Howie would say. Or I would forget to put the water-absorbing paper and plastic "diapers" into the bottom of the boats that we packed quartered broilers into.

But all in all, things weren't going too badly. The dog-food incident blew over. They really weren't bad people. They worked hard, and they took their customers seriously. Once when the kosher tags were missing from a case of boneless chicken breasts, Howie was instantly on the phone, shouting that "You're compromising the integrity of my customers' kitchens!" Yet sometimes when the clarinets on the radio were particularly loud and the blasts of static were shattering the music twice each minute, sometimes when the brain- colored phlegm lay in gobs on the floor like amoebas; sometimes I could feel myself starting to hate the place. I realized that it was essential that I keep listening to classical music on WNCN whenever I was in the station wagon, making deliveries while wrapped in the tragic tenderness of cello and keyboard, to think of Leopold Bloom wandering the streets of Dublin in his black derby hat, his mind humming with music, and to forget for a moment all the other melodies: Howie's loud Marlboro belches, Mack's voice like a mucousy foghorn, the gray, tragic faces of old ladies at the window of the cutting room, asking for "zoop bawns."

One day as I made deliveries in the Pontiac, after having been yelled at for stacking the foam boats too high, WNCN played the symphony from which the Israeli national anthem is taken. I don't know the name of it, or of the composer, since I was out of the car at the beginning and at the end of the piece. It was a warm gray day on Route 59; the main theme rang through the station wagon with its frayed vinyl seats and a slight corned-beef smell everywhere, the strings warm above a chaos of clarinets, like a ship in a storm, enduring, ancient and strong, and infinitely sad; and suddenly everything was radiant, the shapes of houses wrapped in red leaves and brown leaves, tubes of light spelling out the names of stores, the bright yellow school buses; and I knew that no matter what happened, no matter how nasty they acted, I must never descend into hating Howie and Mack, because they were part of the county I grew up with, and to hate them would be to hate a host of other things, like the boxy little shrubless houses, and the sloppy intersections, and the frailness of birch leaves blowing around the houses where I used to play with my old friends from school.

I thought of all the families in the houses around me, the strong and shiny black hair of the little children, kids I've played with all my life, the thick and precise features of their faces, like Cheryl's strong and symmetrical face, full-lipped and dark eyed; and I thought of those children's grandparents and great-grandparents and second cousins who died in boxcars and gas chambers, and of their living relatives who didn't get out of Europe in time, the brave ones coughing today into their gloves in Soviet labor camps, the more malleable ones serving on official anti-Zionist councils. The symphony's theme rolled from the speakers in the car doors, its minor key echoing like an ancient voice in the night, in the desert, in the European winter; and it seemed for a moment that I could hear the voice of an entire people gathered into one choir of cellos. I promised myself that I would never forget that moment, that whenever Howie yelled at me I would silently invoke that melody.

Howie was having trouble with the station wagon. Every few days he would have me drive it to Shlomo's Texaco station in the village of Monsey. I would wait around the station, watching as Shlomo poked at the condensor or sprayed laquer into the carburetor. One day Shlomo said he would have to rebuild the carburetor and that it would be hours before he could even get started on it. I called Howie on the pay phone, which was covered with little stickers from dozens of auto supply houses.

Howie was angry. Shlomo was too busy to come to the phone.

"Tell him to move his fucking ass or he's not going to get paid and all my customers are going to hear what a shitty job he does!" he instructed. He said he would send Lou and his wife Terry over to take me back to the store. Lou was Howie's silent partner, a rheumatologist in private practice. He was in the store that day examining the books.

Shlomo was a young Israeli immigrant who owned the Texaco station in the village of Monsey, doing almost all his business with the Orthodox Jewish communities of Monsey and nearby New Square. Brown station wagons were everywhere, all with Colman and Stanger bumper stickers. Black-coated men peered at the undersides of their old four-door sedans aloft on the hoist. Everybody in the store had a thick accent, from the bearded men questioning the bearded mechanics to Shlomo haggling on the office phone in the rapid airy soft gutturals of Hebrew.

Monsey is not a typical American town. All the males wear long black coats, even on the hottest day of summer. Nothing is ever swept or washed, no building is ever painted, nothing is bright or light or trimmed or pretty or cheerful. An outsider might think Monsey a joyless place, but that's not really true. Religious joy has canceled out everything else; joy has migrated inward, inside the unpainted cinderblock *shuls,* inside the cramped cottages with rivulets of rust running down their white asbestos walls, inside the black coats of the men and the flower print dresses of the women in opaque stockings who push broken baby carriages through the dust of summer and the rank mulch of unswept leaves, up the sidewalk of Monsey Boulevard, from Braun's Juvenile Furniture to Weisberg's Vegetable Store, from Monsey Fish Market to Twersky's Glatt Kosher Meat Market. All the married women wear cheap wigs over their shaved heads. Little boys with thick glasses, yarmulkes, and long sidelocks symbolizing beards, wobble throught the streets on bicycles older than they are. The community bus, which runs six days a week into the diamond district in Manhattan, is divided by a partition of hanging blankets separating the women from the men.

These were the Hasidim, the holiest of the holy, too holy even to shop at Glatt Mart. Howie's customers were the semiassimilated Orthodox Jews, who wore ordinary clothes, but always with yarmulkes. Howie's customers, although they were strict about not driving or cooking or handling money on *Shabbes,* strict in their adherence to dietary laws, and strict about saying their morning prayers, differed from the black-clad Hasidim in that they were allowed to shave, to watch television, to go to college; and their women were allowed to drive cars.

One of the two toilets in the men's room of Monsey Texaco was shattered, the porcelain shards pushed into the corner. I noticed that the holes in the bottom of the urinal were arranged in a random, unsymmetrical pattern, just a jumble of holes, even that small element of design ignored. Moth balls rolled around in the stream. The water was full of loose tobacco shreds. But such neglect and carelessness, when I thought about it, made a kind of sense. To a religious mind, what would be gained by designing things, by trying to make things beautiful? As Howie would say, "What's the point?" Only G-d was perfect; only His beauty was worth considering; and religious joy, that makes men in black coats weep and sing inside synagogues of cinderblock, the only joy in town.

Finally Howie's partner Lou and his wife Terry pulled up at the gas station to take me back to work. They were a dark-haired, serious-faced couple, and both so heavily scented that I wanted to open the window as I sat in the car, bathed in volatile colognes. It would have been impolite to open the window. I tried breathing through my mouth, but I could taste the essences settling on my tongue.

And then I was back in the store, and things were slowing down a bit. Howie was hawking up phlegm and blowing it in the general direction of the fat can. I could smell the distinctive odor of Marlboro smoke passing in a hot column over Howie's grease-smeared fingers as he held the tip of the cigarette below his hand.

I helped him salt the day's meat. As we worked he explained some of the details of Jewish dietary law to me, how there can be no such thing as a kosher cheeseburger because meat and dairy products can never be eaten together or even cut with the same knife. No meat posterior to the next-to-last rib can be kosher; hence there is no such thing as a kosher shell steak or filet mignon or top round—except in Israel, where, by special rabbinical dispensation, hindquarter meat can be kosher if it is carefully deveined. I was glad that he was still willing to teach me about these laws, even though I had made that stupid remark about dog food. I still wanted to do a good job, to make Glatt Mart my gateway to a normal life.

He explained about the designation *pareve*, which refers to foods that are neutral, containing neither dairy products nor meat, and can be eaten with either meat or dairy. Vegetables, grains, eggs, and fish are all *pareve*. I already knew about fish being *pareve*, because of one day when I was stocking the refrigerator case with jars of pickled herring packed in white cream sauce. I asked Howie about this, and he explained that fish was *pareve*.

"In other words," I asked, "fish isn't considered meat, right?"

"Fish," he informed me, "is considered *fish*."

22

Rifle Dance

Sunday is always a busy day in the kosher butcher business. It is the first day of the kosher week, the day every item in the meat case is cut fresh, and whole families go meat shopping for hours together, filling the store with their voices and the squeaking wheels of miniature shopping carts, while in the back of the store the butchers grunt and struggle to keep up with the shopping frenzy.

Sometimes Howie's father would come in to take the place of Mack, who didn't work on Sundays. Howie's father lived in the Bronx, where he worked in Howie's other store, also called Glatt Mart. Mr. Shapiro was a remarkably homely man, his cheeks hanging in great flews, like a bloodhound drained of all cuteness, his large face shiny with a lanolin patina. All day he would bend over the cutting board, saying nothing, a column of smoke rising from the cigarette in the center of his mouth. That face always made me sad. I felt sorry for Howie, for the dreariness of growing up under such a face.

Late one Sunday, I drove Mr. Shapiro in Howie's brown station wagon to the Spring Valley bus station where he would catch the bus back down to the Bronx. I had the World Series on the radio, Kansas City against Philadelphia.

"My son he used to play the baseball," Mr. Shapiro said, "He tell you that?'

"No. He never mentioned it."

"Yankees wanted him to pitch on the farm team in the minor league, but he don't want to go."

"How come?" I asked.

"Have to play on *Shabboes*, and he don't want to break the law. I don't care myself, but his mother, she don't like to see a religious boy play in the baseball."

We were early for the bus. Howie had told me to wait until the bus came and he got on it. "Don't make him wait alone with the *schwartzes*," Howie had said.

As we sat there in the car, Mr. Shapiro took a folded newspaper clipping from his wallet. It was an article about Howie, from the *Jewish Press,* and the headline read, FROM CURVEBALLER TO KOSHER BUTCHER. At a Yankee workout Howie had struck out both Yogi Berra and Bill Skowron. The article went on to explain why he had given up the game, "as a sacrifice to my Faith," and how successful he was in the kosher meat business.

As I drove the station wagon back to Glatt Mart, I thought what a sad choice that must have been. Or perhaps it wasn't, and that made it even sadder. To give up baseball, its precision and geometry and space and the living conglomeration of crowd voices — for meat, for religion. No wonder the guy needed to yell at me.

On Monday I tried to talk to Howie about baseball, but it was a bad day, and the Percodans were on the locker-room shelf, meaning that his kidney stones were hurting and criticism would be incisive and articulate today.

"Your father tells me you were quite a ball player," I said. "I'm impressed. I've never met anybody who struck out Yogi Berra." He said nothing, just bent over his cutting board and let out his breath in a long bronchial rale.

"You must be excited to see how well the Yankees are doing these days," I said.

"The Yankees?" he said. "I wouldn't care if their fucking plane crashed in the middle of the stadium." He was angry.

"How come? What's wrong with the Yankees?"

"George Steinbrenner, that's what's wrong with the Yankees!" he said, as angrily as if he were telling me what a lousy job I was doing. "Steinbrenner's an anti-Sem*itt!*" He pronounced *anti-Semite* in a way I had never heard before, the last syllable stressed, rhyming with *spit.*

I must have touched a nerve that exacerbated his already established kidney-stone pain, because all day long Howie yelled at me. I made the packages of chopmeat too messy, with little crumbs falling out onto the platter.

"What's the *point?*" he said. As I packed chicken legs into boats, I could see his hands, and I could hear him breathing. From the roughness of his breath I could tell that I wasn't working fast enough.

"Hhhhhhhrrrrrhhhh! Hhhrrrrrhhhh! *Hhhrrrrhhhh!*" He was trimming the fat off side steaks and packing the steaks into little number 17 boats. He was in a desperate hurry. I watched his frantic hands, all yellow and twisted and stubby, with anvil thumbs, the pointer fingers flattened at the end, and I could smell the strong dryness of his cigarette breath.

"What I can't understand," he said to Mack, "is why does he get *stupider* on the days when my stones are giving me *tsuris?* I mean, he's got to be doing it on purpose."

"I'm sorry you're in pain," I told him, "but what can I tell you? I'll try to do my best, and I hope you feel better."

"*Leave my health out of this discussion!*" he said, staring at me with pouchy, lightless eyes. "You don't know what pain *is!* You come in here all smiles, like everybody in the world is as healthy as you, and you

213

think people are interested in talking about baseball! How the *fuck* do you expect people to take you *seriously?*"

"I'm sorry," I said, and went to help the Haddar Poultry driver unload his delivery. It was strange to work with someone so ferociously unhappy. I wanted to tell him to cheer up.

Then I was back at the cutting board, across from Howie's hands, and he was watching my exasperating slowness again.

"HHHRRRRR! HHHHRRRRRHHH! *HHHRRRRR-RHHHHH!*" It was strange to think that those same hands had thrown a curve ball that struck out Yogi Berra.

"Is there any reason you're lining up the boats that way?"

"I'm trying to do it smoothly," I said.

"Look at the way the girl *wraps* them!" he said. His daughter Leslie was working the wrapping machine today. "She has to turn them lengthwise. It's just double work."

"I thought I could get more on the tray that way."

"But what's the *point?*"

"To save time and space. I guess."

"It don't make no *sense!*"

In the evenings on the local bus home, I was beginning to hear Howie's voice ringing in my ears. This worried me. I noticed myself sneering at the Colman and Stanger bumper stickers. I'm not crazy about bumper stickers, but I don't approve of sneering at the names of local Jewish politicians. That has always seemed a particularly ugly sort of prejudice, and one that my family, like many Hotchkiss families, has always taken pride in avoiding. You can smell it on people, the way nonsmokers can smell the breath of smokers, can smell the anti-Semitism in the sausage-laden breath of Serbians, can feel it like a film of bacteria over the poems of Ezra Pound. I remembered how huffy I got when my neighbor Heidi, who was born in Germany, asked me how I was getting along with the "kikes." I told her that Germans don't have the right to talk that way. Even though it happened before either of us was born. German people, even young ones, have forfeited all rights to anti-Semitic remarks.

I decided to get back in touch with my old girlfriend, Cheryl Bergman, whom I hadn't seen in five years. If I could see her again, over coffee and dessert, if I could look again into the strong thickness of her features, I would lose all desire to sneer at Jewish bumper stickers. I called up her house, but she wasn't there. She was married and living in Florida.

Her mother remembered me. She told me all about how Cheryl had a master's degree in architecture, about her husband's career in the cleaning supply business. She gave me their address, but I didn't write it down. I thanked her and told her to give my best to Dr. Bergman. After she hung up I sat there, listening to the long hoot of the dial tone. I should have known that she'd be married by now.

I tried calling Neil Horowitz, who had been my best friend through most of my childhood. If I could hear his sense of humor again, his imitation of his coarse and cantankerous Uncle Sidney, it would block out the sound of Howie's loud and honking voice for weeks. His parents' phone was busy. I kept calling for an hour but never got through.

The next day I had to take the station wagon to Shlomo's Texaco station again. The rear door wouldn't open. Howie was angry. Mack followed me over to Monsey in his copper-colored Monte Carlo. Earlier that day he had gotten onto the subject of religion and history, onto the issue of whether Christ was killed by the Hebrews or by the Romans. As he drove me back to the store he resumed the discussion.

He was probably right; it probably was the Romans. The strange thing was how angry Mack was.

"Fuckin' BASTARDS!" he shouted, his face red. I wanted to remind him that it happened almost two thousand years ago. Yet here we were, driving through the sloppy and casual suburbs, past dry cleaners and Chinese restaurants, through stoplights with all sorts of little side-arrows, and I could see puffs of steam coming up from drain scuppers at the edge of Route 59.

I suppose I myself am not perfect about accepting the past quietly. I can still feel traces of anger at Franklin D. Roosevelt for surrendering half of Europe to the Soviets, and at Harry Truman for failing to seize that one precious moment in history when we could have wiped them off the earth; but when I get to something in the area of several hundred years ago, the anger fades, and the past becomes a sort of geology upon which we build our cities and houses, such as they are. That's why I'm confident that I could talk about the Battle of Hastings without raising my voice.

But then that's the difference between a Jew and a Gentile. I don't have to defend myself. No libraries of ideology are howling for revenge against the depredations of Charlemagne; no unwashed councils of scholars forbidden to use their left hands are formulating strategies to blast the old names out of the class benches in the Hotchkiss library, or to expel the British from Britain. Mack's lips were purple with hate as he weaved through the traffic, honking and yelling at other drivers.

"Stupid *ID-JUTT!*" he roared at a young black woman who passed us. Crouched behind the wheel, Mack could barely see over the hood of the car. "Stupid *schwartzes!* I ask a fuckin' *schwartze* who made the rain and the moon and the sun and who put the fuckin' stars in the sky and you know what that fuckin' asshole say? He said Jesus made it all! *Idiot!*"

He started turning the radio dial to find some music that he didn't hate, but all he could find was rock and roll and disco music. He was angry.

"Fuckin' *schwartze* music! Not music at all, just 'YAH-YAH-*YAH-YAH- YAAAHHH!*' Who the fuck wanna listen to that *shit?*"

"It's soul," I said. "You have to understand the feeling, the soul."

"Soul? *SOUL?* I got *soles* on my *shoes!*" he yipped and laughed through fluid and phlegm, and his little eyes twinkled in a red wilderness of sagging flesh.

When we got back to Glatt Mart, it was a swirl of anger and bulletins. A Morroccan airliner had been hijacked. Shopping carts wobbled and squeaked around the store. I forgot to take out the empty chicken crate after I threw the chickens, preparatory to quartering them on the band saw, into a shopping cart that we had stolen from Shop-Rite.

"How long are you *working here?*" Howie said. The siren started up, and its long howling filled the store. I was rotating hot dogs in the display case. Howie was yelling at me, but I cupped my hand behind my ear, pretending not to hear. He came charging toward me.

"You!" he said. "You're wasting my time and my money!"

As I rode the bus home, I thought perhaps I should say the hell with it and quit. But I prefer to stick things out, like a Hotchkiss man who has wandered into a fierce and demanding history class. Anyway, he wasn't always that bad. It was just the kidney stones talking. Any day that the Percodans were on the shelf, I would have to steel my ears against a symphony of anger.

I decided that the next time Howie was in a good mood I would ask him to stop yelling at me so much. All evening I thought and thought about my job. I didn't want to think about my job, but I couldn't help it. I thought about the puffs of steam coming up from the Route 59 scuppers, like tiny geysers, and I thought about cracks in time, about how anger from five thousand years ago can come bubbling up into the middle of Rockland County's green lawns, ancient vendettas behind the wheel of a soft-springed Monte Carlo.

The next day they seemed to be in a good mood. There were no Percodans on the shelf. This would be the right day to ask him to stop yelling. As I changed my shoes in the locker room, I could hear Howie and Mack talking. The subject of the morning's conversation was "People Are Stupid."

". . . and those mutha-fukkas went all the way to the fuckin' union so they didn't have to open up the old books and maybe get dust in their faces to make them sneeze!" Mack's voice was a gargling flugelhorn. Actually the subject of the morning's conversation was *always* "People Are Stupid." To be more precise, the day's People-Are-Stupid *topic* was *"Schwartze Unions Are Stupid."*

"And the frikkin' union says they're right, so they made my wife do it 'cause she's in management and she's not a *schwartze,* so they dump the shit work in her lap!"

"Great country, America," said Howie, his voice sugary with a mixture of amusement, affection, and contempt.

"Good morning," I said, walking into the cutting room.

"*Fleische* in the machine," Howie said.

"Sure, okay. Also, when you have a minute sometime today, I need to talk to you about something. Whenever's convenient."

"Right now," he said. He led me into the office, sat down in his swivel chair, and lit a cigarette. "Yeah, what?"

"Well," I began.

"Not *'well'* . . . What do you want?"

"It's just that I'm . . . a little concerned—"

"About *what?*"

The best way I can describe Howie Shapiro's appearance is to imagine Sandy Koufax with a stocking pulled down over his face, the way Sandy Koufax would look like if he had given up baseball for religion, the sharp, precise Semitic features weighed down, drooping, myasthenic. His nose was all humped over, his lower lip hung slack, his eyes were crinkled with fatigue and impatience. He took a deep drag of his cigarette, as if the smoke could help soothe the pain and stupidity of having to talk to me. He blew the smoke toward the corner of the office, toward the brown cumulus puffs of rusty water stains on the ceiling tiles, and stared into the tumbling shapes of smoke.

"I'm a little concerned that you find it neccessary to yell at me so much," I said. "I mean, I want to do a good job, and I think I could do better if you'd lighten up a bit."

"If you're unhappy you can take off your coat and go."

"That's not really the point."

"That *is* the point. That's *exactly* the point. If you don't like it here, you're welcome to take off your coat and leave right now."

"I don't want it to come to that," I said. "That's why I'm talking to you now, because I'd like to do a good job, and I think I could do better if you didn't dump on me so much."

"I dump because you fuck up! You're cocking around and you're wasting my money; that's why I dump. You come to work all smiles for no fucking reason at all. You put the patties in too many piles. You hang too many London broils on the hook. What's the *point?*"

"Well,"

"Not *'well'*. . . . What's the *point?*"

"I guess—"

"This conversation is over."

"I just think that—"

"This conversation is over!"

The morning quickened in the bright cutting room, to the mixolydian dance of angry clarinets on WEVD, snake-charming music, like the music Vanessa Redgrave had danced to on CBS News on a goodwill visit to a PLO terrorist base, pumping a Kalishnikov carbine above her head as round and round a pile of ammunition they danced. The store began to fill with the people Vanessa wanted to kill. Among the day's infusion of thick floral perfumes and geriatric talcum, Howie yelled and yelled.

We started breaking and koshering the load of shoulders that had come in. Due to the fact that I was never any good at cutting meat, I was having trouble finding the right seam in the broad end of the shoulder where we were digging down to take out the rubbery blood vein before throwing the shoulder in the water.

"How long are you *working here?*" Howie asked.

Mack came back from lunch, furious. I used to think it was something Mack ate for lunch that made him so angry at this time of day, but now I knew that it was the *New York Post.* Every day Mack would eat lunch at home while staring at the terrorist headlines in the *Post,* at the stories of elderly couples murdered in their rent-controlled apartments. I could imagine him there at his kitchen table, wolfing down his corned beef and pastrami sandwiches, his stomach churning like the salty sea, like a storm on the Mediterranean.

"What's the *matter* with you?" Mack shrilled when I failed to take the already-salted pieces away quickly enough. Then I had to go out on deliveries, drifting through the afternoon traffic, into the fragrant kitchens. At one house, when I rang the doorbell I heard the sharp cries of poodles, the dry scrabbling of poodle nails on the floor of the front hall, and through the three little windows in the door I could see them jumping up and down, tense and white and tonsured, with bows at the side of their jeweled collars. I called Howie from a pay phone and told him that Mrs. Geller wasn't home.

"What do you want *me* to do about it?" he said.

It was getting late. We had a lot of work left to do. Mack had gone home. Howie turned the radio to E-Z-Listening music and jacked the volume up. The store lilted with violins playing "Raindrops Keep Falling on My Head" very loud. We worked and worked, wet, sore-handed, cold, hungry, and uncomfortable. My boots were soaked. Howie's dull eyes lay low on his face, within a wilderness of squint lines and fatigue lines. A distinctive smell came from his cigarette, from the hot column of smoke passing over his fat-smeared fingers. He puffed and grunted, silently angry at my slowness.

Soon it was dark outside. I'd never been in the store when it was dark. Everything seemed different, like the special occasions at elementary school when parents came in at night for the Christmas concert, something secret and illicit about the quality of light, as I dredged the wet gray meat out of the water and slapped it down on the white plastic cutting table for Howie to sprinkle the coarse kosher salt on it. My coat was wet, my boots were wet, my hands were white and wrinkled and infected, and the violins fox-trotted through "I Could Have Danced All Night," and into musical commercials for Individual Retirement Accounts. An ocarina tremoloed through "Somewhere Over the Rainbow." Hostages had been taken in Portugal. The Dow Jones was off eight points. An elderly couple in the Bronx had been found dead in their apartment.

As I finished cleaning up and putting things away and throwing down a fresh coat of salt on the floor, it was strange to think that Johnny Carson was already beginning his monologue. The station wagon was being worked on tonight. Shlomo had left his own car for Howie to get home in. Since it was too late for the local buses, Howie gave me a ride most of the way home. As we rode through the dark neighborhoods in Shlomo's old primer-spotted Chevy Nova, the car sputtered and hesitated.

"This car is a piece of *SHIT!*" Howie said.

It was a soft night, warm and overcast, with gusts blowing leaves across the road from both directions. It was, according to the taped Sky Report from the Hayden Planetarium, the night of the Orionid meteor shower, in which up to three hundred meteors were expected to be visible each hour. I tried to make conversation.

"Too bad it's cloudy out," I said. "There's supposed to be a big meteor shower visible tonight, but it doesn't look—"

"Can I *ax* you a personal question?" he said.

"Sure, I guess so."

"Do you smoke a lot of *pot* or something?"

"Sometimes at parties," I said, surprised by the timing of the question. "But no, not a lot. Why do you ask?"

"Because you *forget* things!" he said. "And you're *slow.* I can show you how to cut a piece of meat, and then I have to show you again. So you're saying that you do smoke pot, is that right?"

"Once in a while," I said, "but I'm not some kind of a pothead, if that's what you mean."

"I knew there was something wrong with you, and I figured that might be what it was."

It was strange to think that he couldn't think of anything else to talk about but my faults, strange that after a day when I had worked for him for sixteen hours, he could turn a discussion of astronomy into a criticism session. I was sad for him, and for all the people like him, who lived in a world without meteors, with no stars, no Milky Way, no planets, no comets, no quazars, nothing strange or mysterious; just a crabbed little universe at the center of which responsible people struggled and toiled in a way that other people were too stupid to do. This was Howie's world, a world with no sky; and if he had ever walked far enough out on the beach at Miami to be out of the hotel lights and see the stars, his only thought would have been, "Why the fuck don't people work harder?"

Suddenly everything made a kind of dismal sense, the whole cramped and exhausted world of the meat business, dull knives and rabbis and bumper stickers, old ladies asking for "zoop bawns." It was sad to think of Jews so cut off from the best thing they had, their intellectual tradition, sad to think of Jews who had never listened to a string quartet, who could not even name the instruments in a string quartet, Jews who had never heard of Isaac Bashevis Singer. As for myself, I've never actually read Isaac Bashevis Singer, but by God I've heard of him.

The streets were empty. Everybody had to be up early the next morning. Careers, mortgages, car payments all hung suspended in dreamless sleep. In the darkness of the Grand Atrium Mall, bright Florsheims glinted in the exit light of a shoe store; and downstairs, next to the silent Sears escalator, slept the polyester suits, on sale. I knew that Johnny Carson's suit fit him perfectly tonight. I tried again to start a noncriticizing conversation.

"I bet Johnny Carson's talking about that scandal with the kangaroo meat tonight. You ever watch him?"

"Who has time to watch tele-*vis*-ion?" he said, pronouncing it the European way, with the accent on the middle syllable. He let me off at the far end of Get High Street and doubled back to his house. I began walking the mile to my apartment, over the soft October duff of wanwood leafmeal. Overhead in the darkness I could hear geese flying south, their wild yawping honks joyous and barbaric above the rolling mortgaged and responsible hills where everybody was already asleep, the jack-o'-lantern faces dark.

Strange to think that the center of the universe should be toil, an ancient butcher's bench over which labored tired-eyed old men, for meat and the integrity of kitchens, here among the lawns and music stores, in Rockland County's green and pleasant land; and the whole meat business was like a crack in time from which stale air eructs in ancient steamy belches beneath the avenue bearing the initial of nothing into the Halloween season, the wisdom of the ages, translated from the cuneiform as follows:

Work is supposed to hurt. Days are furrows of poisoned earth to be struggled through. Any man who doesn't hate his job is doing it wrong. Any man who can smile at his own thoughts is a hophead.

23

Mood Flag

Every morning when I got to work, Howie and Mack would already be well into the People-Are-Stupid discussion. The most common People-Are-Stupid topics included: Reform Jews Are Hypocrites, *Schwartzes* Are Stupid, Unions Are Stupid, *Goyim* Are Stupid, and Auto Mechanics Are Incompetent. I would always say, "Good morning," and Howie would say, depending on the condition of his kidney stones, either "*Fleische* in the machine," or simply "Machine." Howie, having been born in the Bronx, didn't know Yiddish any better than I did. To compensate for not knowing the language, he always used as many Yiddish words as possible. Meat was always *fleische,* blacks were *schwartzes.* The gray plastic tubs into which we threw meat trimmings for grinding were *schissels,* a difficult person was a *goniff,* and somebody stupid was a *meshuggener.* This last word was one I came to know well.

After I had put the morning chopmeat out, and had done whatever other odd jobs needed doing, Mack would ask me to feel his knife.

"That's what I call sharp!" I would always say, running my thumb across the honed edge.

"Do you think Shit-Ass could get a knife that sharp?" Shit-Ass was Mack's name for Nathan, an old butcher whom Mack hated who had worked with us for a few weeks until his creditors found where he was working and started calling the store several times a day, at which time Howie fired him.

Mack had a special way of talking, a sort of energetic and confident slovenliness, like a cross between Senator Daniel Patrick Moynihan and Tom Carvel. The timbre of his voice seemed to come from the far end of a narrow mucous-filled pipe.

"That Shit-Ass couldn't work half as fast as me," Mack would say. "Am I right?"

"You're right," I would say.

"Fuckin' Shit-Ass throw all the meat over to my side of the table to make me look bad. Am I right?" He was wrong.

"You're right."

After the feel-my-knife conversation, Mack would tell me about what terrible drivers other people were.

"Some people just too stupid to drive a car. Should give them a mental test to see if they're smart enough. They'd get rid of ninety percent of all the drivers that way! Am I right?"

"You're right."

"Fuckin' *ID-JUTT* drive in my lane don't even look! Then he says he got the right-of-way! You figure it out!"

"Here lies the body of William Grey," I recited, "Who died defending his right-of—"

"Mutha-*FUKKA!*" Should take his license away!"

Halloween came, and they were angry. Razor blades had been found in apples, Ex-Lax in Hershey wrappers. The whole holiday was just a form of extortion anyway. It should be outlawed. The morning after Halloween, I rode the bus to work through a land of strewn toilet paper and smashed pumpkins, to find that the Hereford sentry had again climbed down from Glatt Mart's roof and was mounting the Speedcraft Volkswagen. Now one of his hind legs was broken too.

"The *HELL* with it!" Howie said. "Throw it out!" People passing by in their cars stared at me as I carted the steer around the side of the building to the dumpster in the back. I threw the old fellow in, with his remaining legs pointing stiffly up in the air.

I kept trying to call my old friend Neil Horowitz. I had decided that I would be honest about why I was calling. I would tell him that I needed to talk to somebody Jewish who had a sense of humor. I would tell him about the People-Are-Stupid discussions, about Howie blowing phlegm into the fat can. Neil wouldn't take offense at that. He would come up with some sort of joke, one that I could tell myself on the way to work each morning.

I finally reached Neil's mother. She told me that Neil was in St. Thomas running a charter yacht service. The boat he was living on had no phone, Mrs. Horowitz said, but she gave me a post office box number where I could reach him. As soon as I got off the phone I wrote to him:

Dear Neil,

How the hell are you? I just thought I'd drop you a line at the box number your mother was kind enough to give me.

Remember those imitations you used to do of your Uncle Sidney, pontificating about how stupid everybody in the world was?

I used to laugh like crazy at that imitation. Now, guess what? I've actually met some people who are just like him, only worse. The two guys I'm working for (at Glatt Mart Kosher Meats on Route 59) are an exact copy of Uncle Sidney at his worst. The only trouble is that he was funny and they're not.

And the damn thing is—There's not a soul who would believe me. I want to run out into the street and grab people by the sleeves and say, "Look! Come see! I have discovered wondrous

226

strange creatures existing on Route 59, like a lost tribe on New Guinea."

This letter probably makes no sense to you. But I just wanted to write to you from this strange corner of a planet that I didn't even know existed, if for no other reason than to help preserve my rapidly diminishing sense of humor.

I hope the charter boat business is going well. Drop me a line sometime, or give me a call, collect. Until then, keep 'em sailing.

Best,
Chuck

Every day that we got fresh meat into the store, Rabbi Feiner would come in, with his four-year-old son tagging behind him, and inspect the kosher tags and the killing dates.

"We got a *bear* in the cooler!" Howie or Mack would always say. "Wanna see the *bear?*" They never asked the kid how he was doing in school, or what he wanted to be when he grew up. Just bears. They didn't even know what his name was.

The radio rasped with Yiddish folk music, frantic balalaikas, the clownish clarinets. Sometimes in the station wagon I would try to hum the theme from which the Israeli national anthem is taken, to hear again the tender voice of a people in exile with whom my family and I have always been friends, but I kept hearing the clarinets, like the clarinets in the Laurel and Hardy theme song, snarling and ridiculous ghetto music.

It rained for three days, and they were angry. The roof leaked. Howie was on the phone, cigarette bouncing in his mouth, shouting onto the landlord's answering machine, threatening to sue. The bereaved firemen were called out several times a day, and the store was blanketed with wailing siren sounds. When Route 59 flooded in front of Shop-Rite, and Mack learned that he would have to take a detour home, his face blazed with rage.

At night, at home, I could hear their loud voices ringing through the air, could see their faces, bulbous and gaunt with exhaustion, in the dark shapes of my ceiling. Still, I wanted to stick it out. I don't believe in quitting jobs until I have another one lined up.

Sometimes Howie's father would come and work with us, filling the store with his large and sad face, that huge and tragic Mount Rushmore of a Bronx face, a great mass of flesh at odds with itself, the cigarette trailing off a great lower lip, the plastic-framed glasses tight against the eye cavities, strands of oiled gray hair combed close against the liver-spotted pate. When there was no meat to cut, he would stand at the end of the meat case and sadly survey the vast meatscape stretching across the rear of the shopping area.

One rainy morning, when Howie had already threatened the landlord, I walked beneath one of the leaks, and some water ran down my back. Trying to make conversation, I said, "That's a terrible feeling to get water down your back like that."

"Then don't *walk under it!*" Howie said.

What I couldn't understand was why Howie and Mack had to be so nasty. I can understand pressure, and I can understand greed, I can even understand the pleasure of cruelty, like Sandy at Denny Packing, like Shylock's fierce and evil gusto. But these men didn't even take pleasure in being mean; they just didn't know anything else. Every night now, on the bus, I would be angry, and I would hate them, and all the people from whom they sprang.

There were times, especially on days when the Percodan bottle stood on the shelf like a small-craft-warning flag, that I felt the thing I feared most beginning to happen. I was becoming a hateful person. It would come upon me suddenly, and I would be ashamed, like a little boy with a secret. In the window of the Mange Tree, a collection of cloth dolls called "Shtetlfolk" were on display, each doll illustrating a stock character from Jewish folklore. There was an old babushka'd woman in a print dress, a timid bar mitzvah boy with a Torah and a purple prayer shawl, a shriveled old man with a crooked walking stick;

228

and all their faces were the same, crabbed and joyless, made from drawing the cloth into tight folds around the eyes and cheeks. One day as I walked past the Mange Tree, after nine hours of pointed inquiries as to what the point was and how long I had been working there, I suddenly found myself hating those figurines. I wanted to herd them into a ditch, even the old *bubbe* and *zaide,* and shoot them with a machine gun.

What surprised me most about my anger was how unsophisticated it was. There was nothing that I could have held a conversation about. It was wordless, visceral, and it came steaming up out of me, endogenous, like vapor trapped for centuries beneath the ground, like the vapor from the Route 59 drain scuppers, like the burst of anger that made me almost run an old man over that day last year. The issues are irrelevant. The fact that Howie and Mack were jackasses was irrelevant; it is not normal to want to shoot cloth dolls with a machine gun, and anybody who tries to justify hatred by pointing to the very real faults of those he hates, is taking the first steps on a path that has made this century different from any other century.

On the I-beams that held up the roof over the walkway that ran from the Torture Garden to Speedcraft to Glatt Mart to the Mange Tree to Quik-Chek, the Jewish Defense League had pasted NEVER AGAIN stickers, each with the famous Warsaw Ghetto photograph of a little boy held prisoner by Nazi Storm Troopers, his hands raised meekly above his head, on which he is wearing one of those old-fashioned snap-brim caps. Sometimes I even hated that little boy, especially his hat, an old-man hat, a hat of work and struggle and joylessness.

When I was at Hotchkiss, I learned in biology class about ascaris worms, the foot-long parasitic roundworms that sometimes take up residence in human nasal passages. Our teacher, the brilliant Mr. Gogates, told us that sometimes the first sign that a human victim will have that he is infested will be when one of the worms comes casually crawling out of the host's nose. That's how I felt sometimes, walking to the bus stop on the way home. Suddenly all the anger would come slithering out of me, like a foreign agent. Sometimes I would write I HATE JEWS in Magic Marker on the back of a stop sign, then look around, hoping nobody had seen me.

I knew it was stupid, but sometimes I didn't care. Once, after a particularly bad Percodan day, I started to write, in great big letters in a gas station men's room, JEWS OPPRESS POOR PEOPLE, but I couldn't remember how many *p*s in "oppress," so I just wrote JEWS SUCK. I looked it up when I got home. It was ridiculous. I've always tried to like myself, but I didn't like this man who was scrawling such things on bathroom walls.

I tried to get in touch with Larry Goldstein, who had been my favorite teacher at Quinnipiac. He was a brilliant lecturer and a fine poet. He had even had a poem published in *The New Yorker.* It would be good to hear the measured tones of his voice, which could perhaps drown out Howie's honking vocalizations, would be good to hear the slowness with which Larry talked, a bit like William F. Buckley, Jr., a voice beneath which one could almost hear the pulse of intelligence.

From the phone booth in front of Glatt Mart I called the Quinnipiac switchboard, and they connected me with the English Department secretary, who informed me that Professor Goldstein had been "re-trenched," and was now teaching at the University of Hawaii.

Sometimes in Waldbaum's I would find myself secretly drawing swastikas on the tops of cans of Mother's gefilte fish, knowing as I did it how ugly it was, how soiled, how fallen. I had no excuse. I don't know what I would have said if I had been caught at it. I needed help. This wasn't me. I don't draw swastikas on gefilte fish.

The one thing I could take a modicum of pride in was that I never let myself get serious. I never let my thoughts organize themselves into an ideology that I could pretend to talk reasonably about in a three-piece suit, never gave consideration to the chant of the Left, never sought to begrudge these people that which everybody else in the world takes for granted, the rights to their own land. When I thought about how angry Mack was about things that happened two thousand years ago, I would realize that the difference between him and me was that his history had not firmed into geology; and that made all the difference. The issue of who killed Christ was still a live issue for them, unlike any residual anger I might have had about the Battle of Hastings.

Sometimes when Mack was speaking Yiddish to a customer I could hear how closely his language was related to the German I took at Hotchkiss, but twisted, gnarled somehow, with all the lyrical tenderness bleached and blasted out of it, an ugly language, in which there is no way to say *"Du bist wie ein blume."* Perhaps that ugliness could help explain the astonishing ferocity of Nazi Germany, in that Germans, listening for generations to this clownish, sputtering parody of their own language, would have built up a particularly savage reserve of hatred.

The whole relationship between language and violence is diseased anyway. With Hitler it was straightforward at least, the hissing gutturals, the shreiking cadences of rage. Today, the voice of murder is soft and delicate, mellifluous music of Farsi and Arabic, full of exquisitely soft *ch*s, the precise vowels of a prerecorded ultimatum detailing the fate of hostages if the subject government fails to recognize the rights of the "Pal-e-stin-yann Pee-pool," and on All-News Radio 88, one can gauge the severity of the current terrrorist incident by the softness of the woman's voice that reads the news.

Yet, walking along Route 59 with the voices of Howie and Mack ringing in my ears, I was a Nazi sometimes, for half an hour at a time. By the time I got home, I would regret the swastikas. I was becoming what is known as a crank. Sometimes I would throw my felt-tipped marker into the woods before I could start drawing swastikas, but then I would have to buy a new one the next morning, and that could get expensive. At least I knew enough not to draw them backward, the way most anti-Semitic people seem to; at least I didn't compound stupidity with ignorance.

I finally got a postcard from my old friend Neil.

Hi Chuck!

I just got your letter, and frankly I'm a little puzzled. I don't have any Uncle Sidney. You must be thinking of somebody else, maybe Philly Rabinowitz.

As far as your crazy job is concerned, I'm not an expert in the personnel field, but if you hate it so much, why do you stay there. QUIT, for Christ's sake! I'd offer you a job on the boat, but I just had to let two good men go. Business sucks these days.

So stiff upper lip and all that. Stay in touch. Good luck with your job.

Neil

Every morning at about eleven, Howie would call up the manager of his other store, on Riverdale Avenue in the Bronx. They would small-talk for a few minutes, inquiring about the health of each other's families, thanking God for this and that, listing friends who were currently on "cheemo."

"God Bless America," Howie would say repeatedly, with a sort of tickle of amused and affectionate contempt. At a certain point in the conversation, Howie would say, with a distinctive musical lilt, "What's doin'?" This, I came to realize, was the heart of the conversation. This was Howie's way of asking how much money the store had taken in the day before.

It was getting colder. Everybody wanted to go to Florida. It was getting dark early now, and I would leave the brightness of the store each night, and go into a world of darkness lit by headlights and fluorescent signs. Trucks full of hundreds of trussed-up Christmas trees had begun to appear. Over the dumpster in the back of the store I could see the cold and unwavering light of the planet Venus, now the Evening Star, milky and clear in a sky coming to life with the bright haze of shopping centers.

Every night after Mack had gone home and all the meat was cut and put away, I would sweep the cutting room. Howie and his son Jerry would be sitting out by the cash register, smoking cigarettes and reading the *New York Post* and the *Daily News*.

The floor of the cutting room was sprinkled each day with kosher salt, to prevent slipping on the fat scraps. At the end of the day, among the coarse white crystals, all over the cutting room, lay Howie's Marlboro butts, crushed out. Scattered among the butts and the salt and the scraps of fat, were dozens of little things that looked like jellyfish, soft translucent shapes flecked with floor salt, like macro-amoebas in whom the dirt on the floor formed nucleii and protoplasmic vacuoles. Actually these were globs of mucus that Howie had spit on the floor.

These are the landscapes of another planet, I kept telling myself, but it didn't help, and I would remember last night's swastikas, and those of the night before, and I would putter around Glatt Mart with my secret pulsing inside me, like a little boy desperately ashamed of his masturbation. Neil was right, of course. It was crazy for me to stay there, but somehow I wanted to see it through, through the lonely winter, to the point where the sun rises again and the ice melts and everything is all right, and the clear ringing capo-transposed chords of George Harrison's guitar blend with a faraway calliope melody, pouring down warm as sunlight.

After I had swept the cutting room and thrown the stale salt and the butts and the fat into the dumpster, rinsed the plastic cutting tables with a bucket of soapy water and a white plastic brush, scooped the wet bone-mush from inside the band saw, hefted the fat barrels into the storage cooler, and spread out a fresh coating of salt; I would then sweep out the shopping area of the store. Slowly, with a wide dust mop, I would sweep up and down each aisle, through the residual territories of departed fragrances. Howie and his son would be sitting by the cash register, in the warmth of the hissing electric space heater, smoking cigarettes and reading the tabloids. The music would be soft, and I could hear the hissing of freon coils beneath the meat case, the soft static of the radio, the hissing of traffic that flashed bright across the wide picture window. As I swept the floor, I could hear a soft and continuous hiss as they stared at the headlines of terrorism and crime, could hear the hiss of long drags on cigarettes, the sibilance of Howie's exhalations, the rustle of pages as they traded the *News* for the *Post,* all the huffing and puffing and yelling over for another day, the fierce anger cooling down into a vague, generalized dissapproval, like locomotives resting at the end of the day, the gradual lowering of steam pressure, overheated iron composed at last.

"Good night," I would say.

"*Pssssssshhh* . . ." Howie would answer, not lifting his eyes from the headlines.

24

Izod Amulet

Softly, softly the snow fell outside the great sheet of window in front of Glatt Mart; softly the flakes swirled around the primer-painted I-beams holding up the roof over the walkway. Sharing the beam-space with the NEVER AGAIN stickers were posters saying ELECT STRICT LEADERS. These were actually advertisements for people running for *district* leaders, but the posters were folded over so that you couldn't read the whole thing.

Softly the cars on Route 59 went whispering by, their bumper stickers bright against the mild monochrome of December, and the store was bright with light as I rotated chocolate swirl cookies. Swollen ankles hobbled through the aisles behind wobbly-wheeled shopping carts. The air was thick with perfume. In the little parking lot, mustard-colored station wagons were spinning their tires on the snow, a frantic angry howling sound, and the faces in the store were hard and angry, angry at the weather.

I was feeling relatively good. Thay hadn't been yelling at me lately. I was thinking that perhaps the worst of my initiation was over. I hadn't drawn a swastika all week.

It was Friday, the day we had to be finished in time to close an hour before sundown. The snow came down like dust all day, just a tiny accumulation, but enough to set customers' jaws into a Florida-deprived rictus of anger. As I rinsed the parts of the dissassembled pattie machine, spraying them off with a hose outside the back door of the store, I could see the water cutting delicate branched canyons into the snow, like the branches of a river seen from an airplane; and I thought of all the people who would be getting on airplanes for Christmas, the sky full of travelers, the airports humming with holiday activity; and all the food, gravy-smothered open-face sand-wiches in airport coffee shops, boneless steaks served in flight high above the rolling gray of leafless forests. I thought of all the houses, lined in lights, groaning boards of turkey and ham. Christmas lights were going up along Route 59. The seasonal department at Caldor was a wonderland of synthetic spruce and twinkling lights and the Christmas songs of Johnny Mathis.

"So you like that holiday when they beat up the Jews, huh?" said Mack when I told him I was beginning to feel the Christmas spirit. We were salting the meat together, his shapeless dead white hands sprin-kling salt on the floppy wet meat, and I could hear the yellow Highway Department trucks going by, sprinkling salt on Route 59.

He told me about Christmas in Hungary, how it was an accepted custom to attack Jews. He and his father had been beaten savagely by a mob of *goyim* one Christmas Eve. He showed me the scar behind his left ear, a translucent half-moon of hairless tissue.

"Fuckin' bastards knocked us down in the fuckin' snow," he said, his voice quavering with anger and phlegm, "and after they beat us up they took a piece of raw bacon and stuck it down my throat with a *stick* and said, 'Eat this good *schveina* meat, Jew-boy, make the skin grow back on your *prick!*' That's the only time I ever ate a fuckin' *schveina* meat."

He told me how pigs are cursed animals because they eat their own excrement, how civilizations such as those in the Micronesian Islands, that live on a diet rich in pork, never accomplish anything because everybody gets trichinosis. He told me about the enzyme in pork that causes cancer, and about how he had once looked at a piece of pork under a microscope and seen the tissues riddled with millions of tiny worms.

I thought about the suckling pig we'd had last Christmas at my aunt's house in Baltimore, how the flesh fell steaming away from the tiny bones. I told Mack about the pickled pig fetuses we had dissected in biology class at Hotchkiss, formaldehyded homunculi with distinctive little livers and lungs and stomachs, and arteries full of rubbery red latex. At that stage of their development, I told him, the little pigs are very similar to humans.

"You may be right about those trichinosis worms," I said, "but I think I'll take my chances. I can understand it from a religious aspect, but for myself, I couldn't give up anything so tasty."

"Well, if you think they're just as good as people," he said, his face red as a baked apple, "you might as well eat a *schveina* every fuckin' day, because that means you're no better than they are!"

"I didn't say that. I said we dissected them because their organs are arranged in a very similar way to humans."

"*DON'T TALK TO ME!*" he roared. "You fuckin' snake try to insult my religion. Should go work with the *schwartzes!*"

In silence we finished salting the meat. As I cleaned up in the cooler, hosing the slime out of the chicken bins, I could hear Mack's voice talking to Howie. Later, Howie came bustling into the cooler, his cigarette glowing in the semidarkness.

"Quit cocking around and get this shit *finished!*" he said, scowling at his watch. In the cold damp of the cooler, where *treibored* and koshered shoulders hung in long brown rows, his cigarette had a peculiar smell, rank and illicit and familiar. It was the same smell as the cigarettes in the boy's bathroom at Rockland Country Day School, harsh and wet and secretive.

As Howie held up my handful of money, he wouldn't even look me in the eye, just glared out into the vague whiteness of Route 59, where, in the parking lot of what used to be Shop-Rite, a Christmas tree dealership had been set up, with strings of bare hundred-watt bulbs outlining the perimeter of the sales area, the white lights dancing in the breeze of the darkening afternoon. The *Post* was open on the counter beside the cash register. The Soviets had begun massing troops and tanks at the Polish border.

"Have a nice weekend," I said.

"*Psshhhh . . .*" he replied. He was angry.

On Sunday, Howie yelled at me all day, and the stupid thing was that after all these months it still hurt. He confronted me in the front of the store where customers could hear, making inquiries about what the point was and how long I had been working there. The store was filled with families, all talking at once, about who was getting married, who was a doctor, who was dead, who was in Florida, who was on cheemo.

"Mommeeee!" shrilled a child's voice. "I want *gum! MOM-MEEEEEE!*" Hyperactives dashed among the carts and coats and swollen ankles, and I was a Nazi again. I had thought I was over that stupid business, but here it was rolling back again, all the old anger like a filthy tide coming in.

On my way home, going into Waldbaum's, I looked between the paper window signs saying CANNED FOOD — STOCK UP NOW! at all the faces lined up at the checkout counter, hard angry faces, tightly coiffed, angry at the slow cashier, at the hyperinflation, at the grayness of the day, at the cruel fact that the world was not Florida. The apparition of these faces lined up behind the register; puddles on a wet black aisle, where apple juice has fallen. I tried, among the breakfast cereals, to hear the voice of my old professor, Larry Goldstein, the precise erudition of his words, all spoken with a kind of relentless irony, as if the world wasn't all that serious after all. But I couldn't hear the voice anymore. It had been too many years. The cereal boxes flashed in a hundred colors. I was angry again. I drew a few swastikas on gefilte fish jars, and then I bought a string of Christmas lights for my tree. It occurred to me that I might be the only person in the history of Waldbaum's who had ever drawn swastikas on gefilte fish and bought Christmas tree lights in the same shopping trip.

Alone in my apartment, I trimmed my artificial tree. The lighting of the lights, however, would wait until tomorrow night, when the tree at Rockefeller Center would be lit, there at the epicenter of Christmas, from which the quality of Christmas radiates, and we would light the two trees together. Perhaps in the moment when the switches were thrown, some light might shine into my apartment, bringing tidings of great joy to Cresent Drive Spelled Wrong.

On Monday, Mack was still furious. When I said "Good morning," he sort of keened and burbled with anger and looked away. The day's People-Are-Stupid topic was "Chuck Deckle is *meshuggener*." As I changed my shoes, I could hear their voices at the cutting table.

"Fuckin' *id-jutt* think he can laugh at my religion because they cut up a *schveina* in school!" said Mack through fluid and phlegm.

"Great Country, America," said Howie, and blew a wad of mucus onto the floor.

I "kept a low profile," working quietly and busily. I broke and *triebored* shoulders, quartered chickens, and made deliveries into kitchens redolent with spicy winter soups. I salted the meat all by myself, hoping to save Mack some work, and perhaps even to get back on his good side.

I had decided that from now on I would wear my Martha's Vineyard T-shirt every day, turned inside out so that the Vineyard logo was directly against my heart. On the collar of the T-shirt I had safety-pinned an Izod alligator that I had cut off a worn polo shirt. I told myself that every time they yelled at me I must touch the alligator like an amulet and think of the sound of the quiet surf at night. But it didn't help much. Working at Glatt Mart was like trying to breathe under water. Their voices shrilled through the cutting room like the horns of gridlocked traffic, and the siren howled, and the radio rasped with blasts of static, and walking down the road I was a Nazi again. I stopped in Waldbaum's for a quart of milk. Somebody saw me drawing a swastika on a box of Shofar dehydrated kosher potato soup, and I felt a hand grab me by the shoulder.

The security guard led me into the store manager's office. At first they wanted to press charges. I wouldn't have cared if they had. I would have pleaded guilty. But they just made me pay for the potato soup and told me never to come in there again.

"We don't want your business," the manager said. I walked all the way home. I didn't want to ride the bus. I felt as if the other passengers would be able to smell me, like a child who has defecated into his pants.

That night, the lighting of the Rockefeller Center Christmas tree was carried live on Channel 5. The Seven Dwarfs, and Mickey Mouse, and Goofy, all went skating round and round beneath the dark tree while Ed McMahon told about the history of Christmas in Rockefeller Center. Farrah Fawcett was there, in a hooded coyote coat. Beautiful Farrah. I touched her face on the television screen. The St. John the Divine choir stood on risers above the ice. Then at the appointed time, a crippled boy threw the switch, and the tree winked into light, and the choir burst into "Joy to the World." At the same moment I plugged in my own tree, and it lit the darkness of my living room, although the topmost string of lights was not working.

I watched the Yogi Bear Christmas special. I was tired from all this anger. My head was buzzing. If anybody ever needed Christmas to come, I did. I turned on Monday Night Football. I wasn't paying much attention to the game. Suddenly Howard Cosell said something strange.

"But then we must remember," he said, "that this is only a football game."

25

Brain Furnace

As I walked to the bus the next morning, with my Vineyard logo against my heart and the alligator patch against my neck, and John's death hanging over the land like a stalled weather system with no wind to blow it away anywhere, I tried to think about all the Beatles songs I remembered from Christmas at my first year at Quinnipiac, especially the *Magical Mystery Tour* album, how the bright chords of "Hello and Good-bye" seemed to ring above the snowy hills of Connecticut, the tragic cello lines of "I Am the Walrus," as dark as the land before the lights come on.

I walked past children who stared at my workingman's clothes, as carpool Volvos zoomed by, trailing sulfuric aid and cold oily colognes. I could feel a thin coldness in the wind through the bare trees. I hadn't cried in years. I tried to cry, but it just made my throat hurt.

I stood at the bus stop and watched the traffic flash by in the gray of a December morning, all the hues dull with dust and salt, and I could hear snatches of Beatles songs Doppler shifting on car radios, "I Wanna Hold Your Hand," and John Lennon's new song, "Just Like Starting Over." I thought about all the songs I had grown up with, here in my county, this great dark shape of winter and electric guitars, and all my friends, gone, into careers, to the Caribbean, to Florida. As I sat on the bus, everywhere I looked reminded me of another song.

"Fuckin' New York a fuckin' shit-ass *jungle!*" Mack was saying to Howie. As I changed my shoes, I could hear their voices ringing through the cutting room, above the E-Z-Listening violins of "She Loves You."

"That guy was a *meshuggener* hophead anyway," Howie's voice said. "It's no great fuckin' loss."

Howie actually said "Good morning" to me when I walked into the cutting room, which was a surprise. Perhaps some trace of civility remained; perhaps he would go easy on an old Beatle fan today. I hurried into the storage cooler to grind the morning chopmeat. Howie followed me.

"Can I ax you a question?" he said. "Are you satisfied here?"

"I guess so. Why?"

"I thought you might be trying to get revenge on me for something." He lit a cigarette and took a long deep drag, inhaling as if it were a joint, then blew the smoke in a billowing cloud toward the ceiling. Everything was cold and damp. "Like maybe you wanted to commit sabotage against my store for some reason."

"What do you mean?" I said.

"You broke the law. You defied the *kashruth* law! You have to be Jewish to salt the *fleische,* and you went and did it yourself." His voice rang off the moist walls. I could feel the percussion of his loud syllables, as if we were under water.

"I did it correctly," I said. "I did it just the way you showed me."

"That don't matter. A *goy* is not permitted to salt the *fleische!* If the *rebbe* found out about it he could condemn every piece of *fleische* in the whole store, were you aware of that?"

"I'm sorry. I didn't know. I was just trying to save time."

"Is there something about our religion that you take pleasure in spitting on?" he said. "Weren't you satisfied that you insulted Mack by saying that *schveina* were just as good as people? Do you have to turn around and spit on the *kashruth* law too?"

"I didn't say that pigs were as good as people. The only thing I said was—"

"Are you calling him a liar?"

"What I said was—"

"Are you *calling him a liar, yes or no?*"

"No."

"Because if it comes to the point where I have decide which one of you to get rid of, you can rest assured that you'll be out on the street with the *schwartzes,* because he's worth twice as much as you are."

"I understand that," I said. "I just wish—"

"I want you to remember a few things," he said. "And if you're too stoned to remember them in your head, I want you to write them down on a piece of paper. Number one: you're working off the books here. That means you can't collect unemployment if I decide to get rid of you, and you can't go crying to the Labor Board that I didn't have enough sympathy with your drug problems. Number two: you're on probation here. One more fuck-up and you're fired."

"Look, Howie, I don't know what to tell you. I'll try to do a good job. I'll try not to give you any reason to get rid of me."

"You already *have!*"

"Well, I just—"

"This conversation is over."

I worked in silence, alert, busy, speaking only when spoken to. What I couldn't understand was that if he hated me so much, why didn't he fire me instead of just trying to make the place so hellish that I would quit? Now more than ever it was imperative that I hang in here at Glatt Mart; precisely because it was Hell, and people have to learn to live in Hell. That, after all is what is uplifting and transcendent about the Jewish culture in Europe: they survived Hell. How could I quit? I owed it to the memories of those whose solitary deaths had been part of that survival, owed it to those dead children with thick-featured faces just like the faces of the kids I went to elementary school with, owed it to all of them, to survive Hell, to redeem myself for the potato-soup incident and the pig-fetus incident and the meat-salting incident and the dog-food incident and all the other stupid incidents.

I could feel my hurt and despair turning into a kind of wonder. I felt closer now to Howie and Mack than I ever had before. Now I knew what it felt like to be hated, to be a Jew in Europe. There is a kind of wild alertness in the air where hate lives, where nobody daydreams, nobody falls asleep on the job, a condition of being always on one's toes, on the streets of Kabul and Teheran and Santiago, all papers in order, everyone ready at all times to state their business.

It was just a game, of course. Nothing they did or said could bother me anymore. But why were they so strange? In what crucible were those brains forged, and with what anvils?

Through the morning, the E-Z-Listening station filled in the details of John Lennon's death, at the hands of a Christian, an ex-fan with a concealed weapon who had found the Truth and was serious about it. I remembered how I used to know the Truth, and how the Truth had allowed me to knock the dentures out of an old man's mouth, in the sunshine of Tremont Street.

Mack changed the radio to the Jewish station, where a cantorial tenor intoned a Hebrew prayer, high and wailing. I remembered a time when I lived in the farmhouse in Blauvelt with my friends, and a friend of a girl that was living with us had been killed in the Yom Kippur War, in the Golan Heights. I remembered Judy Mason crying when she got the news, how her voice had rung through the bare upstairs hallway, high and piercing, like the cantor's voice, a woman's desperate grief, the oldest sound in the world.

What I needed to do today was float above Glatt Mart as above a dream, to let nothing touch me but the sadness of losing a friend, to

244

remember after all, that this is only a football game. How well those old songs held up after so long. A whole generation had come and gone in the eighteen years since that February night when I first saw the Beatles on the Ed Sullivan show. I was there the next morning in the bathroom of the Old South Dormitory, the morning we all combed our hair down in bangs. We were part of a day in history. And those chords still ring above the gray hills as loud as they always did, "Eight Days a Week" among the parking lots and film developers, "Please Please Me" bright in the air of a Hallmark card shop all decked out for the holiday.

A whole generation had come and gone, during which time I must have been asleep. And now everything was old, everything but the music, everybody angry about the prices in the supermarket; and on the commercial for the nostalgia radio station a fat lady wiggled and danced with her Hoover to the tune of "All You Need Is Love," a whole new generation, with refrigerators packed with luncheon meats, and a year's supply of canned food in the basement, nostalgia over London broil, fetid playpens adjoining the kitchen, talcum and feces and ammonia, and the television on all day long. I thought about how few good days I'd had since I got into the meat business, back when I never needed anybody's help in any way. But now there were three times as many cars on the road as when I graduated from Hotchkiss, and Pepsi cost half a dollar, and the honking voices rang through the store. I should have been a lawyer. I should have been an Italian meat salesman with my neck bulging and my hands jingling with loose jewelry. Now my life has changed, and there is a slippery film of fat and blood and bacteria over everything, hard as wax on the blades of dull knives, even on the telephone, the insides of the fingerholes crusted with hardened fat, and the plastic surface beneath the fingerholes worn down to bare metal from being dialed so many thousands of times with a pencil eraser for so many angry conversations with angry meat suppliers and angry poultry suppliers, the fingerholes shrunken and fat-crusted like the insides of the arteries of the the swollen-ankled, heavily powdered grandmothers who pushed their wobbling shopping carts around the store in time to the E-Z-Listening waltzes. Telephone dials have always had a whimsical quality to them. When I was a kid, every Easter my father used to hide jelly beans all over the house and there was always a jelly bean in each fingerhole of the telephone dial; but here at Glatt Mart there was so much fat on the inside of the dial that a jelly bean would not have fit. Sad to think about jelly beans. Girls used to throw jelly beans at the Beatles on stage, because George Harrison had said they liked "jelly babies."

Howie and Mack huffed and puffed, in a desperate hurry. The store was getting busy. Howie's daughter Leslie worked silently at the wrapping machine. I started to make the patties, but the machine wouldn't work. Just as I discovered it was unplugged, Howie came charging over.

"What's the problem here?" he said.

"I find that when it's not plugged in it usually won't work very well."

"It won't work *at all!*" he said.

At coffee break I whistled, absentmindedly, "It's Only Love," from the *Rubber Soul* album.

"Stop that fuckin' whistling, you fuckin' *snake!*" Mack snarled, his face veined and red and bloated.

"You're still mad at me too, huh?" I said.

"You're goddamn *right* I'm mad at you!"

"I didn't do anything to hurt you."

"You salted the *fleische,* that's what you did. You spit on my religion, you shit-ass Nazi *schveina!*" He stormed out into the cutting room and tried to slam the door, but it was the wrong kind of door, and it just swung back and forth a few times.

I sat on the bus and watched the Christmas lights and thought about my career. If it was all just a joke, why did it still hurt? Why did my sadness, on this wounded day, here among the streets and stores and cul-de-sacs of a nation of silenced rock-and-roll hearts, have to be complicated by this outside issue of being hated? It was strange to be an American, strange to be hated in my own country, my own town. It occurred to me that I was completely alone with that hate, and that no white American moderate Republican intellectual whose father met Charles Ives and whose mother met Wallace Stevens had ever gone through what I was going through, had ever heard the voices of serious men constricted so. All the more reason to hang tough, never to turn tail and quit, to wear my Martha's Vineyard T-shirt like armor over my heart. The local bus poked through the traffic and the sky pressed down like one of those giant steam irons in women's prison movies, and every street, every store, rang with the memory of music.

26

Crèche Illusion

It was Friday. Hanukkah was over. Howie's mood hung over the little store like a stalled cold front.

"Good morning," I said.

Howie didn't even say "Machine" anymore. He just pointed to the cooler, not looking at me. I had decided that I would continue to say "good morning," as I shall say "good morning" every day, even on the day Nostradamus dictates that the sun shall become a red giant.

It was all just a joke, of course. But it was hard to keep laughing. Touching the alligator amulet helped a little. Every night, with ears ringing, I rode the local bus home with children and servants. Now that I couldn't go into Waldbaum's anymore, I had to walk a mile out of my way to do my food shopping at Grand Union. Each morning I put on my Martha's Vineyard T-shirt inside out, with the logo against my heart, promised myself that I would let no words hurt me, and girded my loins for another day of war. It was what John Lennon would have done, to float above the stink and chaos like the bass line in the final fugue of "She's so Heavy," like the brave and tragic cellos in the Israeli national anthem. All I knew was that I must not let them force me to quit, and I would give them no more reason to fire me; and someday they would get tired of being angry, because being angry takes more energy than being bewildered, and I would emerge victorious, a gentleman, as if with wings, having flown through a thunderhead, friends with everybody.

It had become impossible to eat lunch in the locker room. Every day I ate my lunch outside, with no place to sit, leaning against the I-beams that said NEVER AGAIN and ELECT STRICT LEADERS.

I was in the front of the store, putting a Haddar cookie delivery on the shelves. Clarinets whined through a joylessly jolly hora tune. The air was filled with a multitude of perfumes, thick, rich, desperately erotic, the fragrances of women whose husbands have long ago lost interest. A few empty cookie cartons lay at my feet.

"How long are you working here?" Howie said.

"Is that a rhetorical question?"

"How long are you *working here*?"

"Why don't you just tell me what I'm doing wrong and I'll fix it," I said, looking him straight in the eyes, and he looked two feet to my right, out the plate-glass window into the bright overcast morning. "It's not necessary to be abusive."

"It *is* necessary to be abusive because you're *cocking around!*" A young woman was bending over the meat case, listening, her long black hair brushing against the shoulder roast packages.

"If I'm doing something wrong, why don't you just tell me, and maybe I can correct it."

"Because it *don't help!* You forget things. You're wasting my time and my money." As he yelled at me, I tried to imagine how he must have looked on the pitcher's mound: precise, fierce and gangly, with a wicked curve ball. He really must have looked just like Sandy Koufax back then, and he still did, sort of, but with foxlike Semitic features all weighted down with doom and seriousness, as if in ten gs of gravity, like Sandy Koufax in Hell.

"What can I tell you?" I said. "You've been yelling at me for five minutes and I don't even know why, yet."

"I've been yelling at you for one minute," he said. "*One* minute!"

"Then I guess we have more time than I thought. What would you like to talk about?"

"The boxes. The fucking *BOXES!*" he said. "You leave the fucking empty boxes on the floor. Somebody's going to break their neck and I'm going to get sued." He bustled back into the cutting room, trailing thin blue smoke. The little parking lot was full of horns, everybody trying to get in and out, and the traffic flashed past on Route 59.

There was a strange thing about all these fragrances in the air. They didn't seem to blend, the way they blend at the perfume counter in Bamberger's or in the lobby of a Broadway show, into that generalized elegant modest vagueness. Here at Glatt Mart the fragrances remained separate, refusing to mix, each set of elixirs defining the boundaries of its own territory, like the clotted and curdled mixture of label-coating chemistry at Fasco Labels when my supervisor showed me what would happen if I made the mistake of mixing the 50-50 with the M.E.K. Thus, when I stood up from the cookie boxes, I found myself moving from one fragrance zone to another, from a precinct of marshmallowy talcum in the cookie department, through a border district of powdered apple-blossom extract in the vicinity of the canned vegetables, and when I moved a few more steps toward the door to begin rotating the dehydrated potato soup, I found myself surrounded by strange oily floral molecules. Around and around they hobbled, and the wheels of the broken shopping carts shimmied and squeaked, and the music got louder, and the motions of overweight women stirred the air and moved the unblendable compounds round and round the little store.

We had run out of pickled tongues, so Howie sent me down to his other store to pick some up. The Riverdale Glatt Mart was tiny, no more than twelve feet wide, squeezed between Chef-Ah Kosher Pizza and H & R Block. In the back of the store, Steve, the young manager, bustled around, angry, in a one-size-fits-all Yankee baseball cap with his hair bristling out of the open section in the back where the adjustable headband was, a cigarette sticking out of his little mouth. He helped me put the tongues into plastic bags. Howie's father was there at the table, his huge and solemn face looking out over the tiny cutting board, and the air was filled with a stale and spicy smell of pickled meat, with an undertone of decades of cigarettes.

Mr. Shapiro had been cutting open the boxes of Cryovac lamb shoulders and had put the scissors back on the hook. When Steve couldn't find them to open another case of pickled tongues, he said, "Where the fuck are the scissors?" and Mr. Shapiro pointed solemnly to the wall.

"We put scissors back when we're *finished* with them," Steve said, "Not when we're still *using* them."

As I drove up Riverdale Avenue, in the car heavy with the vinegary pickling smell, to the ramp that led to the Sawmill Parkway, I noticed an enormous nativity scene, with life-sized figures looking out into the traffic. Then I saw one of the Magi move; and as I drove closer I could see that it wasn't a crèche at all, but a bus shelter. The Three Wise Men were old ladies waiting to go to Alexander's, and the manger turned out to be a bench with some Puerto Rican children sitting on it. It made me sad. I tried to squint my eyes and see it as a nativity scene again, but it remained a bus shelter, and the Bronx remained the Bronx.

When I got back to the store, I put the tongues into the pickling barrel; and then Howie, making a point of looking away from my face, told me to drive back down to the Bronx to pick up his mother and father and bring them up to his house where they would all spend *Shabbes* together.

I was glad to be out of the store again, eating lunch on the Tappan

Zee Bridge in the middle of steel-gray water, everybody in a hurry, the toll clerks grim-faced, down the Thruway to the Sprain Brook Parkway, through forests and swamps, past huge red brick high-rises with a thousand blank windows, to the Bronx River Parkway, through a tangle of ramps and cutoffs, and onto White Plains Road, to the neighborhood where Howie grew up, and where his parents still lived, now a little Jewish island marooned in a sea of blacks.

I parked the station wagon on Cruger Avenue, in front of Howie's parents' apartment building. Mrs. Shapiro buzzed me in the front door. Howie's father wasn't home yet. She made me a cup of coffee, lightened with skim milk to a tragic olive drab, and started talking about her son and about hospitals. She was a frail, tightly-coiffed woman with a small serious mouth.

"When I get bad with the pressure," she said, "my son, he help me so I can get in the Suffern Hospital, and not this terrible hospital all full of cullu'd and beds in the hall can't sleep like a human." I was looking out the window, over the elevated train lines at White Plains Road, across gray swampland and tenements with plumes of smoke rising everywhere, burned-out buildings, and far in the distance the ghost-gray shapes of the Manhattan skyline.

"My son, he's a good boy, yes?"

"Yes," I said.

"You Joosh?"

"No. I was brought up an Episcopalian."

"Well, I still know you very religious, and I know everybody worship God in your own church. I'm very religious, and I taught my boy to be very religious. That's why he quit the baseball playing. They make him play against the law, play on *Shabbes,* play on *Yontiff.* He's better be a boocha' like his father."

I was trying not to look at the greenish shade of the coffee, so I kept looking out the window, at the Bronxscape, all its browns and grays and low abandoned shapes. Mrs. Shapiro looked at the Hebrew-lettered clock above the stove.

"He's late," she said. "Maybe trouble."

"I just saw him in the store a few hours ago," I said.

"No place safe no more," she said. "Everywhere cullu'd rob and kill and no policeman enough to help. This used to be so good neighborhood, but now just cullu'd walk everywhere. Ten years I not go in the subway no more."

A few minutes later Mr. Shapiro walked in the door.

"What for you late?" she said.

"I have to work, that's what for. I have a job."

"Fifteen minutes you late, and cullu'd everywhere," she said. "You almost give me a heart attack."

"Five minutes I'm late," he said, hardly moving his bulbous face.

"You valise all pack," she said.

"What you put in it?"

"What you need, that's what I put in."

"I open to see," he said.

"You waste this young man's time. I put you clothes and you medicine in, that's what I put. Clothes and medicine."

I carried their bags down to the car, and we started for Rockland County, driving along Lydig Avenue toward White Plains Road. As we passed the darkened front of Gelker's Kosher Poultry, Mr. Shapiro said, "Benny Gelker, he die."

"Oh, no. What from he die?"

"The heart."

Beside a bridge where Zerega Avenue crossed the Sprain Brook Parkway, I saw a building that I hadn't noticed before. It was painted all over with bright signs and advertisements, like those tourist traps beside the road in Georgia that announce FIREWORKS! PECANS! INDIAN CURIOS! REPTILE FARM! I had been seeing things wrong all day. This garish structure was advertising POLICE LOCKS! ALARM SYSTEMS! TEAR GAS! TOTAL SECURITY COVERAGE!

It was strange to imagine the inside of that store, all the loud sport jackets, men who destroy themselves with work, for their families.

Families, families, families; everybody part of a dreary little family, all the families huddled together against the dark and the stink, clustered around the things the family hates, all the families wishing they were in Florida.

Zerega Avenue: what a perfect name for a neighborhood, from which nothing quiet or blond or Protestant could ever spring; Zerega Avenue, where tires howl on ice-bound Cadillacs, which *everybody* calls "Caddies," the lower-class adjective flying everywhere, where even the richest man in the neighborhood does not own a suit, land of pointed shoes, where garnet studs on a car's mudflaps spell out KISS ME I'M ITALIAN, where everybody has heard of Einstein but nobody has heard of Oppenheimer, where everybody is under treatment for "pressure," and everybody's parents are on "cheemo," land of bumper stickers and long antennae, where deodorant pendants dangle from rearview mirrors, where impact wrenches put wheels on too tight, land where black umbrellas are raised against the hated snow, land without sleds, without dogs or cats, where black-feathered starlings scrabble around on the pavement, fighting over blackened scraps of food, land without baseball, without rock and roll, just cars and families, families and cars, funerals and salted fats, diuretics and beta blockers, hearts hardened with a waxy plaque, land where kites will never fly, where on a clear day a thousand smoke plumes pierce the cobalt sky, a sky beyond which there are no galaxies, no asteroids, just the nonnegotiable demands of an angry God.

In measured tones, Howie's parents argued about the "valise"; they argued about whether I should get gas before crossing the Tappan Zee Bridge. They didn't raise their voices, just kept up a cool, loveless impatience with each other, punctuated by long puffing sighs, like the way Howie would huff and puff when he watched me working.

There was a strange color in the air, a sort of green bright gassiness, and whitecaps were breaking on both sides of the bridge. A patch of brightness blazed in the middle of the choppy river where the sun had broken through, and ten miles upstream across the roiling greenish water, I could see through gassy haze the twin domes of the Indian Point nuclear power plant, a plume of steam rising from the red-and-white smokestack between the two pressure vessels.

It was warm outside. Cars were everywhere, full of families, everybody with a family, family people rushing home, angry at the traffic, angry at the price of gas, angry at the latest news update, hurrying home through the gray afternoon on gray highways choked with family cars. Everybody was from the Bronx. All the cars were going fast. After we crossed the bridge we climbed a long incline; and as we came over the crest of that long grade, and all of Rockland County lay spread out in front of me in a blanket of bare trees and cloverleafs and cul-de-sacs, I had a remarkable sensation.

I was sure that if I could just stop for a minute at that exact spot and stand, surveying the rolling subdivisions, that I would see the whole machine stop, as it stopped once when I was a kid looking down a highway at a yellow dump truck signaling for a right turn; and I would be removed from the struggle, and everything would freeze in time, or out of time, and I could stand there, overlooking the West Nyack interchange, and be lord of it all for one moment, could choose for myself any kind of life I cared to imagine, a life that would have made my father proud, or me proud, or John Lennon proud, could walk into any house and have known the people inside all my life, could walk into the richest, most dynamic corporation in the snazziest landscaped building, behind acres of brown smoked glass, and instantly be named regional sales manager, could win a lovely wife with the right word, buy a new car and a new house with my signature, could walk into any day of my life and lose myself in the busywork of the rolling suburbs; but until that day, life remains what it is, with those beautiful gassy colors in the air when you are driving somewhere in less of a hurry than everybody else; and until that day, or until some other day just as good, I shall go it alone, strange visitor from another planet, who came to Glatt Mart powerless, shall hang in for a few more months at my job, shall walk through the storming store, holding my head up high, unafraid of the dark, shall keep my head when those about me are losing theirs and blaming it on me; and soon, with money in my pocket and hope in my heart, there will be time off for Christmas in Baltimore at my cousin Charlie's house, and an Amtrak adventure through frozen barrens.

I dropped Howie's parents off at Howie's house, amid much discussion about who should carry whose "valise," then drove back to Glatt Mart. Mack was just leaving. He was smiling. His eyes twinkled as he got into his copper-colored Monte Carlo. Howie's son Jerry was smiling as he pulled out in his American Motors Matador. It was a time of smiles. Howie was smiling, and his fatigued eyes twinkled and sparkled, and his lower lip stuck out like a mantelpiece.

"Everything's already cleaned," he said in a honking voice. We were the only ones in the store now. Fresh salt was spread out over the red tiles of the cutting-room floor. As I changed my shoes at my locker, Howie came into the locker room, smirking, twinkle-eyed. I could smell the soft baby-powder fragrance of the case of Charmin bathroom tissue on the shelf.

"Our relationship," he said, rehearsed, "has got to come to an end."

27

Ghost Guitars

I was walking along Route 59, and the cars were going by so fast that I couldn't read the bumper stickers. I could feel that my face was red, could feel the anger rising like steam from the underground drain scuppers as I walked and walked over ground so old that years of exhaust particulates had formed a black rime on the tops of stones.

It was the first time I had ever seen Howie truly happy. We had stood there, Howie and I, in the little locker room, in the humming of refrigeration machinery, in the powdery freshness of Charmin and the residual esters of the day's perfumes.

"As of now," he said, eyes twinkling, "I'm dissolving our business relationship. I've decided that you're annoying to me, and you're just not worth bothering with anymore."

"What do you mean?"

"You don't answer right, and you don't take things seriously."

Everything stood still, as it always does when I'm getting fired. I felt under pressure, as if a great sphygmomanometer were wrapped around me.

"Wait a minute," I said. "I think I deserve to know what I've done wrong."

"You deserve to know that you're not good enough to work here. You salted the *fleische*. You insulted Mack. You said *schveina* were like people."

"In other words you're firing me because I'm not Jewish."

"How can I fire you?" Smiling. "You never worked here. You have no records. You don't exist." He held up a handful of money and looked away, twinkling.

"How much severance pay are you giving me?"

"What you deserve. Nothing." Smiling.

"That is not acceptable," I said, feeling the blood beginning to drum in my ears.

Howie had been smirking before; now he was grinning broadly. "It's not acceptable, huh? What are you going to do about it? Maybe you'd like to threaten me. What would you like to threaten me with?" His voice had a sort of musical lilt to it, as when he was saying "Great country, America."

"Well, I—"

"Not '*well!*' We don't talk like that here."

"I don't know what the hell your problem is, man, but—"

"Not '*man!*' You can talk like that to your friends on the street, but we don't talk like that here."

"I don't have any friends on the street. I'm not a street person."

"Do you have any friends in the courts?"

"No."

"Well, I do. I've helped elect every judge in this county. So if you're going to threaten me, you better be fucking ready to back it up."

"I don't have anything to back it up with."

"I *know* you don't," he said with a sort of musical giggle.

"I just think you should know something," I said. " I don't know who did this to you, but there's something wrong with you, man, some thing really—"

"Not 'MAN!' We don't TALK like that! And anyway, we have nothing more to discuss. Hurry up and pack your things so I can close. It's *Erev Shabbes.*"

"We do have something to discuss." I was rolling my clothes into a bundle inside my green cardigan sweater. My face was flushed, my heart was racing, and all the smells seemed to be getting stronger, baby powder, cigarettes, cigarette-scented breath, residual musk from a late customer, and the general sour, salty, wet, stale, and vinegary smell of a kosher butcher shop.

"I think you should know," I said, "that I'm beginning to understand why there's so much anti-Semitism in the world."

Now Howie was beaming with joy, and he puffed on his cigarette with a Santa-Claus-like twinkle of pleasure.

"*Pee-hee-hee-hee!*" he said, a dry little explosion of laughter and talcum-scented cigarette breath.

"It's *true,*" I said. "Working in your filthy little sweatshop has been a very educational experience."

"I'm glad to hear that," he said, beaming, holding the front door open. With my clothes-bundle under my arm, I walked out the door. Howie picked up the blue nylon People's National Bank deposit bag from the counter next to the cash register, stepped out the door, and locked it behind him.

"It's *true!*" I said. "It's bastards like you, whose mommies didn't want them to play baseball, and who have to take out their frustrations on people who can't fight back, that spoil it for everybody else. It's bastards like you that turn people into Nazis. You can laugh, but it's true."

"I do. I *do* laugh!" He was walking toward his station wagon.

"You *suck,* man! You really—"

"Not 'MAN!' We're not in *Harlem!*"

"Garbage!" I said. "Stinking *Jew* GARBAGE!"

"*Pee-hee-hee-hee!*" he said, eyes twinkling as he got into the car. I hawked up a load of phlegm and spit it across the windshield. I could hear him laughing as he started the engine. He gave the windshield a few squirts with the washer solution, backed out of the parking space, gave a little *toot-toot* on the horn, and roared out into the traffic; and then everything seemed to get very quiet. I was standing alone beside the STRICT LEADERS signs and the NEVER AGAIN signs with the famous picture of that kid with the horrible snap-brimmed hat.

With my clothes-bundle I walked across the parking lot to the road. It was warm. I could smell the rich, sweet, spicy, complex kitchen smells from the Torture Garden. I could feel the ground shake with traffic, could feel the wind of the vehicles, the percussion of loud mufflers; and with every step I could feel the anger jouncing in my stomach, cold and solid. I walked along Route 59, past Caldor, past the Cadillac Manor garden aparments, past Waldbaum's, where I couldn't go anymore, past Black-Eyed Suzie's Restaurant, where, it seemed like years ago, with my paper hat soaked in the swelter of August, I had delivered cases of bone-in shell steaks.

I knew that Howie would be getting home by now, the whole happy family together, the roast in the oven, the week's receipts already deposited in the *Shomer Shabbes* People's National Bank, whose sign was missing the N in National but nobody had bothered to fix it for three months; and I knew he was in a jolly mood, his loud voice ringing through the meat-scented house.

In the parking lot in front of the Hops and Pops discount beer and soda distributor, a pale young scraggly-bearded man in Hasidic clothes was changing a tire on his mustard-colored station wagon. As I came closer to him, I could hear Howie's voice again, his giggle of joy, his tickle of contempt. The Hasid's wife and children huddled inside the car, their faces unwashed and sunless. The man was dressed all in black and white, black pants with the fringes hanging out as required by Orthodox law, black coat, white shirt, black hat, black-framed glasses held together at the bridge by a length of masking tape. I could feel the percussion of traffic, the blood thrumming in my ears, could feel the cold lump in my stomach growing heavy as iron, and the left side of my scalp began to tingle, and I could feel my jaw and throat tightening.

"Dirty Jew!" I heard myself shouting, and my voice was all constricted in the back of my throat. "Dirty stinking lousy Jew *bastard!*" He looked up from his lug-wrench and stared at me. His hands were black with grease. He had a bad cold. The only color in his face was in his red nose, and he snuffled loudly as he stared.

"Fuckin' Jew! Stinkin' Fuckin' *JEW!*" I was yelling at the top of my lungs. "FUCKIN' SHIT-ASS JEW *BASTARD!*" and he stared at me, not in shock or anger, but sadly, it seemed, with what looked like the weariness of five thousand years in his eyes, behind his glasses, staring with his drained face and his red nose. He was young, maybe twenty-five, but the flesh around his eyes was creased, perhaps from years of squinting into the Talmud, and his nose and lower lip seemed pinched, progeric. He seemed to be staring at something far away, staring at something from thousands of years ago, another civilization, across the millennia, as if he could see through the whole miserable abbatoir of our separate histories, as if he could see the faces of all the people who had foamed with hate against his grandfather and great-grandfather, could hear the constricted voices of twenty centuries of furious Kazaks and Magyars. Through his glasses I could see his eyes, sad eyes, dull and empty, like the eyes of a calf that had stared through the slats of the holding pen the day I worked at Hoboken Packing. People getting into their cars were staring at me. From both doorways of Hops and Pops they were staring at me, pointing, their faces blank, as I walked away, along Route 59.

I remembered again the man, years ago, with his bottle of wine, on the steps of the Donnell Library, the spit around his lips as he raged at my friends David Stutz and Cheryl Bergman, saying that he smelled Jews. I remembered the red psoriasis on his hand, how his voice was constricted, like my voice, how his face was twisted with hate, like my face.

I thought about Jill's face, when I had last touched her cheek over a

Big Mac. From the way she had looked the last time I had run into her in the parking lot of her apartment building, she was probably back on a vegetarian diet again. I wondered what she would think of me today as she analyzed electrocardiograms—me, a grown man with spit around my lips, screaming at some poor unwashed priest-ridden bookkeeper who didn't know any better and just wanted to get his tire changed and get the kids home before sundown, when *Shabbes* would begin and to drive would be to break a promise made to God; and me, a grown man enunciating ancient curses, the oldest curses in the world, among the Hallmark card shops and Toys "R" Us stores, among the loose and casual arrangement of houses, where puffs of sewer gas carry the methane stink of fifty centuries of distilled rage, two hundred generations of begats, or maybe even more, because I've read somewhere that anti-Semitism predated the Jews by two thousand years.

As I walked down Route 59, away from Hops and Pops, I looked back, and the people standing around the door were still staring, silent, their eyes cold as Europe in the night.

I wondered what Cheryl Bergman would think of me now, the same man with whom she had spent winter afternoons in the dilled vinegary air of her mother's kitchen, as the snowy light faded and we sat there at the table looking out across her back yard to the rear of another house that was outlined in soft blue lights. I've always loved those blue lights, silent and ghostly, the way when I blurred my eyes I could see a red spot in the middle of each bulb.

I could smell the sharp smoke of hamburgers flame-broiling in the Plaza Diner. Cars were burning oil, trucks belching sweet blue diesel fumes. I could see my reflection walking across the plate glass of a Shell station. I'd forgotten how fat I was, a hulking clumsy shape with shiny cars in the background, or perhaps the glass was bowed out slightly to make everyone look fat, and when I saw that puffy reflection walk across the window, I felt all my anger melting into sadness and shame, felt the rage being let out of me, as from a ruptured football, and I felt as if I would go limp and fall beside the road in a flattened heap, with no pressure to hold me up, like one of the many road-kills scattered around, which no sanitation truck ever cleans up because nobody ever notices the road-kills because nobody ever walks by the side of the road. I wanted to go back and ask the man to forgive me, maybe give him a hand changing his tire, but I knew it was too late. As I looked back to where he was still crouched over his lug wrench, I saw the local bus coming, its dim headlights on.

It's a sad, poky old bus, ridden only by children, blacks, and senior citizens; and when it dipped out of sight in the low ground in front of Rockland Plumbing Supply, I saw all at once how beautiful was the face of my county, a warm wintery gray over the air, school buses like great yellow sound-boxes, tubes of light spelling out MR. KOLD KUTS, children waving at me from the backs of their mothers' station wagons, a dozen strings of tiny lights flashing on and off, spastic, in the window of Tallman Pizza, and the warm, shadowy, dough-colored light that rolls out of a pizza shop window. It was starting to get darker, but I couldn't tell if night was coming or just more clouds in front of the sun.

The bus was almost empty, a few Haitian maids coming home from work, a group of teenage kids in the back, with Iron Maiden and Ozzy Osborne patches on their denim jackets, all on their way to hang out at the Grand Atrium Mall. They were listening to AC/DC's song "You Shook Me All Night Long," loud from a ghetto blaster. I sat down a few seats in front of them and laid my bundle beside me.

The kids were jumping from seat to seat and laughing. When the song got to the line, "SHE TOLD ME TO COME, BUT I WAS ALREADY THERE!" they all sang along, so loud that their voices rang through the bus and made the Haitian maids frown.

"Mr. Deckle!" said one of the boys. "Hey! I know that guy! He was my teacher. Hey, Mr. Deckle!" I looked back and recognized a boy who had been in one of the classes I taught when I was a substitute teacher.

"Steve Jump," I said. "How the hell are you?"

"I'm okay," he said, "How about yourself?"

"Oh, so-so I guess," I said. "A little shell-shocked."

"You don't look too good."

"It's been a weird day. I just lost my job."

"You're not teaching anymore?" he said. The tape player shrilled the song's chorus: "YOU . . . SHOOK ME *ALL—NIGHT—LONG!*"

"How the hell could I teach? You kids know more than I do. You should teach me." One of the other kids was pantomiming the song's guitar solo, swinging an imaginary Gibson Les Paul on an imaginary strap, contorting his face at the high notes the way electric guitar players do for some reason, making lunges with knee and guitar down the center aisle of the bus, and the girls laughed.

"You were an okay teacher, Mr. Deckle," Steve said. "You sent me to the office less than most teachers."

"Yeah, but it's all bullshit. There's nothing to teach, except rock and roll. What the hell else is there? Everything else is just shit and garbage and a bunch of old people with ulcers yelling at each other over the phone."

"You sound like you're stoned! Are you stoned, Mr. Deckle?"

"No, but I wish I were. I'm just shell-shocked. I've seen what happens to people when they get separated from rock and roll. I've seen what happens to their faces when they get too serious. I've seen Hell. It's out there, waiting for you to grow up and get serious."

"Who *is* this guy?" said a girl with stringy blond hair.

"SHE TOLD ME TO COME," they all sang, "BUT I WAS *AL-READY THERE!*" We passed St. Paul's Episcopal Church, where my family used to go when I was a child. White letters in the announcement case proclaimed, WHEN I CONSIDER THAT GOD IS JUST—I MUST CONCLUDE THAT AMERICA IS DOOMED.

"Don't let that happen to you," I said. "Don't lose that music. You know who died this week don't you?"

"That guy from the Beatles, right?" said the boy who had been miming the guitar solo. They were all listening to me now.

"That's right," I said. "My old pal John Lennon. You want me to teach you something: I'll teach you something right now; I'll teach you about history, about how his music is connected to that music on your tape player right now, and it's you kids who are keeping it alive. So when you're in school on Monday, I want you to listen and see if you can hear all the music that's gone through that old school, back when it was the senior and the junior high together. Those halls are full of ghosts, all the people that came before you, and all the music. That's what the Japanese Shinto religion is all about, and that's why the Japanese are the smartest people in the world."

"Now I know you're stoned. Mr. Deckle is *stoned!*"

"I'm stoned on weirdness, that's what I'm stoned on," I said. We were passing the boarded up Jack-in-the-Box, and the Valley Bicycle Shop, and Silver City Appliances. "I've seen Hell, and I've smelled it, and I've heard it ringing in my ears every night, because I let myself get lost, and I forgot to stay high. That's my lesson for today, class. You kids are all right! Don't let your asshole teachers tell you any different. Because if you lose that music, you're *dead,* and I've worked with dead people, and I've been dead myself, and it hurts. So stay high!"

"This guy is really *excellent!*" said another boy. I pulled the signal cord and stood up.

"You kids are *all right!* Don't let your teachers tell you any different, because they don't know *shit!* Take care, Steve. All of you. Stay high. Merry Christmas."

"Merry Christmas, Mr. Deckle."

I got out in front of Fotomat, which was on the high ground that overlooked the Thruway, and as the bus pulled away downhill in a sweet blue cloud, I could hear from an open window, "YOU . . . SHOOK ME *ALL—NIGHT—LONG!*" Through the rear window they were waving at me. I waved back, standing in the exhaust.

I stood beside Route 59, holding my clothes-bundle under my arm, waiting for a break in the traffic. The blank sky pressed down on top of the land, on top of Denny's Restaurant, on top of the Shell station, and Speed King Auto Parts, over the Trader Horn Discount Appliance

Center and Arthur Treacher's Fish and Chips, over the Thruway exit ramps. It was so warm out that most people had their windows open, and above the engine noises I could hear music from almost every car, E-Z-Listening music, soft-voiced bulletin music, and the mellow sounds of smooth California rock, with drug-lubricated guitar riffs going up and down, the vocals embellished with cocaine-soaked sensual quaverings. It struck me what a stupid thing it was to tell those kids on the bus to stay high, even stupider than shrieking ancient European curses at a poor unwashed Hasidic clerk.

Everybody was in a hurry. The bumper stickers flashed by. PRESIDENT CARTER KISS MY GAS . . . COLMAN . . . COLMAN . . . IRAN SUCKS . . . STANGER . . . I♥LIFE . . . IRAN SUCKS . . . COLMAN . . . COLMAN . . .

Nobody ever walked around here anymore. This was a town for people with cars. Even poor people had cars. It was strange to think about how many cars there were, how many millions of crankshafts and bearings and tappets and camshafts and pushrods, all whirling impossibly fast within thousandths-of-an-inch tolerance.

Why didn't everything just fly apart? And why did burned pages of a medical textbook fall from the sky on the day I quit the sales department at Jak-Pak? That was the day I could have been an Italian meat salesman from Brooklyn, in a deodorized Camaro with E-Z-Listening music on the radio. Perhaps if I had studied quantum physics I could understand how those fragile mechanisms held together, and perhaps I could have understood the strong forces and the weak forces that drive careers the way the sun's heat drives weather systems. I know, from what I've read in *Scientific American,* that to understand quantum physics is to give up trying to comprehend it. It incorporates the principle of randomness that keeps all the cholesterol-caked hearts in the meat business from infarcting at the same instant. But then if quantum physics is true—and we know it's true, because here we are—if it's true and everything is really so crazy, why does everything seem so normal? Why don't saxophones grow on trees?

Why doesn't the president of the United States ever turn into a kangaroo?

The traffic was so thick that I couldn't cross, so I just stood there looking east down Route 59, over the low ground where the Thruway runs beneath it, and beyond the Thruway at the Ramada Inn, and Howard Johnson's Motor Lodge with its outside walkway and the soft globes of white light above each of the room doors. To the south of the motels, I could see the subdivided hillside where dozens of bright gray asphalt shingled roofs poked up between the bare trees.

As I stood there waiting for a break in the traffic, watching bumper stickers flash past under the dullness of the sky, I could feel the stupidness of the long day starting to fade along with the white overcast light, the stupidness on my part, on everybody else's part, the stupidness of taking out all those months in Glatt Mart on a poor ignorant Hasid with a flat tire, which event I must remember all my life as a sort of boundary line between me and the professions I was brought up for; the stupidness of having ended up working at Glatt Mart in the first place, the stupidness of having stayed there in the fantasy that it might someday get just a little better; and then the stupidness of telling a bunch of stupid kids exactly the most stupid thing they could ever hear about whether to do something with their lives or to get high instead; all that stupidness seemed to be losing its sharp edges in the long noise of the day, and fading into the memory of other days not as stupid but just as long; and even without a car, even with the cold faces staring at me out of their car windows wondering what a grown man would be doing standing without his car anywhere near him, by the side of the road; even without anything to hold me up against the percussion of air the traffic displaces, I could feel that the ground was still warm under my feet, could feel that the shingle-roofed houses were still my houses, as much as they have ever been. There is a way a man can walk across that landscape if he knows how, a way of walking that shows he's lived with it all his life and goes to sleep thinking about it, and if he holds his head the right way, no dogs will even bark at him. There is a place that stands asleep all night, a place we wake up into a dream of, whatever work schedule we might be on, even on days we haven't gotten enough sleep, even on days when we have just gotten fired and have acted like Nazis. That was my place down there, in the bare trees, and everywhere in every equally noisy direction, my county, my love, silent, rushing, sybilant, monoxidized, fragrant with sweet hydrogen sulfide from thousands of catalytic converters, rich with the chilly morning smell of dog feces, warm breaths of Bounce, the fabric softener that works in the dryer; and lights everywhere, Christmas lights clear above Route 59, the long bright line of train windows snaking north past the Grand Atrium Mall; and in summer the still, purple glow of bug-zappers, the yellow bars of light outlining Carvel Ice Cream stands, clouds of moths around the streetlights. I'm talking about the suburbs; and the suburbs, in and of themselves, are supposed to be boring. Once you understand that, you can begin to build your own interesting life upon the blank matrix that the suburbs provide.

How did we lose each other? All my friends, all my yearbook-mates; may you live an interesting life in a boring decade. May every day be a slow news day, and the road rise gently to meet the tires of your new car. I'm talking about love and freedom and home and money and lights in the night, any kind of night you want, lighted faces around the hibachi, or the Christmas tree, or the Hanukkah bush, or the illegal fireworks nobody gets arrested for; and it was all lost, and it was all nonsense. I knew that now. I'm sorry it was all nonsense. I'm sorry about everything. The slamming of brakes, the guy I pretended to run over. I'm sorry about the swastikas on the jars of Mother's gefilte fish. I'm sorry about all the anti-Semitic thoughts, and about my last little tantrum in front of the Hops and Pops beer and soda distributorship. I have no excuse, except to say that at least I have remained ugly and ridiculous and pitiful, never suave, never articulate. And I promise that I shall never get serious about it, shall never be interviewed in *Rolling Stone,* shall hold no press conferences to clarify my previous statements, shall devise no rhymed slogans, shall not let my voice ring shrill with moral certainty in a three-piece suit, flanked by Moslem bodyguards, shall gather around me no coalitions of rainbow-colored bumper stickers united to save humanity from gutter religions. Let it be known that I am not now, and I have never been, a candidate for president, or vice president, of the United States—although if my party really needs me, I will accept a draft.

Finally there was a break in the traffic, and I dashed across the street, and scrabbled down a gravel embankment into the parking lot of Zenith Kitchens, next to where Get High Street runs under Route 59. The air and the trees and the patches of empty ground, all were full of birds, and the farther I walked from Route 59, the more I could hear them, redwings and starlings, English sparrows and regular sparrows, and everywhere I could hear their tiny, cold, metallic voices, thousands of them, chirping and screeching. There were trees that looked as if they were in a winter bloom of black leaves, but it was just birds. I was walking with my clothes-bundle along Get High Street, toward the one-lane tunnel that cut through a high man-made ridge on top of which the Conrail tracks ran. A flock of starlings burst from a tree in front of Zenith Kitchens and flew, veering in tight formation, to the other side of the tracks, like dry leaves driven before a hurricane.

A line of cars stood waiting to get through the tunnel. Somebody had scrawled SEX PISTOLS in white spray paint on the arch of stone blocks lining the outside of the tunnel. I thought about whoever it was who took the trouble to buy the paint and climb up there and write those words in the middle of the night, how brave and silly and staunch, kids whose parents hated them, whose teachers hated them, kids who would never amount to anything. "You kids are *all right!*" I said out loud, but I knew they weren't, and I wasn't, and anybody who tells them to stay high is a jerk and a criminal, and maybe even the ground such silliness grows from wasn't all right anymore, with its toothless houses and unmuffled cars and kids riding bicycles silently around in a circle, with nothing that they feel comfortable talking about anymore, and when their mothers call them into dinner, nothing to talk about over the dinner table.

I stood next to the tunnel entrance and waited for the cars to stop coming from the other side; then I sprinted through the tunnel, with cars a few yards behind me, like cattle in a slaughterhouse following the Judas goat up the ramp. I haven't actually worked any place where they used a Judas goat, but I have seen it on a PBS documentary.

All around I could hear bird voices, cold, tuneless, like a thousand tiny unlubricated helicopters. A Datsun pickup truck roared past with its lights on, its body jacked three feet above the chassis, paper stickers flashing white on the tread of four brand-new tires. I'd like to invent a kind of tire with a square patch of white rubber set into the tread, so that, for the life of the tire, as you drove past, people would think it was brand new.

From a house set close to the edge of Get High Street, I could hear a family squabble, the high stressed cadences of a mother's voice and the shrill syllables of children. The closer I got to Cresent Drive Spelled Wrong, the louder the birds began to sing. A man was stringing Christmas lights around a dogwood tree. There was no reason for so many birds to be there. They should have flown south or something. It was much too warm for December, abnormally warm, as if the heat from all that molten iron or nickel or whatever it is down there had begun radiating up to the surface of the earth. Far away, I could hear the early commuter train pulling out of Nanuet, with a shrill augmented burst of its horn; and then the Hillcrest fire siren started up again, its long shapeless vowel blanketing the afternoon, and a chained basset hound threw back his head and howled, soulful and ridiculous, and birds were singing and jumping around in the warm air, from branch to branch, from wire to wire, fence to rooftop; birds, birds all over the place.

Edward Allen is a graduate of Goddard College and is at present a teaching associate and doctoral candidate at Ohio University in Athens. He previously participated in the Iowa Writers Workshop program.

Mr. Allen writes poetry and song lyrics. His poetry has appeared in *Mendecino Review, Vortex, Counter/Measures,* and in several anthologies.